DANCING TO "ALMENDRA"

MAYRA MONTERO

TRANSLATED BY EDITH GROSSMAN

FARRAR, STRAUS AND GIROUX   NEW YORK

Farrar, Straus and Giroux
19 Union Square West, New York 10003

Copyright © 2005 by Mayra Montero
Translation copyright © 2007 by Edith Grossman
All rights reserved
Distributed in Canada by Douglas & McIntyre Ltd.
Printed in the United States of America
Originally published in 2005 by Ediciones Santillana, Inc.,
Puerto Rico, as *Son de Almendra*
Published in the United States by Farrar, Straus and Giroux
First American edition, 2007

Library of Congress Cataloging-in-Publication Data
Montero, Mayra, 1952–
  [Son de Almendra. English]
  Dancing to Almendra / Mayra Montero ; translated by
Edith Grossman.—1st American ed.
    p. cm.
  ISBN-13: 978-0-374-10277-7 (hardcover : alk. paper)
  ISBN-10: 0-374-10277-5 (hardcover : alk. paper)
  1. Grossman, Edith, 1936–   II. Title.

PQ7440.M56S6613 2007
863'.64—dc22

                    2006012552

www.fsgbooks.com

2   3   4   5   6   7   8   9   10

DANCING TO "ALMENDRA"

THE MESSAGE

On the same day Umberto Anastasia was killed in New York, a hippopotamus escaped from the zoo in Havana. I can explain the connection. No one else, only me, and the individual who looked after the lions. His name was Juan Bulgado, but he preferred to be called Johnny: Johnny Angel or Johnny Lamb, depending on his mood. In addition to feeding the animals, he was in charge of the slaughter pen, that foul-smelling corner where they killed the beasts that were fed to the carnivores. A long chain of blood. That's what the zoo is. And, very often, life.

Juan Bulgado isn't dead, he lives in an old-age home, he's forgotten that his nom de guerre is Johnny, and the nuns who take care of him call him Frank, later I'll tell you why. When I met him, in October of '57, he was close to forty. I think he turned forty in the middle of the crisis. But I was very young, I'd just gone through the calamity of my birthday party, number twenty-two, celebrated in a way that was very like the twenty-one that preceded it: Mamá on her cloud, a little dizzy because of the Marsala All'uovo, the only liquor she was in the habit of drinking back then; Papá with his arm around my older brother, an engineer like him, both of them smoking their H. Upmann torpedoes; and my sister, seventeen and uncomfortable in her lace-trimmed dress. The three of us were very different from one another, with a father who was similar to my older brother, and a mother who wasn't similar to anyone: ungainly, tense, a smoker, with a voice like hysterical glass and hair that was totally white. As far back as I can remember, she'd had white hair, and probably turned gray even before she gave birth to me. She might have been an interesting woman, but the women who were her friends considered her tiresome. And the children of her friends, some of them my classmates, took care to pass that opinion along to me.

Anastasia died, riddled with bullets, in the Park Sheraton Hotel at Seventh Avenue and Fifty-fifth Street in New York, sitting in a mournful barber's chair, his face still smeared with lather, like a partially decorated cake. The news came in on the Teletype. No one at the paper supposed it would interest me, because my job for the previous year and a half and for who knows how much longer, had been interviewing performers: singers, dancers, actors. Comedians generally are conceited and have very bad characters. I didn't like what I did, I despised that kind of lightweight journalism, but I had no alternative when I began working at the *Diario de la Marina*, on the recommendation of one of my father's friends. All the positions I would have preferred were already filled, and all they needed was some moron who'd be happy to find out what new plans were hatching in the empty little head of Gilda Magdalena, the blondest of our vedettes; or which harem Kirna Moor, a Turkish dancer who packed them in at night at the Cabaret Sans Souci, had escaped from; or which orchestra would accompany Renato Carosone, an Italian clown who sang the absurd "Marcelino Pan y Vino," which played constantly on the radio.

4

I tore the cable about the death of Anastasia out of the Tele-type and ran to the managing editor, an animal with the voice of an overseer, whose name was Juan Diego.

"Did you see this?" I handed him the paper. "I bet heads'll roll. Right here in Havana, I think that—"

Juan Diego put his index finger to his mouth to make me be quiet, took the cable from my hand, and read two or three lines before tossing it on his desk.

"Who cares?" he hissed with disdain. "Who gives a damn if they killed that fat pig?"

He paused, scribbled a note on another cable, and realized I was still there, nailed to the floor, clutching at a final hope that I could cover more substantial news.

"Don't you have anything to do?" he asked without looking up, as patronizing as if he were talking to a child.

"Yes," I answered. "I can write an article about the death of Anastasia. I can go to the Hotel Nacional, or to the Placita de los Judíos."

"Go to the zoo." He raised his voice as well as his head: I saw his porcine face, covered with moles. "A hippopotamus escaped and was killed yesterday afternoon. Don't worry about Tirso, I'll tell him I sent you to cover it. Find out what you can."

Tirso was my boss, and he was in charge of the entertain-ment pages. Skinny, indecisive, with long, thin fingers that re-sembled leftover vermicelli. His favorite pastime was collecting photos of young girls, sixteen- or seventeen-year-old singers or actresses who came out of nowhere and so often had to return there. One attracted him more than any other; her name was Charito, and whenever the photographer from the paper took her picture, he had to make a set of additional copies for Skinny T., which was what they called my boss. Then I'd see him place the photos in a portfolio, and I imagined that when

5

he got home, in the quiet of the night, he'd spread them out on the bed and stare at them, a bachelor who undressed as he looked at them. I liked actresses too, but older ones. Women of thirty or thirty-five who would treat me very calmly, talk without being stupid, and from time to time let me go to bed with them. Several did let me. It was the only really exciting thing about that wretched job.

I left the paper and headed for the zoo. In those days I drove a '49 Plymouth that had belonged to my father, and then my brother inherited it, until he began to earn money and could buy what he called "thunder for two," which was simply a 1957 Thunderbird. I parked a few yards from the entrance. I hadn't been back to the zoo for many years, almost ten years, not since the last time my mother had taken my sister and me there. Back then my sister was a good-natured, enterprising little girl in whom a man's forms, gestures, and preferences were already beginning to make their appearance.

Unlike her, I never had a fondness for animals, not even dogs. The stink of the zoo irritated me, and I didn't see the charm of giraffes or elephants, much less flamingos. I have no idea why there were so many flamingos there. It didn't matter how brightly colored or nice an animal might be, I lacked and still lack the sensibility to feel affection for any of them. Going back to the zoo under those circumstances seemed somehow shameful to me: I had to find the place where the hippopotamus had been killed, interview the director, the animal's keeper, perhaps a few children. Readers, for the most part, are so perverse that they're interested in the opinions of kids. For the moment those were the limits of my brilliant career: to write about a rotting animal and forget that Umberto Anastasia, the Great Executioner of Murder, Inc., had been killed in New York, almost certainly for sticking his nose into Havana's affairs. A wonderful story that somebody else would write. Or nobody else. Newspaper owners avoided getting anywhere near those subjects.

I ran into a groundskeeper right at the entrance to the zoo, and he took me to the director's office. As I walked through the park, certain images from my childhood came to mind: paths full of puddles, cotton candy, a badly hurt monkey dying inside a cage, all of this colored by my mother's ridiculous reproaches as she made useless attempts to correct my sister's behavior. When she failed, she blamed my father. "I'm going to have a mannish daughter," she'd complain to him in my presence, perhaps in my brother's presence, never in front of the girl, "and you, Samuel, you don't seem to care at all." My father didn't respond, he behaved as if he hadn't heard her, in his heart he knew there was nothing to do about his daughter. Lucy was his third son packed into a robust female body. A misfortune like any other.

The director of the zoo didn't look like the director of any zoo, at least I wouldn't have imagined one looking like this: well-groomed and distant, a withdrawn little man with a soft face that wore half a grimace of disgust; I knew right away he was disgusted, but I had no idea why. When I walked into his office, he was holding his hat; I assumed he was about to put it on and go out. We spoke for a while, he gave me some information about the hippopotamus: he said it was a male that recently had emerged from adolescence; it had been born in a New York zoo and had been in Cuba for about five years, fairly restless, that was true; according to the keeper it had always been a nervous animal. If I wanted to take a photograph, an employee would be happy to accompany me to the place it had fallen and where it was still lying, waiting for an examination by the forensic veterinarian. As for the rest, it was too soon to determine if it had escaped because somebody let it out or if the animal on its own had charged and trampled the

7

fences, since they were inclined to wander at night. As he was speaking, I suppose he guessed my boredom at being there, and he changed his tone, looked me up and down, and asked, with some sarcasm, if I wanted to take the animal's picture or if what he'd told me was enough. I replied that it wasn't enough, I wanted to interview the keeper and take a few photographs.

"I'll have someone go with you," he said.

He went to the door and called for somebody named Matías. A bearded, toothless old man, whose stink caught in my nose like a fishhook, responded. Without introducing us, the director ordered him to take me first to the pond that had been occupied by the hippopotamus and then to the edge of the wood that surrounded the zoo, where the animal had been cordoned off. The old man looked at me with curiosity; I carried a notebook in my hand and had a camera hanging from my shoulder.

"Come this way," he said, and I followed him in silence, swearing to myself that I'd finish up as soon as I could. When we reached the pond, I saw another animal wallowing in the water.

"It's the female," the old man announced, "she's a poor widow now."

He repeated "poor widow," perhaps hoping I'd laugh at the joke, and I looked at him with absolute contempt. I took a couple of photographs and signaled that we should go on. The worst was waiting for me: confronting the huge bulk that I imagined as discolored, suppurating, disfigured by swelling. When we arrived I saw that the spectacle went far beyond any horror that might have crossed my mind: the hippopotamus's guts were coming out of its body, and in the sunlight, from the spot where I was standing, they had an intense iridescent color between green and light purple. A handful of mean-looking turkey buzzards circled overhead, forming something called a black halo.

"There's the wanderer," the old man said, showing me the obvious, because it was impossible not to see the hippopotamus lying on its side, surrounded by men in gray coveralls who, I supposed, were zoo employees, looking on in silence. One was a kind of guard who kept anybody from getting too close.

"Let this man through." The old man's voice vibrated with a toothless authority, and its register reminded me of a little Chinese trumpet. "He's from the *Diario de la Marina*."

Everyone turned to look at me. I had the impression they expected a typical sleuth, a tough guy with his sleeves rolled up and his hat pushed back. Instead they saw a thin, blond kid with an altar boy's down on his face and two-toned shoes that looked as if he'd inherited them from his father. And that's exactly what they were: shoes I inherited from Papá.

"First I'll take some pictures," I proposed. "Stand to one side, as if you'd just found the hippopotamus."

It's a device that never fails: people like them adore being in the papers. As I focused on the animal, and on the crowd facing me and smiling at the camera, I began to think of what original question I could ask anyone about the beast's stampede and subsequent death, what new angle could be revealed, what detail would be worth digging up. Though I was bitter at having to write the piece, it wasn't something that could just be tossed aside. You never could tell where the lucky stroke might come from, the one that would smooth the way for leaving the entertainment section for another, juicier part of the paper: court news, for example, or feature articles about the airport.

I began with the animal's keeper: a taciturn, ebony black man, about fifty years old, with the air of a stevedore and a gold tooth that I saw when he bit down on his cigar. He also had an enormous cyst in the middle of his forehead, like an embedded Ping-Pong ball. There wasn't much he could tell me, only that when he arrived at the zoo, before dawn, some soldiers were already tracking the animal, and they stopped him from getting close. He was sorry he hadn't gotten there earlier, because the animal knew his voice, and more than his voice, the howl he always gave to let it know he was bringing food. Then he emitted the howl so I could hear it, and I was struck that nobody found this silliness funny, nobody started to laugh. I realized that the fauna whose job it was to take care of the animals were more fauna than the beasts themselves. I asked him to go up to the hippopotamus so I could take his picture, and he did what I asked without protest. In fact, he kneeled next to the animal and rested his hand on its dry back. It was all I needed. I knew an image like this was worth more than any paragraph I could write about the situation of this black who'd suddenly been orphaned; the poor man projected orphanhood. I took other photographs in which the man opened his mouth and narrowed his eyes in an expression that resembled weeping but wasn't. Much later I understood that zookeepers never cry for any animal. They mustn't, and they can't.

When I began to put away the camera, a new Kodak Retina, a birthday present from my brother, I noticed one of the men in the group walking toward me. He had coppery skin, with nervous, almost feminine eyes, and he was wearing a convict's cap that had nothing to do with his uniform. I thought he wanted to ask me something about the camera, and I hurried to put it back in the case; I wasn't interested in having a conversation with anyone, least of all a monkey keeper or whatever he was. I looked up briefly and saw that the man was smiling; he had dark lips and yellow teeth. With his head he gestured toward the hippopotamus's defeated corpse.

"That's a message for Anastasia."

It took me a few seconds to understand this simple statement. To understand it in the sunlight, at the border between the zoo and the wood, facing the animal's immense open belly, which was beginning to release fast-moving bubbles. Suddenly I reacted, turning my gaze away from the camera to look into that man's eyes. Among all these people seeing me for the first time, who could have known that less than two hours earlier I'd tried to write a story about Umberto Anastasia, shot to death in a chair in the barbershop of the Park Sheraton in New York?

"Anastasia's dead," I replied.

The other man was somewhat disconcerted and looked down at the ground. "What a waste," he murmured. "He didn't get the message."

I began to laugh, trying to gain a few minutes. I betrayed a beginner's nervousness. I looked at my watch, I looked at the man again, and he in turn was observing the arrival of the forensic veterinarian, an impassive bald man who made his way with great pomp, accompanied by three or four assistants and followed by a large wagon pulled by a mule and loaded with boxes and pulleys.

"Are we talking about the same Anastasia?"

He shrugged, and I had a premonition. I looked for my cigarettes, thinking I had a pack in my jacket pocket. There was nothing there, and I couldn't come up with an idea that would allow me to resume the conversation. We were silent for two or three minutes while we both watched the forensic veterinarian, who was walking around the hippopotamus.

"An Anastasia died today in New York," I said finally. "He was shot."

"He's the one," he specified, not blinking and not looking anywhere but straight ahead. "That's why they killed the hippopotamus."

I tried to act naturally, like a surgeon with a cold heart, and covered in cold sweat too. One of the veterinarian's assistants asked us to step back so they could began the autopsy. The pulleys had been taken down from the wagon, along with a sign that said "Silence," which was hammered into the ground.

"Why don't we talk about this somewhere else?" I suggested but immediately regretted it because I saw him smile. I was afraid, perhaps absurdly so, that he'd confess it was all a joke.

"Whatever you say," he replied.

"How's tomorrow?"

He didn't answer right away, and I thought he was thinking it over, but that wasn't it, he was simply enjoying the pirouettes of the veterinarian, who'd climbed a handheld ladder and was doing a balancing act in order to see inside the animal's open belly.

"It'll have to be at night," he murmured, "about eight o'clock. I live in Neptuno, but I like going to Sloppy Joe's."

Sloppy Joe's was a bar for Americans; I was surprised that a man like him would go to that kind of place. Still, I dug into my pocket and took out two pesos.

"Here . . . have something to drink while you're waiting for me. What's your name?"

"Johnny," he answered, showing no interest in knowing mine. Still, I told him my name was Joaquín, and didn't give my last name either.

I turned to leave the zoo. The stinking old man who'd led the way to the hippopotamus ran toward me. "Aren't you going to take more pictures?"

I made a gesture with my arm that meant no, or maybe, but in any case he shouldn't come closer. And I achieved my purpose, because he kept his distance, bewildered, probably feeling dirty, humiliated by my attitude. In those days I was generally repelled by old people, I couldn't help it. I didn't like their lined, excessively dry skin, and the scaliness that kind of skin generates. If the old person was also in rags and smelled of shit like that man did, my revulsion was infinite.

I drove away in the Plymouth, which was green, and named Surprise. I drove slowly along the narrow street lined with palms and concluded that this was the real surprise: I'd come to the zoo totally irritated, and now I was leaving filled with hope. I was in no hurry, I even had an appetite. I went straight to the Boris, a Jewish restaurant on Calle Compostela. In the past, I'd run into certain individuals there; I supposed many of them had reason to celebrate that day, and maybe they'd have lunch in a discreet establishment. Boris, the Polish owner, always reserved a table for Meyer Lansky, regardless of whether the client showed up or not. At that table, and at every table, there were bottles of wine that had been uncorked and closed again with caps topped by silver crowns. On the crowns he'd put an inscription in Hebrew, but I didn't know its meaning; that very afternoon I intended to find out. I parked the Plymouth on Callejón Porvenir, next to a tobacco kiosk where I bought cigarettes. I'd never gone so long without smoking, and so I lit one with longing and finished it before I reached the restaurant. At the door of the Boris I lit another.

My eyes were clouded by smoke when I pushed open that door.

HEY, KIDS . . .

It was the dead afternoon of Christmas Day. The year was 1946, and Julián was still my best friend and had been since kindergarten. He was almost twelve but looked younger, he was so short and conceited, and had a round baby face. His mother, Aurora, was a young widow whose work was decorating dining rooms. I don't know any other way to say it. She brought the tablecloths and candles, arranged centerpieces with natural flowers, orchids for the most part, some entirely purple and others striped like candies. Frequently she was hired to decorate the tables at banquets for the military and other prestigious dinners at clubs or private houses. Mamá, who was her close friend, used to say that Aurora didn't need to work, since Julián's father had left her enough money, but it seems she enjoyed giving orders and managing her small army of colleagues: two silent women, so identical they looked like twins, and five or six mulattoes, who ran back and forth, taking care of the heavy work, moving chairs and hanging fabrics, and sometimes large signs frosted with glitter.

Aurora had suggested we go with her that afternoon. I'm

sure she included me so that Julián wouldn't be bored by him-self. But I didn't care, I'd been wanting to see that hotel, peo-ple said it was the best in Cuba. At the time it wasn't open to the public, it was closed for a convention, a meeting of rich Americans, that's what Aurora told us. A little while after we arrived, we followed her to the kitchen. She went up to the chefs to introduce herself and in passing to learn the details of the menu; I always heard her say that the meal and the deco-rations ought to go hand in hand and resemble each other a little. The gigantic kitchen was crowded with hurrying men, some wearing cooks' hats and aprons, others simply in their undershirts. There were impassive women in uniforms, peeling pineapples or chopping meat. In a corner, next to the sinks, breathing lightly and quivering from time to time, were the flamingos. There were ten or twelve of them, intensely pink, piled on top of one another. Julián and I went closer, and he murmured that he felt sorry to see them like that, almost dead but not so far gone they couldn't tell they were in a hostile place, hearing voices, hearing above all the boiling water that would be used to strip their feathers; the boiling was the worst. I didn't feel sorry, but I did feel repelled, especially because they opened their eyes and looked around, and it was incredi-ble that their throats weren't slit once and for all, that they were allowed to see the knives. There were long knives right next to them.

A boy a little older than we were squatted beside us; later we learned he swept up the feathers and scales that fell to the floor. He told us his name was Pancho, I said we didn't care, he became furious and added that if we wanted to see turtles that were already gutted we had to follow him. I proposed to Julián that we go see them, and he agreed, a little reluctantly, and so we began to follow the boy, slipping past the legs of the cooks, invisible to everyone. I remember shouting something like that to Julián, that we were invisible. We reached the far end of the kitchen, Pancho opened a door, and we came out into an interior courtyard with washtubs. There were buckets, hoses, a terrible gleaming machete with a curve that looked like a smile to me, and there was blood, above all blood, clotted pools of it, and an odor of shellfish. We saw the opened turtles and dozens of live crabs, some trying to climb up the wall. Oysters were piled in an enormous basin.

"It's what Americans eat," Pancho revealed. "They hardly eat anything else."

Julián and I looked at each other, and the other boy picked up a crab; he showed us how to do it with two fingers, from the back, fast so the animal couldn't pinch with its claws.

"They're all in this hotel," he whispered, pointing his index finger at the upper floors. "Gangsters, like in the movies."

He threw down the crab and ran away. Julián was pale because he was tenderhearted about animals. I was pensive, perhaps a little pale too, but for another reason: when I heard that word, "gangsters," I thought of a picture my family had just seen, one of the few times Papá and Mamá took the three of us to the movies. Now, after so many years, it seems like an omen that George Raft played the lead in the film, though "played the lead" is very broad, all he did was play cards, he'd been accused of murder, had a shoot-out with the police, and fled to St. Louis. His girlfriend, who was Ava Gardner, left him for a nightclub owner, but in the end she discovered it had all been a trick: Raft was wounded, and she hurried to be with him, to change his bandages, put a cigarette between his lips, cook him some broth, those little things that magnificent women do. After seeing the movie, my sister spent the night saying Ava Gardner was her girlfriend. She was still a little girl, but she knew what being somebody's girlfriend meant.

I asked Julián if we could go look at the Americans. I could tell he was relieved: all he wanted was to get out of the kitchen and not see that stream of guts. We went back to where we'd started, slipping past people again; nobody noticed us, only Pancho looked at us from a distance, the broom in his hand, there was some envy in his eyes, and some resentment too, a kind of adult curse. Just then Julián's mother called us, and the three of us left the kitchen. She said she'd begin to decorate the ballrooms, and in the meantime we could go to the gardens, without going too far, of course, and without being loud, the Americans couldn't stand noise. She kissed her son, she often kissed him, and she smiled at me, she wasn't my mother to give me a kiss, though I thought I saw the impulse, as if she'd been about to put her lips to my forehead and at the last moment something stopped her. It was a shame, because Aurora had a husky voice and a pretty face. Without a single gray hair, she was just the opposite of my mother. I'd begun to love her a long time ago, when I spent a few days in her house right after Julián's father died. They lived on the Paseo del Prado, in an old house with a lot of rooms, and even though Vedado had become fashionable, she never wanted to move. I remember the bathroom, the one she used, with an old bathtub covered with drawings, and the dressing table that was a hundred years old, her perfumes lined up on it like little soldiers, several glass powder cases, and a small rococo box of rouge, a box that I opened once and smelled, rubbed a little with my finger, and then put the finger in my mouth.

Julián and I walked around the lobby. Once he'd left the dying animals behind, he recovered his usual tone of voice, a tone of command. As soon as we went out to the gardens, he saw that boring panorama, stopped, and signaled to me that we should go back. "Hey, let's go upstairs. They must be up there."

I agreed, and we went back to the lobby. Since he already knew the hotel, we walked straight to the elevator; we had that air of superiority, we were well-dressed and had gold watches. Julián's was better than mine, much better; it was a man's watch, it had belonged to his dead father. I inherited mine from my brother, but it never failed to attract attention. The elevator operator didn't say a word, he took us to the second floor, and when he opened the door he said, "Gentlemen," and bowed with what looked like mockery to me, but Julián knew how to respond, midgets always know: he gave the elevator operator a gangster's look, an authentic look of contempt that seemed more like a gunshot to me. That's the kind of look that boy could give. We walked with a good deal of confidence, passing more or less normal fauna: waiters walking back and forth, carrying trays; husky guys, with distrustful faces, we imagined they were bodyguards; and two women who, after so many years, I can still remember because of their shoes: high-heeled sandals at whose tips some ambitious toes peeked out, their nails polished.

"I bet it's there, there's a room . . ."

We went up to the door and pushed it without consulting anyone, without first knocking. In fact, Julián pushed it; he always had the recourse of becoming smaller, putting on his baby face, and pretending to be a little boy: seven, eight, maybe nine years old. The door opened onto a corridor, and at the end of the corridor there was, in fact, a large conference room. At first we could make out only the enormous table with men sitting around it, smoke floating over their heads. We also heard voices, very discreet, and I thought it was suspicious for gangsters to speak so quietly, so courteously. I told Julián that.

"Well, it's them," he answered, "they're the only Americans here."

Suddenly he crouched down, his back against the wall, and pulled at the bottom of my trousers so that I'd crouch down beside him. From there we had a better angle for spying on the men sitting around the table. I knew a little English, and Julián knew much more than I did, but neither of us could understand what they were saying. They were talking too quickly, and really, all we cared about was to look at them, see them move, scrutinize their gestures through voluttas of smoke, all of them smoking their H. Upmann torpedoes, or who knows what kind of cigar that could burn that way, as if performing a little piece of music. After a while we realized they were all wearing rings as a secret sign, star sapphires on their pinkies and only on those fingers. Each one of them exuded luxury, and more than luxury, authority, a perfume that overpowered any other. Julián and I understood this on the same day. That's why he said that when he grew up, he was going to be like them, and in a way he kept his word. But for the moment, we were only a pair of idiots breathing in other people's smoke. A couple of well-combed boys wearing winter jackets and lace-up shoes. Mine, inherited from my brother, but Julián's worn for the first time on Christmas Eve.

This image, I assume it was fairly offensive, was precisely what the man coming down the hall saw. He smelled the difference, we weren't exactly intruders in the hotel. "Hey, kids . . . ," he said as he passed and continued along to the meeting, but he stopped at the door, turned to look at us as if he had a doubt: he was short and big-eared, he had sleepy-looking, unassailable eyes, the kind of eyes that don't lose their calm, that never open wide, not even at the sight of a revolver. He said another sentence in very rapid English; maybe he'd had second thoughts and was asking who we were, or what we were doing there. We didn't move, just in case, and he rejected the doubt, rejected it or felt too lazy to argue with two kids. The fact is he turned his back on us. Inside there was the clink of glasses, it seemed to be a recess, some Americans left the room and passed us, talking among themselves. I remarked to

Julián that we were still invisible, and he answered with a statement that I kept turning over in my mind for many days afterward.

"That's not it, Quin, they're the invisible ones."

A fat man with leaden feet also came out of the meeting, chewing gum. He had curly black hair, an oily wave of hair that he combed to one side. He wiped his forehead and didn't put back his handkerchief but kept it in his hand, and as he passed us he shook the handkerchief, releasing a rank, slightly bitter perfume. That bitterness went down my throat; in a second it rebounded to my tongue.

"Anastasia!"

Someone had called him from the room, and he turned. All his clothing was white except for the red bow tie around his neck. It seemed incomprehensible that a man his size would have a woman's name. I mentioned this to Julián, who replied that very often Americans gave themselves broads' names, he used the term used by kids in the street, and I began to laugh. My laughter was a mistake, because at that moment the fat man discovered us, looked at us as if we were two unexpected flies, opened his mouth to say something, but closed it again when he heard someone calling him a second time. We looked toward the door to the conference room, which was where the voice was coming from, and we saw a man who looked Chinese, had gray hair, and wore a dark suit. In one hand he had a cigar, and in the other he held a dog; he held it against his chest, and it looked more like a rat than a dog. The fat man said something to him, and the other one replied with icy words. I felt the cold on top of my head; the dog must have felt it too because it began to bark, or rather to screech, not only are those miniature dogs disgusting, but they're fairly hysterical too. The fat man named Anastasia walked back toward the room; he did it unwillingly, and the man with the dog waited for him, smiling. He smiled as if he were Chinese, with an enigma playing around his lips.

Two months later, on a Sunday when I was looking through the paper for the comics, I came across the photograph: it was the same man with the same little dog, impossible to forget his face. In the newspaper it said that the day before, Saturday, February 22, Havana's chief of police, Benito Herrera, had ordered him arrested at the Vedado restaurant, where he usually went at night. I tore out the page to show to Julián: there was the American, the asshole let himself be caught and didn't even put down the dog to shoot it out with the police, which was what gangsters did. What we saw George Raft do: shoot till he had no damn bullets left so he could get away to St. Louis.

Julián bent over the newspaper clipping and began to laugh, and I still remember what he said: "He doesn't have a broad's name."

I shrugged, and his expression changed. He pronounced each word very carefully: "Charles 'Lucky' Luciano. I'd like to have that name."

BORIS

Empty. That's how the Boris was on that strange afternoon. All you heard was the sound of the fans, and noises from the street, which seemed somehow muffled and indistinct, as if they'd stopped being real. I sat down at one of the tables, instinct told me to, and I remained there, my eyes fixed on the door to the kitchen, expecting to see the owner, who almost always was in the restaurant, tending to his patrons, or Constantino, the Russian waiter, a haughty bear who exuded vodka and would offer the soup of the day and the off-the-menu specials in Yiddish and Polish, never in Spanish.

It was Julián who took me to the Boris for the first time. By then we'd become men. He'd just returned from a university in Boston where he spent some time, pretending to study architecture but learning other things. That day, during a lunch to celebrate our seeing each other again, he told me the truth about the so-called convention of Americans, and about the afternoon of gangsters that we'd had at the Hotel Nacional. Anastasia wasn't a broad's name, as we thought, but the last name of an important capo. Not long after that, the Cuban police put Lucky Luciano on a Turkish ship and deported him to Genoa. And as for the one with the drooping lids and sleep-walker's ears, the one who greeted us with that insipid "Hey, kids"—that was Meyer Lansky himself, who'd soon become boss of all the businesses, a real empire to which new cabarets and hotels were constantly being added. According to Julián, the only one missing from that Christmas conclave was Bugsy Siegel, the strongman of Las Vegas, and for very good reason: it wouldn't have been a good idea for him to hear how they were planning his execution. At the meeting in the Nacional, they concluded that Bugsy was a hindrance, they decided to wait six months, and then they raised their glasses to signal agreement. He was eliminated on June 20, 1947, while he sat on the sofa in his house in Los Angeles, reading the paper and waiting for his dear friend the actor George Raft, with whom he was sup-posed to have dinner at Jack's. That's what they discussed at the "convention" while Aurora, Julián's mother, was placing or-chids in the centers of the tables, removed from everything, radiant because she was in love, she'd just fallen in love again, though her son suspected nothing and neither did I; it was a secret between her and the man who'd won her. I saw them once, some time later, dancing to "Almendra," the *danzón* about the almond. It seemed to me that listening to "Almen-dra" was like watching a pendulum; it was a melody that could hypnotize the people who danced to it, those two people in particular but also the ones who had the experience of seeing them dance. Aurora and that man, like a single seed, satisfied at last and for that reason strong, their passion spent, I understood this despite my youth. There was something solid and distinc-tive in the way they connected, in the honored way they fol-lowed the rhythm. There was no hope for anyone else.

After that lunch, I developed a liking for the food at the Boris, or for the atmosphere, I'm not really sure which. Maybe

it was only curiosity, and at heart something much more intimate, something that had to do with a morbid urge to punish
myself and that absurd dream of mine: I'd have the chance to
see my rival, and rivalry is a guiding principle like any other.
Julián assured me that Meyer Lansky ate there too. Before
lunch, he'd come to the neighborhood with his bodyguards, go
to the bakery on Calle Luz, buy the bread the Jews ate, and stay
for a while talking to the baker. Sometimes they'd be joined by
the owner of a nearby jewelry store, also named Meyer, and
famous because he obtained the best *stones*, and when I say
"stones" I'm talking only about the star sapphires they all wore
on their little fingers. Lansky would go out to the street, followed by his men, and stroll around the Arco de Belén, and
during his walk he'd pinch off little pieces of bread and put
them in his mouth. At one or two in the afternoon, when the
bread was half eaten, he'd return to Calle Compostela between
Merced and Bayona. Boris Kalmanovich would be waiting for
him there with the table set and a recently opened bottle of
Pernod, which was the only liquor Lansky liked to drink.

The food at the Boris—boiled chicken, gefilte fish, kreplach soup (that's what Constantino called it), and a soup colored by beets that had a sweet-and-sour aroma—was good.
These smells would float out to the street. Because of that, and
because of the pleasure I took in nosing around that universe of
bowed profiles—the tables were arranged so that all you could
see were profiles—I'd stop in at least once a week. I almost always was there with the owners of the stores on Calle Muralla,
men who ate quickly but not insulting the food, not that, they
had good manners, they kept their distance, they drank tea and
then went back to work. Several times I saw Meyer Lansky,
who had a sleepy look. Anybody would have taken him for
a simple watchmaker—he was as subdued as a good watchmaker—or the neighborhood dentist, or the bookkeeper at

one of the fabric stores. By this time I'd begun to organize very rudimentary files with the names, relations, and activities of the Mafia in Cuba. I dreamed about writing a great article that in my heart I knew no paper would dare to publish. Sometimes Lansky came in with his brother, who was named Jack and nicknamed "El Cejudo," or "Brows," and the two of them would eat in silence, smiling at no one but Dimitri, the Ukrainian cook, who'd leave the kitchen only to greet them, a little bewildered, humble down to his bones, carrying small dishes of gelatin, I don't know what kind of strange, copper-colored gelatin it was, or the serving dish of rice and lentils, which was Lansky's favorite dish. "El Cejudo" devoured nothing but red meat; he wanted it bloody, and he'd put yogurt on it.

"No tables today."

I was so caught up in my memories I didn't even hear him approach. Constantino, the Russian waiter, stood in front of me, chewing on the end of a sinister cigar, looking at me with his narrow blue eyes, sticky with secretions.

"What do you mean no tables?" I looked around the deserted room with no sounds of its own, as if it had been placed in the middle of a dream. "They all look empty to me . . ."

They didn't generally use tablecloths at the Boris, but that day they had, white ones, rather good ones, with embroidered initials: *B* for Boris, and *K* for Kalmanovich.

"It's full." He'd taken the cigar out of his mouth but still spoke as if he were chewing on it. "There's a lunch soon. All reserved, you can't eat."

The last sentence was like a telegram. He was brusque by nature, especially with those of us who didn't belong to his kingdom of cloth merchants from Calle Muralla, or casino operators.

"Come back tomorrow."

He stopped looking at me, fixed his eyes on the door, and

crossed his arms: it was obvious he was ready to shove me out. Before he could, I stood and walked to the door, thinking after all it was logical that Lansky had given orders to close the restaurant so he could talk in peace. I bet most of his lieutenants—Luigi Santo Trafficante, Joe Stassi and his son, "El Pequeño" or "Little" Stassi, Nicholas "Fat the Butcher" DiConstanza, Dino Cellini, maybe Amleto Battisti—would be there this afternoon. And for dealing with a delicate matter, certainly Lansky would be accompanied by Milton Side, a man with a cool head, I don't mean cool, I mean totally icy, though in one of fate's ironies this man would burn to death many years later in the casino of a hotel in Puerto Rico.

But now, on that late October afternoon, they had to talk about strategies, organize for the complicated days ahead of them: days of caution, eluding the detectives who'd come down from New York to nose around the Nacional and the Sans Souci (the Sans Souci was Trafficante's cabaret) and, above all, to look through the papers at the Riviera and the Capri, two hotels that were about to open. I was surprised that none of the businessmen who usually came to the Boris had shown up that day. I concluded that the store owners had been told the restaurant would be closed for lunch. I stood there on the sidewalk, lit another cigarette, and began to search mentally for a place where I could have a few beers and at the same time observe the movement around the Boris, the people who went in or came out. But at that moment I felt someone smack me on the shoulder; it was a fearless approach, deliberately obscene, and when I turned around I was confronted by a narrow face covered in little beads of sweat. He had a scar on his chin, a low forehead, and graying eyebrows that seemed glued on by a clumsy hand.

"I know you," he said in a thick voice; some dried mucus

hung from his nose, and I had a hunch his feet hurt. "Aren't you the reporter from the *Diario de la Marina*?"

I took a step back and discovered that on the opposite sidewalk another guy, a brawny mulatto, obviously armed, was watching us.

"Beat it," added the one in front of me. "Beat it right now."

I shook my head; it was a gesture of disbelief, though everything was perfectly believable, perfectly logical. And then Boris, so fat and ashen, appeared at the door; it was a theatrical appearance, the kind attributed to the hand of God.

"They already told you we're closed, kid," he said, panting. I assumed he'd run out from the kitchen, a major effort considering he suffered from gout.

"And I was leaving," I lied, staring at the guy with the mucus. "The truth is I don't know what's going on here."

"Yes you do, fella," he said. "How's Skinny Tirso? He's your boss at the paper, isn't he?"

He passed his thumb under his nose in a defiant gesture, the bit of mucus fell, and I noticed his scaly fingers, bony but pitiless, surely accustomed to hurting, to causing uncommon pain. I turned and walked to my automobile, the '49 Plymouth, which suddenly seemed distant and tiny, like a little toy car. I felt my face flush when I started the motor. The entire street was crawling with bodyguards and the police that always accompanied Lansky, bloodthirsty, irascible mulattoes, selected and paid for by the Ministry of the Interior. I thought it very strange that I hadn't noticed the presence of this small army before. When I arrived I'd looked all around and hadn't noticed anything special, so in all likelihood they'd just positioned themselves; they tended to do that an hour before the boss showed up. I could see Boris go back into the restaurant, and those men in suits who were keeping guard didn't even bother to make sure I left. They knew very well I would, that I wouldn't dare stay even a minute longer in that neighborhood, on those streets that suddenly had become unrecognizable, false within their routine, as if the buildings were a stage set and the passersby perfect accomplices.

I went back to the paper. I sat down in front of the typewriter and rubbed my hands together. It was a puerile gesture, the useless display of someone trying to persuade himself of his own thirst for vengeance. I typed out the article without stopping and gave it this title: "The Dead Hippopotamus: A Message for Anastasia?"

I still remember the first line:

> The hippopotamus killed yesterday in the Havana Zoo might have been the innocent victim of a message sent to the men of Mafia capo Umberto Anastasia, who was also murdered yesterday in New York City.

Then I filled a page and a half with information about the animal and its keeper (another animal of smaller girth), the comments of a few zoo employees, the extremely solemn arrival of the forensic veterinarian, and the reactions of some children, these last totally apocryphal. In short, a string of stupid anecdotes and expressions of grief. I saved for the end the small, delicate lines that were the reason for the existence of my article:

> Late in the afternoon, an unimpeachable source assured this reporter that the death of the hippopotamus probably was carried out by elements of the Havana underworld who intended to send a message to the New York capo Umberto Anastasia. The message, apparently, came too late.

I rushed it over to the managing editor. He wasn't at his desk, and I left it for him on a pile of papers, like a cherry on the top of a confusion of cables and submissions. I had to go back to Entertainment, back into the claws of Skinny T., who still hadn't said a word to me because he knew I was writing a story that didn't concern him.

"Did you finish the thing about the bear?" he finally asked, not looking up as he drooled on the photo of Noemí, the exotic dancer at the Nightandday.

"It wasn't a bear," I told him, "it was a hippopotamus. And I think the one you have there is the girlfriend of a certain Fat the Butcher."

I put my finger on the photograph, specifically on the pubescent little belly of Noemí. I'd seen her perform a very obscene number that didn't go with her schoolgirl's mouth, not at the Nightandday but at Mandrake's Cave, literally a cave where a black with three balls stripped for tourists. Skinny T. gave me a rancorous look, but I pretended not to notice. It wasn't my fault the gangsters had taken over the best hips in Havana.

"Well, you'll have to interview this one," he mumbled resentfully, putting the photo of a much older *rumbera*, that is, one who was twenty-five or twenty-seven years old, in front of me. He'd just thought up the interview and assigned it to me: it was my punishment for having ruined his interlude, for not minding my own business, for reminding him that Noemí had a problematic boss. Contrary to what he expected, I almost reacted with enthusiasm: the vedette he was sending me to interview was the star of the show at the Sans Souci, and ever since I'd learned about the death of Anastasia, I'd been playing with the idea of dropping in on Trafficante in his own lair. I was about to tell Skinny T. that I'd interview her, what could I do, but just then the managing editor, that worm Juan Diego, interrupted us, waving the two pages I'd left for him.

"Don't let this boy go out in the sun," he said to Skinny T. "This morning the poor kid got sunstroke. He went to the zoo, and it did him the worst damn harm: he really doesn't know what he's writing."

"Yes I do," I dared to answer, caught between the two of them, two rotten guys who were suffocating me.

"No you don't, damn it. I told you to leave Anastasia alone, nobody cares about that fat pig. I'm taking all that shit out of your piece. I probably won't even publish it."

Then, turning to my boss, who was still fingering the picture of Noemí: "Skinny, I'm giving this dumb jerk back to you."

Juan Diego walked away, and Skinny T. let go of the photo and sat looking at me. I think he felt sorry for me. "Things don't mix," he said. "Not here in Entertainment, not anywhere else on the paper. If you want to survive, you have to learn that."

He had the cheekbones of a corpse, sunken eyes, and a witch's chin that scared little girls. He gave me information on the vedette at the Sans Souci, whose name was Kary.

"Interview her and don't fuck around."

SANS SOUCI

It was like a premonition of what would come later. The sensation of having reached a dead end, or an inexplicable point of departure. In the half-light of that living room crowded with so many disparate objects, I looked back, looked at the years of my life, the way I conformed, the useless hours I spent at the paper and in the routine of my house, with a mother who was an ironic lizard, a father who was another kind of distant reptile focused on my brother, his faithful reflection, and a renegade, sleepwalking sister who now got up at the crack of dawn to put on a tie and pee standing up. I embraced it all, and what I had left was smoke. From the depths of that smoke emerged Juan Bulgado, the animal keeper at the zoo. First we went to Sloppy Joe's, had a few drinks, and talked about the hippopotamus, the rumors he'd heard, the absurd way the animal was killed. Later we went to his house, which belonged to his mother-in-law. I never imagined the wretch would live in so big a house, a place that in the past had possessed a certain splendor, but not now, dust and vicissitudes had brought it down: a sinister reception room, even more sinister hallways, many closed doors on both sides, and a melancholy prison tempo pervading everything. At the back, like the end of a story, was the chaotic living room, where I was offered an ancient armchair to sit in. Bulgado's mother-in-law, whose name was Sara, carried a stamp of bitterness on her face; she tried to keep up appearances and was courteous when she saw me come in with her son-in-law: she welcomed me and then left immediately to prepare coffee. She looked at Juan—she called him Juan, not Johnny Lamb or Johnny Angel—with weariness, with the expression of someone contemplating the ruins of her house after the fire has been put out. I thought it was logical, wasn't it? No moderately well-off woman could feel proud of seeing her daughter married not only to a zoo employee but to an employee at the bottom of the repugnance ladder, the one who spent his time cleaning up lion shit and cutting up horses for their breakfast.

Elvira, Bulgado's wife, was fat and cheerful, a blonde in her thirties with very thick glasses, orthopedic shoes, and large, unexciting breasts: all the elements of a discreetly retarded woman. I understood immediately that it had been impossible for her mother to marry her to a boy of their class, and so she'd had recourse to Juan Bulgado, alias Johnny Angel or Johnny Lamb, an astute individual who didn't express himself badly, and who perhaps could have obtained a better job but who turned to the zoo for his own amusement, to defy the world and his mother-in-law. A piece, however, was missing in his skull: people don't waste their lives by accident. In Bulgado's case, there were certain indications: his obsession with a Hollywood actor, that was first. He told me he knew George Raft's pictures by heart, and when he was young he'd learned the actor's most solemn statements, he'd learned them in English, though Bulgado didn't speak the language. He was convinced that only a journalist of my stature, an entertainment reporter on the *Diario de la Marina*, could lead him to Raft when he came to Havana, which would happen any time now, since he'd been hired as a "greeter" at the Capri, a hotel that was about to open. The deal Bulgado proposed to me was this: I'd take him to the opening party, and in return he'd reveal the connection between the death of the hippopotamus at the zoo and the death of the capo in the barbershop. He'd give me only one piece of information in advance: three men had been involved in the animal's stampede, three common criminals who at the same time gave a warning to Anastasia's emissary, who'd been staying in a small hotel in Miramar. He didn't call the criminals by their names but by their aliases: "Buzzard," "Jar Boy," and "Turtle." They were forbidden to enter the zoo because in the past they'd stolen leopard cubs to sell to medicine men and other sorcerers, and they were suspected of occasionally stealing flamingos for the same purpose.

Bulgado's mother-in-law offered me a cup of coffee, which I drank with apprehension. I remembered that my mother had warned me, at a time when she still bothered to warn me about things: you take in evil with coffee, coffee can hide everything. You should never drink it in a strange house. And Bulgado, alias Johnny Angel or Johnny Lamb, was precisely that: totally strange, half a madman who claimed to know the keys to a murder that interested me.

I looked around. I'd never been in so crowded a room, where you could barely walk without tripping over china closets and end tables, and I asked myself where those paintings had come from, those glass cabinets and wall clocks, and in particular the half-mutilated piece that rose in the center of the room, several feet above the disorder: a Statue of Liberty, the most incomprehensible piece of junk, apparently made of galvanized metal.

"My father-in-law found it during a hurricane," Bulgado said proudly when he realized I was looking at it. "That was in 1903, wasn't it '03, Sarita?"

His mother-in-law pretended not to have heard him. Bulgado hadn't taken off his cap, and he raised it slightly to scratch his head, I could see he was a little embarrassed by the old woman ignoring him.

"It was in '03," he went on, "before I was born and before you were born. How could you have been born if you're still a kid?"

I lit a cigarette, as I usually did after coffee. For the moment, I'd survived the brew. Then I heard Bulgado say that the statue had been on the Paseo del Prado for many years, but the winds of that hurricane knocked it down and then kept pushing it through the streets. When it was all over, his father-in-law, who was a boy at the time, left his house, saw the statue, took it inside, and hid it in his room. Bulgado didn't know if anybody had claimed it, or if anybody took the trouble to look for it; maybe they thought it had shattered when it fell to the ground. He invited me to look at it up close, but I didn't have to get very close to realize it was an awful reproduction. It was hard for me to believe it had ever been on Prado, and I proposed to find out in the paper's archives if any statue like it had ever been lost. Elvira went up to it with a feather duster in her hand and began to dust it. I realized she was doing it for me, a show for the visitor; she was trying to attract attention with gestures that corresponded to her mental age: five or six years old. And at that moment, surrounded by those self-glorifying and to a point inexplicable creatures, I began to ask myself what I was doing there, but not only there, in the house of Juan Bulgado, his wife, and his mother-in-law, but here, in this country and this city, working for a paper where I was allowed to interview only comedians and whores. I had a feeling of nausea and blamed the coffee; I had another, less dramatic feeling: it occurred to me I'd become invisible, everything was so unreal, it was a passing moment and, to a point, a pleasant one, I'd never felt anything like it before, and I'd never feel it again. I imagine I turned pale, because Bulgado kept looking at me; he bowed his head, and I swear he was about to move his hand in front of my eyes, the way you do with people who've been hypnotized. After a minute, when I recovered, I got to my feet and promised him I'd arrange things so we could attend the opening party at the Capri. Once we were there, I'd take care of getting him together with George Raft.

He tilted his head back and narrowed his eyes, he turned them into a pair of inhuman slits. "You better not think I'm a faggot," he muttered in a threatening tone.

"Why would I think that?"

"I don't know, but just in case: there's nothing queer about me."

I said goodbye to his mother-in-law, who stared into my eyes, giving me an immense, grief-stricken look, as if she were saying: "Have pity on my decadence and my family's, forgive us for ending up like this." Her daughter, Elvira, shook my hand (she'd been trained to shake hands and greet people like a grown-up), and she also stared at me, her eyes full of happiness, of course. Only stupid people or killers are capable of giving that kind of brutally joyful look.

Bulgado accompanied me to the door, and we walked out to the street together. Suddenly he said he'd give me another piece of information, he was giving them to me with an eyedropper. He looked all around to make sure no one was watching and took a paper out of his pocket. There wasn't enough light on the street, but I managed to see the letterhead: "Hotel Residencial Rosita de Hornedo." I also saw the hotel's address and a phone number.

I looked up and discovered that Bulgado had become tense. I thought it was a joke, and I was going to say something, but he didn't let me. He raised his hand and used a funereal tone: "Wait . . . Now I'm not Johnny Lamb or Johnny Angel. For you, I'm Nick Cain."

If I'd known then that all those names corresponded to characters played by George Raft, I'd have felt calmer. But I didn't know or suspect anything. A madman with information is a hand grenade: pull the pin and you can explode along with him, that's what I thought. And still do.

"All right, Nick, let me see what you have," I murmured as I tried to take the paper. But he moved it away and kept it there for a few seconds, and then, suddenly, he put it in my hands. I discovered that it had writing on both sides, in block letters, in English. I didn't have the slightest intention of reading it there, in the middle of the street, and for the sake of courtesy I asked Bulgado if I could keep it.

"We have a deal," he muttered coldly. "For now that letter's yours, and you should know I'm giving you a treasure, but don't say my name. I don't know anything, I haven't given you anything."

He assured me that the letter came from the room of Louis Santos. He imagined that someone like me had to know who Santos was.

"Of course I know," I answered.

"Well, he lives in that hotel. With his one-armed girlfriend; he has a cutie who's missing an arm up to here . . . What do you think of that?"

I laughed out loud as I folded the paper and put it in my pocket. Bulgado followed what I was doing, his lips tightening in an expression that looked to me like rage, or regret. I tried to pretend that the letter didn't mean very much; as if, when I put it in my pocket, I was taking the first step in forgetting about it. I asked him to call me in a few days, which would give me time to find out about the party at the Capri. I got into my car and drove to the Sans Souci. The cabaret was on the outskirts of Havana; it had a casino and a bar that curved the entire length of the stage, much of it outdoors. I didn't know the club very well, I'd been there only a couple of times, the first time with my brother and his friends, giving the models the eye and trying our luck at roulette. On another occasion I went with my boss, Skinny T., for the opening of Edith Piaf. That night, a little while after she began, Piaf collapsed onstage, and people jumped from their seats. She was taken to her dressing room and brought back a few minutes later with her hair uncombed, her face livid, and she was just as livid when she finished the show, looking like a dead woman. They said it had been heatstroke, but Skinny T. told me not to believe it. I wrote an article based on the confidence of a guitar player: Piaf had fainted when she saw a former lover in the audience. It was the only one of my pieces my mother ever mentioned to me. She said she loved it and that maybe it suited me to be a reporter. I never knew if she really thought so or said it only to ingratiate herself with me and get the support she needed. She had her reasons. At that time, Papá had set up an apartment for Lidia, an employee at El Encanto, the famous shop where he bought his shirts. Lidia was young and docile, a girl my brother approved of; my father depended totally on the opinion of his son. I don't believe he ever trusted anyone else the way he trusted Santiago. My father told him about his life; they were identical, they were accomplices, and they had a good time together. I always envied that relationship, how could I not?

Before I went into the Sans Souci, in the half-light of the parking lot, I took out the paper that Bulgado had given me. If those notes had actually been stolen from Louis Santos (the nom de guerre of Santo Trafficante), the great irony was that I was about to go into his lair carrying them in my pocket. I read in a hurry, skipping lines: Trafficante was ordering somebody named Cappy to make a hotel reservation, three rooms and a suite, and to get women for four Cubans who were coming to New York. The four of them were going to negotiate the casino concession at the Havana Hilton, and the paper showed every sign of being authentic. I blessed Bulgado, and George Raft in passing for having dazzled him; there was no limit to my gratitude or my stupefaction.

The woman I was going to interview had made an appointment with me for ten, before the first show, which began at eleven-thirty. I went straight to the courtyard of dressing rooms. A bald, doglike individual with protruding eyes blocked my way. He said his name was Jacobs, and later I learned he was second in command at the Sans Souci. I showed him my press card and explained that Kary Rusi was expecting me; he forced a smile and pointed to the door of her dressing room, which had a star, and her name beside it. I knocked, and a woman opened the door, but I hardly noticed her because I immediately saw Kary Rusi, sitting at her dressing table, wrapped in a white robe, looking at me in the mirror. For the moment she couldn't or wouldn't hide her surprise. I was used to causing that kind of disappointment: the women all expect a hard-bitten reporter, a cynical guy who'll tear out their souls, and what they find instead is this cherubic-looking boy who detests writing about repertoire and wardrobe more than they can imagine. After their initial amazement they move on to pity: I look so young to them, beardless, almost childlike. And so, in the end, they forgive me my life and tell me about fantastic situations. They spend all the time in the world with me, something they don't even bother to give to more seasoned reporters.

"They're taking me to Las Vegas," she declared as soon as she saw me take out my notebook. "That's the most important thing that's happened to me."

The woman who opened the door for me also had the courtesy to pull over a chair so I could sit down next to Kary Rusi. It was then that I noticed her: a light-skinned mulatta, between twenty-eight and thirty, bony, downcast, with a mysterious birthmark on her forehead and another small one, much darker, on her chin. She had a black woman's cheekbones (we have to say everything), greenish, somewhat sunken eyes, and that natural pout, a plump, candid mouth that suggests slow, exquisite agony.

"This is Yolanda," said Kary Rusi, "the aerialist's mother."

I held out my hand, not really understanding the detail about the trapeze and her maternity. I felt the contact of her fingers, she gave me only her fingers. Very humble women, or very timid ones, tend to shake hands that way. As I pressed those fingers, I realized she was missing the other arm, or a good part of it. I saw her sleeve pinned up at the elbow and understood: there was no hand or forearm or elbow, what the hell was this? I was hypnotized and looked at her cleavage to become even more hypnotized; from there I moved up to her face, I looked at her eyes again and noticed that she was looking back at me; we had made an easy connection, with a little thread of fiery longing. Kary Rusi turned into the perfect stone guest, serenely watching us.

"Sit down," said Yolanda. "I was just leaving."

Everything I'd sensed in Bulgado's house, that feeling of having reached the limit, suddenly became solidified there. She didn't give me time for anything, she said goodbye to the performer, and to me she simply said "Pleased to meet you." I followed her with my eyes. I saw her walk out of the dressing room and into the night at the Sans Souci, and I sat there wondering if she could have her arm bent, hidden for some reason. It made me furious to think it might be a joke, a cabaret performer's trick. But the same fury that so frequently can blind us often throws light on the most unexpected points. Didn't Bulgado say that Trafficante's girlfriend had one arm? I looked at Kary Rusi. I know I should have asked her about Las Vegas, but I asked her something else:

"What aerialist are we talking about?"

"Yolanda's son's the one who jumps from the tree," Kary replied. "Haven't you seen the show yet?"

I shook my head. It was hard for me to believe that a woman so young could have a son old enough to take those kinds of risks.

I assured her I'd stay that night to see it. Then I shot questions at her, the ones I supposed she wanted to hear. It wasn't in my plans to challenge her or get any information from her that she might prefer to save for Don Galaor—"Ron Galeón" or "Galleon Rum," as we called the most famous of the reporters, a mature god who dazzled those women, a pretentious man who pretended to be incisive. I didn't give a damn about the interview, and so I let her shower me with facts, let her shine as she told me about the invitation she'd received to dance at the Stardust. I applied myself to taking notes because I was thinking about something else, about Yolanda: how had she lost her arm, and how long had she been involved with Trafficante? There were a couple of light taps on the door, and a man looked in. It was Jacobs, who saved my life by warning Kary that in just a few minutes she had to be ready to go onstage. I took the opportunity to tell him I needed a good table; I promised I'd also write about the show, a complete report, the Sans Souci in the eye of the hurricane. Jacobs stared at me;

he was a suspicious ox, he said he didn't want to mix the cabaret into politics. I assured him I never talked about politics or mixed into anything, the hurricane I was referring to was the nocturnal one, teeming with cabarets and hotels. He made a gesture of relief, muttered "Come with me," and I said goodbye to Kary Rusi, wishing her good luck in Las Vegas. I followed Jacobs like someone following a hippopotamus; his devastating advance ended in front of one of the maître d's, he told him to put me at the table set aside for the press.

He was about to leave when I decided to take the plunge. "Just a minute," I said. "Would it be possible to ask Señor Louis Santos a few questions?"

"Santos?" He dissimulated like a bull; he had beads of sweat on his bald head. "I don't know who you're talking about."

"Trafficante," I specified. I felt my mouth go dry. "Just a few questions about the cabaret."

Jacobs shook his head. "There's nobody here by that name."

He left, and I ordered a Tom Collins. I looked around for Yolanda. It was impossible to find anyone in the crowded room. I'd stayed to see her son, a boy who leaped in place of a dancer, an aerialist whose mother, delicate and one-armed, was a sign in the place of exile. I was nothing more than an exile in the Sans Souci or anywhere else. I lived uncomfortably in an invented house (my parents' house), in a bare city that at night was populated by corpses, bodies without eyes, without nails, often without tongues. I was pondering all this when the room grew dark and I heard the sound of drums, that's how the show began.

After an hour, the dancer disguised as a woodcutter climbed to the top of a tree—a real tree, one of those that grew near the area of the bar—pursued by the dance troupe, each of them disguised as something, a devil or a leafy branch. Exhausted by his pursuers, the woodcutter reached the edge of the abyss, and in an obscure exchange the aerialist replaced the dancer and threw himself into the void. Shouts and applause. The boy fell into a net the public couldn't see. I thought about his mother, who probably was frightened. It occurred to me that in a situation like this, someone ought to embrace her. I'd never embraced an unsymmetrical body and hadn't ever been embraced by someone who could do only half of it.

I finished the last of the Tom Collins and left at two in the morning.

Hotel Residencial
Rosita de Hornedo

Ave. PRIMERA Y CALLE O
MIRAMAR - HABANA

PIZARRA ROTATIVA
B-6561

THURSDAY AFTERNOON
WARWICK HOTEL
3 BED ROOM AND 1 SUITE.

THE MINISTER OF PUBLIC
WORKS WILL BE THERE
WITH MR MENDOZA, MR
SUAREZ, AND MR AGUIRRE
WHO IS THE HEAD OF
UNION WELFARE FUND WHO
IS BUILDING HOTEL.
CAPPY HAS TO GET THEM
WOMEN AND WHISKEY AS
THESE PEOPLE LIKE TO LIVE
IT UP. RAUL WILL BE
ALONG WITH THEM. THEY
ARE COMING THERE TO TALK

WITH HILTON SO HAVE YOUR
PEOPLE READY WITH
NAME OF PERSON WHO IS
TO FRONT PLACE AND
RUN IT ETC ETC..

THIS IS IMPORTANT: WE HAVE
TO HAVE COMPLETE CONTROL
OF CASINO: RAUL IS NOT TO
HAVE ANYTHING TO DO
WITH RUNNING CASINO. WE
HAVE TO TAKE CARE OF
RAUL IN SOME SMALL WAY
AS HE HAS BEEN VERY
INTERESTED IN THIS DEAL
WHICH I HAD TOLD HIM TO
WORK ON WHEN HE WAS
WITH ME AT SANS SOUCI.

THE KEY

I asked Santiago, the brother I hardly ever saw at home except for Sunday lunch, for help. Sunday was when Mamá cooked chicken and rice, a tradition her children despised and her husband was indifferent to; my father boasted of eating anything, even stones. Santiago led an intense social life. He was only on loan to us, he barely swallowed two mouthfuls because somebody was always waiting to have lunch with him someplace else, he'd tell me about it in a quiet voice. Often he hid the food in a napkin and then threw it in the toilet. During those lunches, Lucy looked like a corpse, pale and teary-eyed, not because of the food, which after all was merely a passing revulsion, but because she felt uncomfortable in her clothes and had to sit there in front of the entire family, especially in front of my mother and father, who separately were sarcastic but together became binomial acid, above all when they attempted to overlook the ambiguity (the great ambiguity that was Lucy) and called her, not without a certain irony, señorita. Won't the señorita have more rice?

At first Santiago said he had no idea who'd know about invitations to the opening party at the Capri, but he'd look into it. Two days later he knocked at the door to my room. "Lidia," he said, "has a sister who's a friend of somebody who'll let you in. She says you should call her next week."

Lidia was my father's mistress, whom I'd met not long before when I went to a restaurant in Chinatown late one night and ran into them, in the company of other couples, drinking beer and eating the soup of people who are up at dawn. When he saw me, Papá invited me to sit at the table with them and said: "I want you to meet Lidia." We were men, after all, and I shook hands with her and realized she was warm and whorish, with short nails and a sixth-grade education: the perfect companion. I felt very sorry for my mother, but the future of the family was a mass exodus.

When Bulgado called me at the end of the week, I told him we'd almost taken care of getting into the Capri, and then I'd introduce him to George Raft. But a deal was a deal, and when we left the hotel that night, he'd have to tell me everything: who hired the thugs that spooked the hippopotamus, and how he obtained the letter allegedly written by Santo Trafficante. Bulgado would only say: "Remember, I'm Nick Cain, and Nick Cain keeps his promises."

I let a few days go by before I called Kary Rusi. The interview I'd done with her at the Sans Souci ran an entire page, and she hadn't even bothered to call me at the paper to thank me, the way other performers usually did. When she heard my voice, she offered an excuse, but I said that wasn't why I called, I wanted to find out how to get in touch with the aerialist's mother.

"Yolanda?"

"That's right."

A woman who works in a cabaret doesn't need many explanations. Kary Rusi told me to wait a moment. I sat there like an idiot for a couple of minutes, holding the phone; I assumed she was looking for her friend's number, but I became impatient and was about to hang up when I heard another voice: "Yes, hello . . . This is Yolanda."

I had an English teacher at La Salle Academy who used to tell us that the most important quality in a boy was not his courage or his intelligence. None of that mattered if he didn't have reflexes, and reflexes were a savage attitude.

"This is Joaquín Porrata, from the *Diario de la Marina*. Where can we see each other?"

Yolanda, in her way, must have been half a savage too, I knew this as soon as I heard her laugh. First she was evasive, asking me if I'd enjoyed the show the other night, and then she said we could meet at the tables outside the Hotel Saratoga, back then they were called Aires Libres, or Open-Air Cafés. We agreed to meet the next day, at about ten in the evening, which was the time I left the paper. I felt a vague, awkward happiness. I'd taken the risk of calling a woman who was missing an arm, an undecipherable creature, half a person in the strict sense of the word. I haven't known a single one-armed person who wasn't violent, violent or stupid, it amounts to the same thing. But besides that, if what Bulgado said was true, then chances were she was Trafficante's girlfriend. There couldn't be another one-armed woman around the Sans Souci, she was the only one; I had to be cautious when I looked into that.

That's what I was thinking when I left the paper that night. I was thinking about Yolanda—precisely the person I was going to meet—about the possibility that the stump wouldn't let me concentrate in the way I should. I tried to imagine her naked, without her left arm. I wondered if it wouldn't have been better if she'd been missing a foot, for example. I was cutting off her limbs in my mind, as if I were getting rid of the evidence the way some criminals did; I tried to carve her up before I saw her again. Those little tables in front of the Saratoga were the perfect place for a meeting like this, the best anybody could imagine. If, when I saw her again, I discovered she was different from what I'd expected, I could get up and disappear without any fuss. That atmosphere made everything easier.

I got into the car and had just started the engine when I heard someone tapping at the window. It was dark, and all I saw was a hat. I hesitated a few seconds but then I lowered the window. His parrot's voice reassured me: "Don't tell me I scared you, Joaquín honey. How are things?"

It was Berto del Cañal, he covered entertainment for *Prensa Libre*. His colleagues called him "lily in a can" because he always dressed in white and drove a Packard the color of café con leche whose interior smelled of perfume, he claimed it was Germain Monteil's Fleur Sauvage, the only scent his wife used. He had a wife, though it might sound illogical, and a son as well, a lily bud about fifteen years old who often rode with him in his "can."

"They want to see you on Manrique, doll. I told them you were very happy at *la Marina*, but they insisted. I said I'd tell you, and that's what I'm doing."

Manrique was the street where the editorial offices of *Prensa Libre* were located. Berto handed me a card: it was the managing editor's, and a phone number was written along the side.

"Call them, you've nothing to lose. They want you for something, so they'll probably make you a nice offer."

I thanked him and headed for my meeting with Yolanda. For the moment, I couldn't think about anything else. I got there early enough to choose a nice table, have a couple of drinks, and watch her come along the sidewalk. There was a chance people would turn to look at her: Yolanda attracted attention, she looked something like the sweetheart of Tamakún, the Wandering Avenger, a character from my childhood, an adventurer on a radio serial who wore a turban, a mustache, and a sword. His sweetheart was a Circassian slave who was described as having dark skin, light eyes, and a beauty mark on her forehead. I ordered rum and tried to concentrate on the music; an all-female orchestra was playing a *danzón*. As it happened, the *danzón* was "Almendra" of happy memory. Something about Yolanda reminded me of Aurora, the mother of my friend Julián. Not physically, of course, the resemblance was on another plane, a level that may have been slightly allegorical, that originated in my head, and depended entirely on the way I perceived them and, in a sense, spied on them. I was considering this when I saw her cross the street, look around the tables, and see me when I stood and called her name. She was taller than I remembered, a little less bony, and she wore a very tight flowered dress that, to my horror, was sleeveless.

"I wasn't sure I'd recognize you," she said, extending her only hand. I replied that I, on the contrary, was certain I'd recognize her no matter where I saw her again. Yolanda made a gesture of disbelief. I asked her to sit down, and began by speaking to her about the aerialist, he had to be very young, almost a boy, how old was he?

"Eighteen," she said with a sigh. It's a mania of mothers: they always sigh when they mention the ages of their children. "I had him very young, I was sixteen."

I made the calculation in a second: thirty-four, maybe thirty-five. I didn't think she was so much older than me. It was perfect.

"And a year later I had the accident . . . they had to cut this chunk off."

She indicated her mutilated arm. I thought it pathetic that she dismissed everything she was lacking with that stupid word:

"chunk." Her fingers, her hand for pressing and caressing, her soft forearm were a chunk. Almost nothing. I called the waiter, and we ordered two drinks. The all-female orchestra was playing another *danzón*, "Isora Club"; it was a hot night, extremely hot, the absurdities of November. It seemed to me that Yolanda was accustomed not only to referring with great naturalness to her lack of an arm but also to drinking rum. I asked her straight out how the accident happened.

"It was because of my profession," she said with a dramatic inflection, "it was a deadly profession. Now I'm a secretary. I help artists like Kary Rusi, I take care of their correspondence, I organize their wardrobes, I go with them when they shop, and sometimes when they take a trip."

She paused, and I suggested going to Chinatown for something to eat. I usually was hungry when I left the paper and generally stopped off at some cafeteria and wolfed down a sandwich, but sometimes my body demanded an undecipherable soup, the kind of soup Cantonese cooks reinvented every night. We left the Aires Libres, I showed her to my car, the green Plymouth named Surprise. She asked if I was a bachelor, a pointless question because it was obvious in everything about me, in my manner and disposition. When we turned onto Zanja, the main street in Chinatown, we heard an explosion in the distance.

"Another bomb," Yolanda murmured, as if one had gone off earlier. "I'm afraid to go out at night."

"Afraid?" I asked, and took my hand off the steering wheel for a moment and placed it on hers, the most solitary hand I'd ever seen, and maybe the real survivor.

A short while later, arm in arm, we walked into the Pacífico, teeming with Chinese waiters and night owls. The Chinese never look straight at their patrons. But the night owls do; they looked at us from their tables, we weren't a very digestible couple, I'd say we were absurd. To begin with, Yolanda ordered "butterflies," tiny pieces of fried food that she dipped in sauce before putting them into her mouth. She chewed as if they were real butterflies, with a concealed fury that was like a key to a puzzle.

THE CIRCUS

Fantina. That's my real name. I know it sounds ridiculous, like an acrobat or a bearded lady, that's why, after the accident, I wanted to be called something else. I picked Yolanda because that's the name of my older sister, I don't know her, I don't even know where she lives, if she's still alive. Before she fell in love with my father and had me, Mamá had another family: a husband, some kids, a mother-in-law who lived with them and was a seamstress. But then a circus came to town—the town's named Coliseo, in Matanzas—and the magician traveling with the circus began to ask people if the place had a seamstress good enough to repair an important item for him. They said my mother's mother-in-law was the best in the area, they gave him the address, and the magician went there, with his cape under his arm. He was Portuguese, pretty old, about sixty, bald, with funny ears and a little red beard, the typical illusionist's goatee, a perfect Beelzebub. When he came into the house, Mamá was preparing lunch, but she felt as if the soul of that man had snared hers with a very thin hook and an invisible line that he used to pull, pull, pull her in until he caught her in his hand and put her in his mouth. She told me she'd seen it all: the man moving his hands as if he were pulling in the line, and then tasting, chewing on the soft little fish, her entire soul, like candy. Mamá would say that her mother-in-law hadn't noticed because she was busy mending the cape, and her children didn't either because they were too little. Yolanda, my older sister, was three then, and the boy, whose name was Fico, was less than a year old. Two days later, Mamá ran away from her home and her town. Her husband, who was a pharmacist's assistant, was desperate and went to find her, but on the way he ran into someone, a cousin, a girl my mother had asked to tell him that she'd never come back and that he should forgive her. She traveled with the circus until the magician fell sick and died. When he died, they looked through the man's papers, and that was when Mamá learned his real age, which was ninety. She told the circus people at the wake, but nobody could believe it. Next to her, crying for the dead magician at the coffin, was the woman who'd been his partenaire for years, a Chinese woman. The Portuguese called her "Chinita." He always called her that, when he put her in the case with the swords, or when he sawed her in half. Chinita here and Chinita there, nobody ever called her by her real name. Mamá suspected that this woman had once been the old man's lover, and maybe she still was, but she couldn't do anything because the Chinese woman was silent and respectful, she lived alone in her roulotte and walked looking down at the ground. My mother's mission was to cook and keep his traveling home clean, but she also had to brush his capes and the hats the rabbits came out of—they'd be covered with hair, shit, and sometimes piss, nothing smells worse than the piss of those animals. The magician and another man, the master of ceremonies, were the owners of the circus, and when the first one died, the second wanted to keep the entire show—the chest of swords and the chest of mirrors, which was wonderful, and even the books that taught the art of escape, though they were written in old Portuguese— for himself. My mother rebelled and said those things belonged to her; the Chinese woman helped her, she stood beside her and didn't let anybody touch anything, not even a magic wand. That softened my mother, she asked her what she'd do now, and Chinita said she'd have to find another magician to saw her in half, but that wasn't easy. With Chinita's savings, and the little the Portuguese had left them, the two women rented a room for themselves and another to store the chests; they spent a few days in mourning and then they went out to look for work. At the first circus they visited, the owner was as interested in the equipment as he was in my mother: she was so pretty she could dance the rumbas that closed the shows. The Chinese woman wasn't pretty or ugly, she was a bean, or a gnome, with scars on her legs and arms. Even so, she was taken on as a substitute partenaire, because the magician was an understanding man, a Panamanian who passed himself off as a Hindu and used the name Sindhi. Mamá didn't last very long as a dancer, because she got pregnant by a man who trained dogs (in an environment like that, there wasn't much to aspire to), and that was my beginning, that pregnancy brought me into the world, with a mild case of rickets and my eyes stuck shut so they thought I was blind, but no, they used some oil to open them, and I laughed when I saw the light. I grew up in the circus, my father teaching me about dogs and Chinita teaching me her profession, which was more difficult. When I was six, I performed my first routine: the magician covered me with a sheet, touched me with his wand, and when he pulled back the sheet all that was there were my clothes, my empty little shoes. When I was eight I was sawed for the first time. At the age of ten I did my first "Chinese torture": twelve swords and the spear, with me huddled inside the chest, hearing the screech of the sword edge against the wood, but I wasn't afraid and my mother wasn't either. Little by little she was separating from that world, and I traveled in the care of my father and Chinita, until Mamá faded away altogether, Papá died of a heart attack, and Chinita took charge of me; she disguised me as herself and taught me to say phrases in Cantonese. They thought up a kind of comic skit between the magician and me: Sindhi would ask me questions in Spanish and I'd answer in Chinese, and the people in the audience found that funny, the kids would double up with laughter. We traveled half of Cuba, once we passed through Coliseo, the town my mother had left. I was thirteen or fourteen and knew my brother and sister lived there, a girl named Yolanda and a boy, Fico. Unfortunately, they'd named me Fantina; it was the circus owner's idea, he was also my baptismal godfather. Chinita asked around town and went to the house where my mother had lived; she knocked on the door, the pharmacist's assistant answered, and she told him straight out that Tula's daughter was working in the circus (Tula was Mamá's name) and that meant she was the half sister of his own children. The news hit the pharmacist's assistant like a bomb; his eyes darkened with anger, and he shouted at Chinita that nobody even remembered Tula in that house, and his children didn't care if they had one sister or two, an acrobat or a roustabout, it was all the same to them. And he slammed the door in her face.

She didn't tell me about it right away since she knew I lived with the hope that my brother and sister would come to the matinee and be proud to see me work, not as an acrobat or a roustabout (roustabouts are the men who put up the tent), but with the magician, performing the most popular numbers. But it didn't happen, my brother and sister didn't come to the circus, and when we left Coliseo, Chinita put her arm around me and advised me to forget about them; they had to be sad because my mother left when they weren't even old enough to remember her face, and there was nothing crueler in this life than not being able to remember a mother's face, she knew that, she didn't have a mother or a father, and the only thing she saw in her mind when she tried to remember was the face of the Portuguese magician who brought her up. I asked if the magician had stolen her. And she said no, she was sure her parents gave her away when she was born, it was something they did in China: parents, when they were very poor, gave away females, and it didn't matter that they lived in Cuba, they'd gone on being poor and little Chinese girls were a burden.

Not long after that, there was a disaster at the circus. During the night performance, as he was beginning his number, the fire-eater started to retch, he got dizzy or lost his mind, he never could explain the reason, but before he should have, he spit out the flammable liquid in his mouth and his clothes caught fire, some sparks flew over the audience and fell on the seats, which were folding chairs, so dangerous when they're overturned. There weren't many people in the audience, which is why the tragedy wasn't worse, everybody managed to escape, but the fire-eater was in tatters, alive and conscious but roasted down to his soul, that's what the poor man was shouting. They took him to the clinic, and he died that same night. Then two policemen came to the circus to investigate, and when they asked who'd seen what happened, I stepped forward. They were asking me questions, some of them very stupid, you could tell they didn't know how a circus worked. The next day the show was canceled; in fact, we were leaving for another town, and one of the policemen followed me there, he waited for the show to be over and looked for me behind the tent: he asked me to marry him. Chinita grew sad, she said I was ruining my career, my future would be just like my mother's, and my children, the ones I'd have with that man, wouldn't remember my face either, because sooner or later I'd leave when a magician showed up on the street: magicians always come back and almost always have the same kind of woman with them. "You're just like Tula," I remember Chinita telling me, "you're not made to stay in one place." I thought it over and asked him to wait a few months, I'd have to pass through that town at the end of the tour, before we went back to Havana, and then I'd decide whether or not to get married. He wanted a romantic farewell; we saw each other every night, three in all, and on one of them I got pregnant. I'm light-skinned, and he was white. When my son was born, he had dark skin. That scared me, but Chinita calmed me down, saying that the boy—we named him Daniel—had almost been strangled by the umbilical cord, and the dark color, it was really purple, would fade. The midwife, to tease me, said: "What a nice throwback." I didn't know what a throwback was, but she explained it was what they called children born with skin darker than their parents'. Throwback or not, you can see what kind of boy I have, a phenomenal artist, terrific in the air, *almost a miracle, and I like to watch that miracle, stare at him when he's going to jump until my eyes start to hurt, I swear everything hurts, I want to die but I always watch. Daniel was little when the thing happened to my arm. It wasn't Sindhi's fault, I was distracted when I went into the box, and my heel caught, I tried to get free just as the doors were closing. I thought I'd be all right and so I didn't do anything to stop the show, but the sword came in, I couldn't put my arm in the right position, a good part of it was cut, I screamed, nobody in the audience heard me, but the world fell in on Sindhi. His voice trembled when he whispered, "Are you hurt, are you hurt?" I asked him to go on, I didn't want the kids to see me gushing blood, I didn't want to ruin the number. Sindhi kept putting in swords, but none of them could hurt me now. When he finished and opened the doors, there was a puddle of blood on the floor. The audience thought it was part of the trick. I had disappeared and wouldn't come out again because they'd taken me straight to the clinic. They treated me and bandaged me, but the wound got infected, and I was in a lot of pain. I almost died, and I told Chinita to take care of my son. Then I passed out. I was unconscious for a couple of days, and when I woke up my arm was gone. Chinita was beside me with the boy in her arms, Sindhi was there too, and the owner of the circus, my godfather, both of them crying, and they promised they'd never abandon me. I was sixteen, and I remembered my mother's face; I thought I remembered it. She heard about my accident and showed up again, then I realized that her real face had nothing to do with the face in my dreams, or with the face I guarded so carefully in my memory. Mamá left a little money for me, and during the afternoons she spent tending to me in the hospital bed she told me things, the whole story about the Portuguese magician who pulled her in with the little invisible hook. She advised me to find the father of my son, leave the circus and the Chinese woman too; it was time I stopped wandering around with strangers. I didn't listen to her. I stayed for several years with the only people I really considered my family, doing different jobs, like helping the owner of the circus with bookkeeping.*

I couldn't be sawed anymore, in a way I already was sawed. My son showed a liking for the trapeze; nobody gave him the idea, it was something he chose on his own. People should choose their lives, at least choose their names. Can you think of a shittier name than Fantina?

FISH AND EYES

Sometime later, I managed to interview Anastasia's bodyguard, errand boy, and occasional driver, a man nicknamed Cappy. He was rotting in jail, literally rotting. He was tubercular and had been abandoned to his fate. Anthony Coppola, which was his real name, agreed to write in my notebook, in his second-grade handwriting, the words Anastasia would growl when anybody contradicted him: "*Chi boni su li paroli de li muti.*" (The words of mutes are so pretty!)

He also told me that his boss, when he cleaned his revolver, or got ready to go out to settle accounts, used to sing an old Calabrese song. Cappy hummed it for me, and I still remember the plaintive way he sang the refrain: ". . . *sangu chiama sangu*" (blood calls for blood).

I wouldn't have known any of this if I hadn't gone to the interview with the people at *Prensa Libre*. And I almost didn't go. I didn't like the idea of working with Berto del Cañal in Entertainment. I had enough with my own cross, which was the pervert Skinny T., but at the *Diario de la Marina* at least they paid me a good salary, they weren't too fussy about my schedule, and I had a couple of nefarious colleagues with whom I could shoot craps on Thursday nights and then slip into the Mambo Club, one of those places that had photographs on display, though we never chose women using that system, we went there only to drink and let them cater to us because we wrote where we wrote: at the most powerful paper in the country.

The interview didn't take place at the editorial offices on Calle Manrique. They were very discreet; I suppose they didn't want it known ahead of time that they were recruiting a reporter from another daily. They made an appointment with me for midnight at the Mercado Único, another very popular place with night owls. The managing editor asked me to wait for him at one of the food stalls; he gave me explicit instructions regarding the stall, the arrangement of the stools at the semicircular counter, and even the name of the cook, a certain Aquino, whose specialty was fish and eyes soup, he called it that because along with pieces of fish, he put in the eyes he removed from the heads of the porgies and also added black olives, that was the joke. I arrived at a quarter past twelve and sat alone for a fairly long time, but as soon as Aquino brought me my soup, a man sitting a few stools away, who'd already finished his, stood and came to sit down next to me. He was carrying a copy of *Prensa Libre* under his arm.

"You're Joaquín Porrata, aren't you? I'm Madrazo."

We didn't shake hands, he didn't extend his hand and I felt I shouldn't force it. Later I thought the scene must have seemed pretty ridiculous. I quickly swallowed spoonfuls of soup without looking at anyone, like a child being forced to eat.

"We're interested in the story about Anastasia, it has a lot of loose ends."

An eye moved at the bottom of the bowl, a real eye, not an olive. It occurred to me that it came from another animal, that it wasn't from any fish; it was a sudden insight, something I'd have liked to rule out when I was alone. I'd never seen the managing editor at *Prensa Libre*, this Madrazo, before. I noticed his nose, which damaged his looks; he had acne scars, thin lips, and a movie star's smile, his teeth were very well cared for, there was even a gold edge on one canine. That surprised me: according to my father, gold on one's teeth was synonymous with pimps or hoodlums. And unconsciously I'd inherited his opinion.

"You were going to write something and they censored you, or is my information incorrect?"

I wondered who could have told him about the incident with Juan Diego. It couldn't have been Skinny T., he was like a tomb where the paper was concerned, servile down to the marrow of his bones, an obsequious rabbit capable of kissing the part of the desk where the editor of the *Diario de la Marina* rested his big two-toned shoes.

"I mixed two stories," I began warily. "The truth is they sent me to write up the shit that happened to the hippopotamus, and I found something else."

"You found gold," said Madrazo. "Listen carefully: Santiago Rey has forbidden the publication of a single word about Anastasia's death. Castillo is being watched and threatened, because we found something too."

Santiago Rey was minister of the interior. Castillo was the best investigative reporter in the country, a bloodhound who presented himself as infallible, that was his great defect. Recently he'd become melodramatic and lost his coldness, the last thing one should lose in this profession. Madrazo fell silent, because at that moment Aquino came over to serve us another two bowls of fish and eyes soup that nobody had ordered but that we didn't send back. On the side he set down a small plate with sliced lemons and plantain fritters.

61

"They say you have good files," Madrazo continued in a joking tone that infuriated me, "and that you know a lot about those people, I mean the big fish, who gives the orders and who takes them, who's in charge of each casino, where they live—"

"I don't have anything," I answered as quickly as I could. "I cover entertainment, with Skinny Tirso."

Madrazo lost his smile. The steam from the soup bothered him, or maybe it was the odor, period. The fact is that he pushed the bowl aside and turned to me, leaning forward until his nose was two inches from mine.

"Don't be a pain in the ass, Joaquín. I said for us to meet in this pigsty so we could talk. Did you know this is the only place where people can talk? That's how much I trust you: Aquino's on the *Prensa Libre* payroll. I know you're being wasted in cabarets, that's why I sent for you. Move over to Manrique."

The conversation made me hungry, or worried, I'm not sure which. I picked up a couple of plantain fritters and put them in the soup. I thought the fritters were like the eyes of some other monstrous animal, a larger fish, blinded on a whim.

"The offer is this: we'll pay you the same salary you get now, though you'll have to travel; we want you to go to New York."

He turned back, recovered his bowl, and began to eat soup, his second bowl of soup, without apparent enthusiasm, his mind focused on the next thing he was going to say. Madrazo assured me that Anastasia had moved heaven and earth to obtain control of the casino at the Hilton that was about to open in Havana, and had even asked for help from his brother, "Tough" Tony Anastasia, considered the master of the Brooklyn docks, to pressure the Cuban Gastronomic Union, whose funds were being used to build the hotel.

"They're already at war," Madrazo said, and as he chewed he made little cracking noises, as if the fritters were bursting between his teeth. "They're beginning to kill each other and nobody even knows if the hotel can be ready by March. But it's going to be a gold mine."

I looked up, I couldn't swallow more soup.

"Now you choose. Either you come over to Manrique and work on this story about important people, or you wash your hands and keep on interviewing Kary Rusi. You did interview her, didn't you?"

I burst into laughter—pure nerves. "I went and asked for Trafficante. Nobody knows him at the Sans Souci."

Madrazo guffawed, and a shower of saliva fell over his own soup. Then he gave me a condescending smile. I can't stand those damn smiles.

"Listen to me, kid: Trafficante's in New York. He's been there for days. That's what Castillo found out: our Santo left on the same flight with four Cubans, big fish who don't plan to give up an iota of their interests in the Hilton, do you get it now? They all stayed at the Warwick Hotel, celebrated that night at the Copacabana, invited Anastasia out to eat, and pumped Cappy for information—do you know who Coppola is?"

No, I didn't know, but I'd already seen his name in that mysterious letter Bulgado gave me: Cappy had been charged with getting women and whiskey for some guys accustomed to the high life, the letter said.

"They said they're bringing in Joe DiMaggio as the 'greeter' at the Hilton. Anastasia agreed, and they all went out to supper at Mario's. That happened three or four days before they shot your favorite hippopotamus to death."

Madrazo wasn't fat but he had a fat man's voice, that way of gasping and losing his breath after certain phrases. I was stunned; at that point I felt as if I didn't understand anything, it was too much information for my indecisive brain. I signaled to Aquino so I could order some rum, I needed a strong drink.

"I promised the man who works at the zoo that I'd take him to the opening of the Capri."

Madrazo didn't get it. He looked at me as if he were waiting for something else, another little clue.

"He's a guy who works there taking care of the lions, and he has a half-queer longing to meet George Raft. I want him to tell me what he says he knows about a message for Anastasia . . . I don't know, I don't think I lose anything if I take him to the Capri, and maybe he'll give me a good tip."

It was after two in the morning, and the owners of the daytime stalls were beginning to arrive at the market. There was a din of crates banging into one another, voices different from the voices of those who stayed up all night. Aquino yawned several times, and Madrazo and I drank down our rum in silence. Then he took out a couple of bills, he didn't even ask how much he owed, he put them on the counter, and Aquino picked them up right away.

"What the hell," Madrazo mumbled, "I'm thinking right now about one of Raft's movies, it's one he made with James Cagney, I saw it when I was a kid."

I thought about Bulgado, it was the kind of conversation where he'd shine.

"They put Raft in prison, and he meets Cagney, who's a reporter but he's in jail, and Raft goes to him and says: 'Write a piece about me. I like my name in the paper.' Sometimes I say that to fuck around with the boys at the paper. It's a pretty old movie, you must have been very little when it came out, or probably you weren't even born yet. How old are you?"

"Twenty-five," I lied. "I just had my birthday."

After that, Madrazo suggested we leave. "Each one separately," he recommended in a low voice. "Think about my offer."

"All night," I promised. "I'll let you know tomorrow."

"All night" was just a figure of speech, in no time it would begin to grow light. In any case, my decision was made. And my time, the rest of the night till dawn, was free, so I could give myself over to a single thought: Yolanda, the chest with the swords, a stream of blood trickling into the corners of that damn trick. A dangerous love was beginning; I knew because I didn't feel sorry for her at all, there was no pity in the way I wanted to shelter her, in my passion for holding her. I was going naked to the sacrifice, without the consolation that later on coldness would save me, or disdain. There can be no disdain where there was no compassion first.

When I got home and turned on the light, I saw my mother and was startled, though I didn't want to show it. She said she was waiting for me because she'd heard sirens and bombs exploding. I told her I knew how to take care of myself and she could sleep easy. I said it in a tone that left no doubt: I was excluding her, I always had, who knows for how long, ever since I came out of her womb. Probably ever since then.

"Your brother hasn't come home yet either," Mamá added.

"Don't worry about him. He's probably in bed by now, he's always in some bed with somebody."

Mamá nodded with an expression that was unusual for her, I had the impression she was going to burst into tears, but no. She got up and left. It was impossible to tell if Papá was in the house or not. He was pretty unpredictable about that: for a week he'd come straight home from the office at six in the evening, and for another week, day after day, there'd be no sign of him until three or four in the morning.

I went to the kitchen and opened a can of anchovies. I ate

without hunger, for the pleasure of spearing the little rolls with a toothpick and washing them down with beer. I had to tell Papá I was going to another paper. After all, it was thanks to him that I'd gotten on the *Diario de la Marina*, but now I was leaving it, going away. Never again would I wait in the reception areas of radio stations. No more going to the airport to greet Juanita Reina or Renato Carosone, what did I care about them? No more competition with Pacopé or Don Galaor (alias Galleon Rum), much less the Gondolier, that scarecrow who went up and down the canals picking up the best exclusives. I was ending it there, saying goodbye to Skinny T. and turning my efforts to the mystery surrounding the death of Fat A. It was the journalism I'd always dreamed of writing. The opportunity I'd been looking for for so long.

A hippopotamus had done it all.

APALACHIN

It was my second day at *Prensa Libre*. For the moment, my work consisted of organizing and classifying information about an enormous hotel project that was being cooked up in the shadows: fifty hotels at different sites in the country, opening into a fan of perfect places, from the banks of the Jaimanitas River to the beach at Varadero. The first would be the Montecarlo, to the west of Havana. They told me to go over the documents and open a file with the names of the shareholders. I was doing that, whistling a Frank Sinatra song because I'd just found his name among the future owners, when Madrazo came over and said: "What's doing?" I held up the paper, showed him Sinatra's name, and while I was showing it to him I stopped whistling the tune and sang it very softly: "How little we know, how much to discover . . ." I really enjoyed digging through those documents. Interesting names from here and from up there would surface, my file grew fatter by the minute, and still there were too many loose ends: the song fit the situation like a glove. That's why Madrazo's indifference annoyed me. He tossed the paper aside and took a breath with an expression that was weary, or very studied, or perhaps cynical: cynicism is sheer exhaustion. He looked around to make certain no one could hear him.

"Trafficante's been arrested," he said quietly, in a very soft tone. "That's what they're saying, it has to be confirmed. There was a meeting in New York, somebody tipped off the police, and they got them all."

The song froze on my lips. The little bit I had, the little I'd been able to find out through Yolanda (who, incidentally, was offended when she denied any amorous link to the owner of the Sans Souci), was that Trafficante had gone to New York to get some dice tables, the most modern on the market, a design that had already been tried out in Las Vegas. But I didn't buy it. I had a hunch Trafficante had been sent by Lansky, an old fox who pretended to be semi-retired from business, to warn them that interlopers wouldn't be tolerated in Havana. What happened to the hippopotamus had been an error in calculation: it was assumed they'd frighten and kill the animal in mid-October, so that Anastasia's scouting party, which was in Havana at the time, would get the message before it was too late. And the message was that they should back off and stop pressuring and bribing. Anastasia had come in like a bull; his enormous nose had smelled the aromas of an impossible stew: fifty hotels in a row, on an imaginary line overflowing with power, extravagance, inconceivable sums of money. I supposed that Trafficante was carrying the message in order to deliver it in exactly the right place, to two or three representatives of the New York Mafia. What I didn't imagine was that he'd go to a full-fledged convention of notorious families from various states in the house of Joseph Barbara, a man who'd always known how to sit squarely on the fence.

"Get ready." Madrazo hurried me along. "We'll find out if there's a flight this afternoon."

They wanted to anticipate the censorship. Their aim was to have the report ready in a couple of days. In that time I'd have to confirm the arrests, especially that of the owner of the Sans Souci, and compile the facts necessary to connect a meeting of the underworld with the casino business in Havana and the construction of the new hotels. Madrazo said the magic word:

"Apalachin. It's a village northwest of New York, near some lakes, or a river, I don't really know. It must be near something. That's where they held the meeting."

I collected my papers and called Bulgado. His mother-in-law told me he'd just left for the zoo. I hung up and called Yolanda. She answered on the first ring, and that detail moved me: a woman missing an arm will try to compensate by reacting quickly, especially to the small details of daily life. I explained that I was going on a trip and wanted to have lunch with her. She asked when I was leaving. It was what I wanted, the melodramatic effect of a sudden departure.

"This afternoon," I replied. "It's almost time."

I was putting her on the spot, and she must have been thinking about the next thing she'd say. Certainly she bit her lip, wondering if this lunch would be decisive.

"The paper's sending me to write some articles," I added, "and since I just started here I can't refuse."

She stopped biting her lip and asked where they were sending me.

"New York, just imagine. Are we having lunch or not?"

After the meeting that led to our eating at the Pacífico, we'd seen each other twice, both times to go to the movies, very guilelessly, because afterward we had ice cream at the América Cafeteria or El Carmelo. On both occasions she insisted on how much she disliked her name. I consoled her by saying that Fantina was an easy name, thought up so children would learn it right away, but really it was enigmatic, depending on the person who said it. I took the opportunity to say that in time maybe she'd help me understand what happened in the circus, which I'd despised since I was a kid because it seemed absurd, and my sister reacted in the same way. Except that, for her, a halo of illusion had remained. I didn't know it then; I found out many years later, when Mamá died, during the depressing night we spent alone in the funeral home. That was where my sister told me in whispers that the first woman who seduced her was in the circus, and she wasn't a dwarf or an acrobat but someone in the audience, a lady like our mother who'd brought her little son. Lucy calculated that she must have been about twelve, she wasn't sure if she was twelve or thirteen, what she was sure about was that she already had breasts. The woman said she was going for some cotton candy and asked Mamá if she could watch her little boy, it would be only a few minutes. And then, as if she'd just thought of it, she asked Lucy if she wanted to go with her. Lucy looked at Mamá, and Mamá said she could, since the woman probably looked like a good person. It's true they bought cotton candy, but instead of walk-ing back to the tent, they took a path that went behind the cages, where it was very dark and smelled of elephant shit. The woman suddenly bent over and kissed Lucy on the mouth. I believe my sister must have seemed happy, because after the kiss they embraced, touched each other a little, returned in silence to the tent where Mamá was uneasy, waiting for them. The cotton candy was dirty. Lucy felt transformed and the woman triumphant for having hit the bull's-eye.

"I'll fry you a steak," said Yolanda. "What time will you be here?"

It was something new. We wouldn't eat out. A Cuban woman getting ready for sex prepares steak. I suspected it then and have proved it over the years. Yolanda emphasized "steak" and on the other end of the telephone my face burned. I promised I'd be at her house at one. I gathered up my papers and left for the zoo. I found Bulgado with his assistant, cutting up a mule. He wore high boots and a rubber apron. His face was spattered with blood.

"I need you to do me a favor," I shouted at him unnecessarily; there was no noise and I could have spoken in a different tone, but the mule's blood, the butchered meat, it all shocked me. Bulgado asked me to wait for him outside. I said I'd take a walk and be back in half an hour. I took off my jacket and walked for a while in the sun; my shirt became soaked, and I decided to sit down. In front of me was a pool, and I realized that by sheer chance I'd stopped at the place where the murdered hippopotamus had lived. An unmistakable stink was in the air; it wasn't the ordinary stink of excrement but something else, a distant odor of rot. Another hippopotamus, I suspect it was the inconsolable female, raised her head out of the water and snorted. I took out my notebook and began to write a kind of plan. The first thing would be to get to Apalachin, find a boardinghouse to stay in, and gather impressions. Later, when I returned to New York, I'd have the chance to learn new angles on Anastasia's death. Before anything else, I wanted to interview Cappy, the man arrested the day after the murder on the strange charges of "vagrancy" and being "a material witness." Then I'd try to talk to the barber who was shaving Anastasia when they shot him—it wasn't his usual barber—who, according to the information that had come over the Teletype, answered to the name of Anthony Arbissi and lived in Brooklyn.

I didn't have to go back to the slaughter pen because Bulgado came out to meet me. He had a suspicious air and asked if something had happened. I shook my head.

"I know we have a deal," I began carefully, "but something has come up, and I leave tonight for the United States."

Bulgado gave me a grief-stricken look.

"Then you won't be here for the party with Raft."

"Of course I will. That's not for a while, at least ten days, and I'll be back in five or six."

With hands still stained by mule's blood, he lit a cigarette. I didn't want to let up on him.

"You have to understand, Nick, Johnny . . . what do you want me to call you today? The paper's sending me because of what happened to Anastasia. They're asking me to find out more, but I can't find out anything if you don't tell me how you got that paper, the letter from Trafficante. I don't even know if it's real."

"A woman gave it to me," said Bulgado, smoking solemnly and looking very serious. "She's a friend of mine who cleans rooms at the Rosita de Hornedo hotel; my wife and my mother-in-law can't know about it. From time to time we get together, and I help her out with something. She has a husband, but he's in jail."

A love story, and a repulsive one, considering that the adulterous passion between a chambermaid dedicated to spying and a brutal lion keeper, a mule hacked to pieces in the middle, had to unfold in a distinctive way, with different rules and a different kind of courtship.

"The same thing happened to me that happened to George Raft," Bulgado boasted. "Didn't you see that movie where he works as a bail bondsman and falls in love with a woman whose husband's in jail?"

I shook my head.

"Well, this one hid a few things from me: that she was married and her husband was serving a sentence for robbery. I tell her my name is Vince, like Raft in the movie, and the bitch laughs, she knows it isn't true."

Bulgado pronounced the name "bean-say." I felt that I was running out of time.

"And how does the hippopotamus fit in?"

"At a zoo you can do a lot of favors," he mumbled, confessing. "I've done them myself, not very often, two or three times at most. I never killed anybody, no, but horse meat is easy to mix, understand what I'm saying? There's Lázaro, the black who helps me, he takes care of bringing in certain packages, large packages, from the neck down, you follow me? We don't see anybody's face, he brings them in without heads, he cuts them up and mixes them in with the pieces of an animal, a horse or whatever, that we feed the lions for lunch. I've told you this, but now erase it. I didn't say anything."

I erased it in part. I was still concerned about the letter attributed to Trafficante. I hadn't completely swallowed the story about the zookeeper's chambermaid lover who instead of calling him Bulgado, Johnny, or Nick, called him Vince, which she surely pronounced "bean-say" too.

"We've talked a lot," I said, as if I were becoming resigned, "and you still don't trust me. You haven't even told me who gave the order to let the hippopotamus out."

Bulgado smiled. His smile was shrewd, or completely mistrustful, only a very vague and indistinct line separates one thing from the other.

"Somebody named Raúl," he revealed suddenly. "They say he worked at the Sans Souci, but I'm not sure about that. He has a club called Club 21, I've never been there. He was the one who hired Buzzard, and Buzzard found himself some helpers, two blacks who are always with him: Jar Boy and Turtle. The three of them arranged for the hippopotamus to escape, those animals like to run at night, they shit while they run and scatter all the shit with their tails. I don't know who called the soldiers, but they came and shot the angel. I say he must be an angel, an innocent that died for no reason."

We fell silent and sat looking at the pool; the heat was growing worse and the "poor widow" stayed under water. I told Bulgado I'd be in touch with him as soon as I got back and wouldn't break my promise to take him to the opening party at the Capri for anything in the world. Then I rushed to my house to pick up what I needed and throw some clothes in a bag. My mother was on the phone and saw me pass by as if she were seeing a ghost; she gave a start, she wasn't expecting me at that time of day, much less expecting to see me leave again after a few minutes with a raincoat over my arm and an ancient suitcase. She didn't even finish her conversation. I heard her say: "I'll call you right back, Aurora." I shivered. Aurora was a thorn in my memory (the part of memory that you keep in your lower belly). I hadn't seen her for a long time. I estimated a couple of years had gone by since I was last in her house, when Julián had an accident, or not exactly an accident but a fight with a jai alai player. In those days he lived and died at the frontón, and he tried to take a girlfriend away from one of the players. He used a very human trick: he told the girl that in his free time the player was seeing another man. She didn't believe him, no girlfriend is prepared to believe the truth. The player, who'd just broken off with the other man, a well-known architect—maybe that's why he was devastated—took his revenge on Julián; he hit him more times than he deserved for so small a thing. I remember that Aurora was grief-stricken when she received me, and I remember too that Julián, motionless in his bed, admitted that one of his ribs had been knocked all the way into his cracklings, that's the phrase he used, and it was a miracle he was still alive to tell the tale. When it was time for me to go and Aurora walked with me to the door, I threw myself at her and tried to kiss her. She shoved me away and told me never to come back to her house; she was suffering too much at seeing her son in that state to let another person do the same thing to her friend's son. That other person was undoubtedly the man I'd seen with her dancing to "Almendra." They were still together, they had been for years, and recently he'd taken to spending the night at her house since Julián was hardly ever there. Aurora had just realized there was very little left of the boy she used to invite to the movies so her son wouldn't feel lonely. Or what was essential was left: a spasm in time, a painful way of spying on her, nothing that wouldn't have survived with courage and desire.

"Where are you going?"

Mamá was frightened, I could hear it in her voice, see it in the way she opened her eyes wide when she understood that everything in the house had gone too far.

"I borrowed Santiago's raincoat," I answered. "Tell him for me, I don't have time to wait for him."

"I asked you where you're going," she said slowly, as if she were talking to a wall, the suddenly unknown wall that was her son who'd just turned twenty-two.

"New York. You know I began at *Prensa Libre*, and they want me to do an article there."

"An article about what?"

"About a meeting, and some people who were arrested."

I told her the truth because I was in a hurry and too lazy to tell her anything else. To say, for example, that it was no concern of hers, which supposed an effort, a determined tone of voice. And I was too lazy to tell her a lie, to set my imagination working to invent an excuse that had nothing to do with reality.

"When are you leaving?"

Mamá was beginning to drive me crazy. I put the suitcase down and loosened my tie. I wanted to go to Yolanda's house with my tie loosened.

"This afternoon. I'll call you from New York. I'll be at the Park Sheraton."

I said it for no reason, but the idea excited me, why hadn't I thought of it before? I'd ask Madrazo to make my reservation there. When I said Park Sheraton, flashes in the barbershop passed through my mind, two shots, one of them sounded sharper, and Anastasia collapsed, still alive. He dragged himself from the chair where he was being shaved to the one beside it, and there he made a final effort to stand, but it was useless, he slipped in his own blood and instinctively felt his pocket. In his wallet he carried the small print of St. Francis of Assisi that his wife, Elsa, had given him, and photographs of his four children: the youngest a girl eight months old, and the oldest a man my age.

"Park Sheraton?"

"Yes, Mamá. Fifty-fifth and Seventh."

I closed the door delicately and got into the car feeling cheerful, happy at having controlled myself and behaved like a sweet son. For his part, Santiago would be happy to know that his brother was traveling to New York, a city, he said, that had excited him from the first moment he set foot in it. I was sure he wouldn't give a damn that I'd taken his raincoat; on the contrary, he'd be glad it fit me. That's how my brother was, generous with what he had plenty of.

I headed for Yolanda's apartment, located on the fourth floor of a building near the university. From the street I looked up at her balcony; one door was closed and the other open. I supposed she'd been there waiting for me, uneasy because I hadn't arrived at the time we agreed on, until she caught sight of the big green Plymouth that wasn't called Surprise for nothing. Only then did she go back into the apartment and take out the pan to fry the meat. I was thinking all this in the elevator, and suddenly I realized I hadn't bought her anything, not even flowers or candy, not even a bottle of Marsala All'uovo, Mamá's favorite liquor, it would have been so easy to take one from the bar. All I'd brought was the melodrama of having to leave in an hour, an hour and a half at the most. That shakes women. That tension involving the clock.

A little later, as she was getting up from the bed where we made love for the first time, Yolanda had a strange reaction, a kind of female phosphorescence, a hybrid between rancor and intuition.

"What an odd name that place has."

I asked her what place she was referring to.

"The one you're going to write about."

"Apalachin? I don't know, does it seem odd to you?"

She chose to remain silent. I heard her moving around the kitchen, and I heard the hot fat sizzle. I looked around and saw that I was in a clean, cared-for apartment; it moved me that she could do everything with her one slim arm. I closed my eyes. From that moment on, Apalachin was a better place.

IN AN ASIAN PARADISE

Just a while ago, while I was seasoning the meat, I thought about Chinita. When I was fifteen and wanted to marry that policeman, she advised me not to, she said I was too much like my mother and wasn't made to stay in one place. Later, when I lost my arm, I didn't dare reproach her for anything, I didn't say that if I'd gone to live with that man, like he asked me to, I'd have left the circus and the accident wouldn't have happened. The past is past, and I didn't want to hurt her, she was the one who brought it up. After a few months, when I was adjusting to the idea that I'd never again be the woman I used to be, Chinita came and begged my pardon. She began to cry and blamed herself for having given me bad advice. "You'd be in that town today," she said, "with both your arms, and you'd probably have more children." I said that was true, but she ought to remember what she'd said to persuade me: magicians always come back, and generally they bring the same kind of woman with them. Maybe if I'd married that man— he did get me pregnant, though he never found out and never met his son—I'd have made him unhappy, I might have left him and my son too, and today the boy wouldn't be able to remember my face. When I least expected it, a circus might have come to town, a magician might have walked down the street, and just like my mother was caught, I'd have been caught with an invisible hook and an invisible line, and even my invisible soul would have left my body and gone to the newcomer. And then it did leave after all, not because of a magician's illusion but because of Roderico Neyra.

Ten years after I lost my arm I was still with the circus, helping out wherever they needed me. I even fed the lions once when the lion tamer was sick. Chinita wanted to stop me but I didn't listen to her, she was terrified that the animals would bite the only arm I had left, but here it is, I still have it. Lions respect women a lot, I realized that, they can tell the sexes apart. Other animals can't.

Daniel, my son, was growing up, Chinita treated him well, she was like his grandmother. The principal aerialist in the circus caught him one day by the arms and began to teach him; he and his wife had no children and they did some wishful thinking about mine. But at some point it seems they realized the boy really had talent; they stopped cold and talked it over with me, it all depended on me: if I wanted them to, they'd go on training him. If I didn't, they'd leave it there and just teach him some tricks. I said I wasn't afraid, and if my son liked the trapeze I'd like it too. And so they went on, with serious training every day, and when Daniel began school they prepared routines for him to practice in the afternoon, exercises that they showed me how to supervise. This was when I decided to leave the circus and find work in Havana. History seemed to repeat itself, because Chinita insisted on taking care of Daniel, like years earlier she'd insisted on taking care of me. Except I wasn't like my mother, I had no desire to separate from my son, he was staying because of the trapeze, at that stage he couldn't stop practicing. Chinita promised me she'd take care of him and feed him, though I thought it would end up reversed and my son would take care of her, because lately she'd become very thin; one night she went to bed a young Chinese woman and the next morning she got up an old Chinese woman, just like that, with no warning. It really affected me, but I hid it, she had to have felt the change, that great blow of the years. I found work with Loretta, from the dance team Loretta and Johnson; in those days they came to the Tropicana more often and stayed in Cuba for several months. I did for her the same thing I do now for Kary Rusi: I organized her wardrobe, kept her accounts, occasionally answered letters for her, and most important, I kept her company and got her out of difficulties, the kinds of difficulties that are bound to come up in cabarets.

I'll never forget my first day of work. I close my eyes and see the girls, the dancers rehearsing, the models waiting their turns, wearing rollers in their hair, and the employees in their undershirts sweeping around the tables, cigarettes dangling from their lips. I have it all etched in here, down to the last detail, because on that day Roderico didn't throw me a hook, it was a harpoon that flew straight from his heart to mine, though he wasn't aware of anything, his mind didn't know, it was concentrating too hard on the show. Loretta had to rehearse with Johnson and was there for a while, watching a dance with little Chinese lanterns, because the new production was called In an Asian Paradise. *When the number with the lanterns was over, she told me she was going with Johnson to settle something about his wardrobe, and I should wait for her at one of the tables. That's what I did, I sat down and looked around, I'd never been in the Tropicana. I liked that world, it was so similar to the circus—sometimes they drew back the roof, sometimes not, that day you could see the sky—and the sounds and voices of the rehearsal were so different from the sounds and voices of the real show. And at that moment Roderico spoke, but didn't speak, a roar came out of his throat: "Odalys, you damn whore, you never gave anybody your ass? Well, move it like you were giving it away." All my blood rose to my face, I gasped for air and felt like I was dying of embarrassment, because even though I'd given birth to a child, I was basically very innocent, I'd never heard anything so disgusting, so insulting, people didn't talk like that in the circus. One of the dancers stopped her number, walked to the front, to the very edge of the platform: "Rode, my love, can't you see I* am *moving it?" Roderico took a few steps forward, stopped in a spot where the sun shone on him, I saw him very clearly, this is the image that opened my eyes, a profile on a melted coin that disturbed my sight, as if the light had bounced off him and was blinding me. You know him, you must have seen him so often, you know he has that nose, half eaten by tigers, just like one of his ears, he has an ear that's all chewed up. Then I looked at his feet, I noticed the tips of his shoes, they turned up, like he was a little elf, I thought it was intentional. "Don't fuck with me," he shouted again. "Move your ass, girl, and you too, Olguita, do I damn well have to diddle you to wake you up?" My mouth felt dry, I looked around to see if anyone else was shocked, but no: the men sweeping around the tables kept sweeping and didn't even look up. Onstage, none of the dancers protested, in fact, the rehearsal continued and it seemed to me they were obeying him and moving better than before. They left the stage, and the models paraded by with their necks held straight, like they were carrying great weights on their heads, though rollers were all they were carrying. After a while I learned they had to do that, pretend the rollers weighed a lot, since in the show they were decked out with crests of feathers and jewels and as much extra ballast as the designers could think up. Loretta came back, gave me instructions, I had to put her dressing room in order (she was handing me the key very solemnly) and get her some sodas to drink after the rehearsal. I didn't say anything to her about the impression the overseer had made on me, he reminded me of an overseer, I still didn't know he was the creator of famous productions, a powerful artist in Cuba, the god of the Tropicana. I didn't know anything, but I had a hunch that somehow he was the magician that fate had in store for me. It was a feeling of horror but also of relief, and when I went into Loretta's dressing room to organize her things and become familiar with her tastes, I was hopeful, because I thought that in the next few days I'd have the opportunity to see him again, that ugly, really ugly individual, a kinky-haired mulatto with a mouth like a sewer, who for the moment had only one quality: knowing that the thing that moves us most is the memory of what we've given. That was the point that changed me. I admired him from the moment I saw him, or from the moment I heard him, I don't know any other way to talk about it. When Loretta came back from rehearsal, covered with sweat, her plush robe over her shoulders, I asked her who the man was who was shouting at the dancers. She thought about it for a few seconds: "Ah, you mean Rodney?" She spoke Spanish pretty well but she called him by his stage name, she thought Roderico was unpronounceable. I wanted to know if he'd had an accident, I said that because of his nose. Loretta took a few sips of warm soda, took off her robe, I handed her a towel, and she said "leprosy." I don't know English but I'm not that stupid, and when I heard her say "leprosy" in English I thought of St. Lazarus, of the sick people I'd seen around the sanctuary. I thought it was a beggar's disease. Then it occurred to me that it was a joke and Loretta might be kidding. I went up to her and said, seriously, "Is it really leprosy?" Even more seriously, she nodded. "Yes, leprosy, leprosy, leprosy . . ." She repeated the word in Spanish, maybe to memorize it, and she didn't say it again in English. I felt strange and asked if I could drink one of her sodas. How do you approach a man who's crumbling away?*

The first days passed and I would come to the Tropicana punctually, an hour before Loretta and Johnson arrived. When she came into the dressing room, I had her clothes ready for rehearsal, and then at night I did the same thing, but for the show. A week later, when I was going to get sodas one afternoon, I ran into Roderico at the bar. He smiled when he saw me, told me to wait, and I realized he wanted to talk to me: "If you weren't missing that arm, I'd hire you as a model." He was sincere; we looked into each other's eyes, and he gave a little laugh, I saw his teeth for the first time, they were dark, I don't know if it was because of cigarettes or his disease. He asked me how it had happened. "It was an accident," I rasped, my voice wouldn't come out. "I used to be in the circus . . ." He smelled of perfume, I liked his twisted face, the sad way he held his cigarette: he still holds it that way, far down, near the base of his fingers, so that when he lifts it to his lips, his entire hand covers his face, like a lean, slow-moving spider. He invited me to have coffee. I realized that everyone treated him with respect, the artists because he hired them, but the employees too because they were sure of one thing: the great Rodney, a man who came from nothing, from some godforsaken village in Oriente, can help them when he wants to; he can get them a raise in salary, but he can also crush a person, destroy him, simply because he catches that person looking at him with revulsion. We had coffee, he became interested in my story, it didn't embarrass him to keep repeating that I'd have made a good model in his productions except for my arm, it wasn't possible to put a woman onstage in a situation like that—he said "situation"—unless, he added, and his face lit up, he created a production with the theme of Greece and the Venus de Milo. He told me it was a famous statue missing both arms. "For the production I'll cut this one off," he joked, pressing the only one I had with his damaged fingers, which didn't feel like fingers on my skin but like something else, like a bird's claws, a stuffed bird that only seemed to be grasping something. I sensed he felt comfortable with me; after all, we shared an emotion, a sorrow, we were disabled, he in his way and I in mine. I realized that the lit end of the cigarette was beginning to touch his fingers, though he might not feel it. I told him he was burning himself, and he put it down right away but lit another one, and as he was lighting it he stared at me. "You have the look of a Siamese wolf." I took this as a hint, a little hook that suddenly left his mouth and headed for mine. When each of us went back to work—he was rehearsing In an Asian Paradise and I was taking care of Loretta's things—I realized we were connected, hooked on a plane that wasn't of the spirit, or the soul, or any of that foolishness, we were hooked in the flesh, in misery, in the language known only to a damaged body. The next day, one of the seamstresses came to Loretta's dressing room to fix her outfit, it had ripped during one of her leaps—Loretta would leap into Johnson's arms, it was almost like the circus—and while she was looking at the tear, she lowered her voice to say: "Rode is taking gold injections, real gold, they say it cures his disease." I was looking through some magazines for photographs or articles that mentioned Loretta and Johnson, and I stopped cold. Without turning to them, I decided to ask a question: "Who's Rode married to?" I could hear the silence, as if I'd opened a bottle of smoke and the smoke had filled the dressing room. "He's not married to anybody," said the seamstress, "can't you tell he's a fag?" I kept looking through the magazine, but I felt my stomach contract; it was an extreme sensation, no pain or vomiting, just that stone here, spinning around a bottomless well. "No, I didn't think he was." It was my voice, my own stone defending itself. The seamstress gave me a mocking look but didn't say anything else.

The days that followed were all the same, the routine of rehearsals and Roderico's impatience, he was always dissatisfied, always shouting insults. He didn't look for me, and we didn't run into each other again. When I could, I'd stop to watch him from a certain distance, I saw him smoking, walking back and forth with his strange gait and misshapen shoes, he looked as comical as a clown. But he was the boss, the man in command of an army of dancers, choreographers, singers, and dance teams like Loretta and Johnson, or Ana Gloria and Rolando, or Peggy and Ruddy. One afternoon I heard him tell one of the models: "Walk like a whore, Dinorah, don't you realize you're walking like a flaming queen at the Aires Libres?" I looked at this Dinorah, who started to laugh and responded with a disgusting wiggle of her hips. I looked at him: he didn't look like a flaming queen at the Aires Libres or anywhere else. He looked like a man. Very ugly, that's true. Very foulmouthed. I thought about the gold injections, the yellow liquid going into his veins. The most unlikely people sometimes make us feel tenderness. It's logical to feel it for a child, for example. But I felt tender toward a mulatto who was eaten away, poisonous, sad. I must have been sick: I only wanted to embrace him, kiss his melted nose, his crystallized ear, his fingers that couldn't feel flame, much less affection. Late one night when he was leaving with his driver, he saw me standing there, outside the cabaret, waiting for a cab. He ordered his car to *stop and asked if he could give me a lift anywhere. I said he could, I was going home, and on the way he wanted to know if I'd eaten, I said I almost never ate at the Tropicana, then he suggested we go to a restaurant. We were very tired, he kept yawning, and I said that if he preferred I could fix him something light in my apartment. He closed his eyes, his expression turned dreamy, and he murmured that he could eat steak and potatoes. I said that was my specialty. Close up he wasn't the ogre who threatened the company, he looked like a solitary man. Later, while I was cooking, he looked at the photos of Daniel, which were everywhere, most of them of him dressed for the trapeze. I told him the boy was still with the circus, he promised that one day he'd use him in one of his productions. When we finished eating, we went out to the balcony because dawn was breaking, Roderico smoked constantly, looking at the roofs of Havana. "How sad this city is becoming," he said suddenly. "Would it bother you if I slept here?"*

"DEATH IN THE BARBERSHOP"

That night I slept in the hotel at the airport. "Sleep" isn't the word that best defines the state of furtive drowsiness in which I spent the hours between one in the morning, soon after I landed at Idlewild, and six sharp, the moment when the telephone rang and a woman's voice murmured: "Good morning, Mr. Porrata. It's six o'clock." I tried to fall into a normal sleep, but I couldn't. I was obsessed by the thought of Yolanda, and that immediately became intertwined with Aurora's face and features, and her voice and two arms. I've said two, what more can a man aspire to?

I had breakfast in the cafeteria next to the hotel and headed for the train station. First I had to catch the train to Binghamton, and once there take a taxi to drive the twelve miles to Apalachin. I bought a couple of newspapers, and as soon as I sat down in one of the cars I began to read them and take notes. Joseph Barbara, the liquor distributor in whose house the "conclave" had been held, stated that he was at a loss to explain why his friends, sixty-five in all, had decided to visit him on the same day and at the same time, simply because they were interested in the state of his health, weakened after the grippe he'd had the week before. "Coincidence," he said, laconically. There was one problem, however: his eighteen-room house couldn't accommodate all the men—they'd come from as far away as Ohio, California, Texas, Colorado, Puerto Rico, and Cuba—which meant they had to look for lodgings elsewhere. Almost all of them found something in the Apalachin area, either in the one small hotel or in rooms they rented from the owners of nearby houses. From the beginning, the strangers established that price would not be discussed, and, in fact, rather than haggle, they paid double the rate they were asked for. But among the residents not blessed by this bonanza, that is, by the thrilling tips of Don Vito Genovese, Joseph Profaci, or Frank Cucchiara (the cheese manufacturer who attended as Lucky Luciano's representative), there was one who revealed the true nature of the meeting. It seems this was enough. On Thursday, November 14, a few minutes after twelve noon, half a dozen police cars and a truck filled with federal agents and state troopers advanced stealthily along the private road that led to the mansion. The "delegates" had just taken a break to stretch their legs and eat lunch outdoors at the tables on the patio: grilled steaks and potato salad. Everything was fine until Michael Genovese, who didn't own a car wash for nothing and could smell police cars the way dogs smell hares, stood up and shouted the alarm: he could see the feds. Fifteen men panicked and ran into the woods behind the house, but the others remained impassive, sitting under the trees, chewing tender pieces of steak, while the police, four in each vehicle, got out with weapons drawn.

Forty-eight hours had passed since then, and in that time I'd managed to get to Apalachin and was standing in the center of town, a gloomy, totally deserted square. On one side stood the wooden church; diagonally across from that was the tavern, which had an old-fashioned look. The cabdriver hadn't been able to give me directions to Barbara's house; he claimed he almost never drove anybody to Apalachin. I'd checked my bag at the train station, and all I was carrying was the brand-new Kodak Retina. I'd used it for the first time when I took pictures of the dead hippopotamus, and this was the second time it would see action, tracking down more refined hippopotamuses. I went straight to the tavern and ordered coffee. Two patrons sitting at a table barely looked up. I asked the owner where Barbara's house was; he said he didn't know, he didn't know anybody around there by that name. I paid for the coffee and started walking, looking for a police station, a police officer, anybody with authority in the town. Life in Apalachin was life in the suburbs, and a Saturday morning in any suburb is a morning without style. I found the nerve to stop a few passersby, they refused to answer any question related to the raid at Barbara's mansion or the arrests, they refused flat-out, no matter how trivial or insignificant the question was. Finally, on a two-story building, I saw the sign: "Sheriff." The door was locked, but through the open window I saw a desk, papers in disorder, signs of activity. I decided to wait, and while I waited the first line of my article came to me: "Apalachin is not a ghost town, although these days it is bent on seeming like one." I didn't need to write it down, I wasn't going to forget it because that was just how I felt, disappointed, slightly ridiculous, for I'd imagined something else, I thought people would talk to me openly about what had happened; I supposed that somebody would offer to be my guide and take me to Barbara's house, that's how naïve I was.

I saw a man coming down the street toward me, his identifying badge clearly visible, a fat little man with the face of a corpse. Generally, the face of a corpse is associated with thin, emaciated men. But that isn't always the case. The sheriff of Apalachin was fat, not bad-looking, but I realized right away that it was easy to imagine him stiff; it was a kind of strangeness in his eyes, maybe it was a premonition of mine. He took off his hat and asked what he could do for me.

"I'm a reporter," I said, showing him my credentials. "I just came in to cover that roundup at Joseph Barbara's place. I understand that one of the men arrested is Cuban."

Up to a point, my imperfect English came out clear as crystal, and nobody was more surprised than me. The man asked me to come in, but we remained standing; he already knew the interview would be brief.

"Cuban? I don't know. You'd have to go to Endicott, that's where the court is and that's where they booked them. But I think they were released."

My ear was imperfect too. I assumed I'd misheard him.

"They let them go?"

"Of course they did," the sheriff replied. "It's no crime to visit your friends, or is that a crime in Cuba?"

As far as he was concerned, I must have had the face of a corpse too. A future corpse. A blond, skinny Cuban, breathing like a beginner, wearing his older brother's coat, sticking his nose into the Mafia's business. A damn idiot wasting his time on a Saturday.

"Can you tell me how to get to Joseph Barbara's house?"

"I can," said the sheriff, "but let me warn you, you won't be able to get close to the house. It's on a hill, they'll make you turn around as soon as you begin going up because it's a private road. Yesterday they punched a photographer from the *Journal-American* down the hill, and Barbara's son smashed his camera.

See, that's what happens. They arrested young Barbara but he paid the fine, and since last night he's been back in Apalachin with his mommy and daddy."

He used those words, "with his mommy and daddy." Irony irritated me, especially irony in English.

"If what you want is a photograph of the area, ask them in Endicott, the police took some and maybe they'll give you one."

I felt like an imbecile, and above all I felt humiliated.

"There's a bus leaving in ten minutes. It stops in Endicott and then goes on to Binghamton."

This was how intruders, sleuths without influence, poor bastards were thrown out of town, and I was all three. I'd seen it a thousand times in the movies. I thought of Bulgado and his beloved George Raft, who surely had been thrown out of places even shittier than Apalachin.

"I'd like to go to Cuba." The sheriff said goodbye amicably when he realized I was going to do what he said. "Good casinos, right?"

I went back to the square and saw the bus. A couple of women in hats were about to board. Three adolescents were going to board too, and a man holding a newspaper; he carried it rolled up as if he were going to punish a puppy, a nervous old man who couldn't stay still on the bus and changed his seat a couple of times before he opened the paper. From where I was sitting I could see that he was reading an article that disclosed new angles about the police raid. I'd already read it: it said that the men who hid in the woods behind Barbara's house took more than eight hours to surrender. It wasn't until nine that night that they came back with their tails between their legs, thirsty, their clothes muddy, guided by the flashlights of the police. I thought about my files, about something I'd discovered shortly before I left Cuba: November 14, the day of the meeting, was also Santo Trafficante's birthday. His forty-second, and who knows if Joseph Barbara's wife, a woman meticulous about details, had ordered a cake for him. Cake came to mind, and I felt hungry; I hadn't eaten anything since breakfast. I also thought about Yolanda. I'd call her later from Binghamton, or if everything turned out as I expected, I'd call her the next day from New York, I wanted to be back in New York.

I got off the bus in Endicott, went straight to a cafeteria and had a fast lunch, thinking about the information I needed: I had to find out if Trafficante had been arrested, and if Joseph Silesi, another big fish in Cuba, was with him. If I could confirm that, it would prove that both of them had been at the meeting representing Lansky, so quiet and retiring in Havana. A second fact was that, together with Lucky Luciano's representative, they'd been dividing up another delicious cake: the fifty hotels that were going to be built in Cuba along an imaginary line that opened into a fan of perfect places. The entire operation had been revealed, with Lansky at the head, indisputably the one in charge, and with President Batista and his brother-in-law Colonel Fernández Miranda helping him from the shadows.

At the police station in Endicott, they took the trouble to look over my credentials and hold my passport, which was reassuring. They had me go into an office decorated with little cactus plants, where an elderly lieutenant who resembled Buster Keaton with a disconsolate expression, or to be precise, Buster Keaton in *Sunset Boulevard*, asked how he could help me. I explained that I needed the names of the men arrested in the Apalachin raid, and he said he wasn't authorized to release them all but could help me if I was looking for one name in particular. I said: Santo Trafficante. He looked at the long list, sixty-five Italian names, last names like Bonanno, Evola, Falcone (the famous Falcone brothers), something that can immediately confuse a person accustomed to the simple family names of upstate New York.

"It isn't here."

I said Joseph Silesi, alias Joe Rivers.

"It's not here either."

My mind went blank for a moment. I took out my cigarettes and realized my fingers were trembling. The old lieutenant, who also noticed the trembling, gave me a fatherly look. I made a mental bet he had a son my age.

"They might have used other names," he murmured. "Think about it for a minute."

I looked up, I wanted to hug him. I believe I smiled.

"Louis Santos." It gushed out like a torrent, and he looked at the list again.

"Santos, Louis," he read, happier than hell. "Forty-two, resident of Havana, Cuba, operator of the Sans Souci nightclub. Place and date of birth: Tampa, November 14, 1915."

Trafficante had a record. He'd been convicted of bribery in 1954 and again, in 1956, for conspiracy to violate the tax laws as they applied to games of chance. In that mad year, which was 1957, he'd been subpoenaed on two occasions by courts in Florida.

Encouraged by his find, the officer asked me if I could remember any other alias for Silesi. I said no, I couldn't. Maybe he'd stayed in New York, waiting for instructions from Trafficante, who undoubtedly had the job of explaining Anastasia's death to the men who'd gathered in Apalachin. In any case, after a few brief procedures, the sixty-five men had been freed, and Joseph Barbara complained that his best friends, wary after what had happened at his house, would not want to visit him again. I asked the lieutenant if he could let me have a photograph of Barbara's mansion, and he shook his head: for the moment, the photographs were also restricted material. There was a silence, and to break it I risked throwing a small stone; the man inspired me with confidence.

"I've heard that the meeting was called in a hurry, to discuss the death of Anastasia."

He didn't move a muscle. He was Buster Keaton in the wax museum.

"Anastasia?" He smiled serenely. "The Lord High Executioner! . . . Listen, I'm going to give you some advice."

He got to his feet and said that, in my place, the first thing he'd have done was go to the office of the district attorney in New York. It wasn't a secret, because it had just been published in the papers, that one of the investigators in the Anastasia case had been in Apalachin the previous day, probably looking for some connection.

"There you are." He opened the door, showed me the exit; maybe he thought he'd spent too much time with me, maybe he no longer saw me as someone who could be his son. "Go to New York and ask them there. The detective who was in Apalachin is named Sullivan. I wish you luck."

On the train, on the way to New York, I rested the case of the Kodak Retina on my lap. I hadn't been able to use it yet, and I wondered if taking it hadn't been a waste of time. Tomorrow at the latest I had to call the paper and dictate a piece that would have a New York byline. Under my name they'd put: "Special Correspondent for *Prensa Libre*," and that made me happy. I imagined Skinny T. reading the first line: "Apalachin is not a ghost town . . ."

When I got to the train station in New York, I caught a cab for the Park Sheraton. I felt an adolescent excitement, totally inappropriate for a mature sleuth, when I walked into that luxury hotel. As I filled out the registration card, I stared at the sign: "A. Grasso, Barber Shop." It was closed, but I refrained from asking what time it opened. I went to my room and called the paper. I explained the fiasco in Apalachin to Madrazo, and at the same time I confirmed that Trafficante had been arrested. With the little I had, and especially with what I'd be able to find out the next morning, I could write a couple of pages and dictate them in the afternoon.

"Do it fast," Madrazo ordered. "*Carteles* came out today, and it has a good article. Do you want to know what it's called?"

He paused and deepened his voice to fuck with me even more: " 'Death in the Barbershop.' "

I cursed. Madrazo heard and jabbed at me again. "In *Bohemia* they prepared one that's fairly long, it'll be in the next issue. I think they interviewed the barber. But neither one mentions business in Havana or that little matter of the hippopotamus."

I was silent. Madrazo asked if I was listening to him. I answered with another question: who the hell had scooped me at *Carteles*?

"That Chinaman Cabrera Infante," he said. "He was in New York interviewing a movie director, he was passing the Park Sheraton and he had to piss—you know the Chinese piss a lot—he went into the lobby to use the bathroom, and they blocked his way because there was a dead body in the barbershop."

"That bastard" was what I managed to stammer.

"You do it better" was Madrazo's goodbye. "You go take a piss too, hurry, and send us something good."

"Sure," I promised before I hung up.

I went out to arrange the interview with Cappy. I took a taxi to Bellevue Hospital, filled out some papers at the prison ward, and left him a note. I didn't know it at the time, but Coppola was longing to complain to reporters. They told me to come back the next day, they couldn't promise me anything, but there was a remote possibility I'd be able to see him. When I went back to the hotel, I stopped in front of the barbershop and looked in through the glass. The killers, according to the papers, wore hats, aviator glasses, and black gloves for holding their weapons: a Colt .38 that was tossed away right after the crime and a Smith & Wesson .32 that was found in a subway trash can.

There was silence and bottomless depths in the area. Up to a point it was understandable; it was less than a month since the murder, and the soul of Anastasia was still afloat, condemned to wandering. The Church had refused him final absolution and prohibited any Mass or prayer for the dead, and not even his brother, the priest Salvatore Anastasia, had been able to keep the nine-hundred-dollar coffin from being lowered into unconsecrated ground, in the most apostate corner of Green-Wood Cemetery.

I went up to my room and asked the operator to connect me with a number in Havana. Yolanda answered at the first ring. I could tell she was excited, I don't think anyone had ever called her from New York. Not anyone from a bed in a luxury hotel. And, of course, not anyone from the scene of the crime.

GORGEOUS HAVANA

I read it dozens of times before dictating it. I revised the order of sentences, changed adjectives, polished it as much as I could, trying at all costs to make it a piece that didn't have too much or too little. I wanted a paragraph that would be like a bomb, and in a certain sense I succeeded. But I was concerned about how the paper would react, and especially about the expression on Madrazo's face when he saw my article, which began like this:

On Saturday, October 19, a few days before he was cut down in the barbershop at the Park Sheraton Hotel, the Mafia capo Umberto Anastasia had lunch with four prominent Cubans who traveled from Havana to New York for reasons unknown. The four men, identified as Roberto "Chiri" Mendoza, Raúl González Jerez, Ángel González, and Alfredo Longa, met with Anastasia at Chandlers, a well-known restaurant on Fiftieth Street. It was the last Saturday for Anastasia, who was shot dead the following Friday.

Two of these individuals had sufficient pedigree to enjoy a privileged place in my files: Roberto Mendoza, nicknamed "Chiri," an intimate friend of President Batista, had significant interests in sugar and in construction, and Raúl González Jerez, the former manager of the Sans Souci and Santo Trafficante's right-hand man, was the owner of Club 21, a few steps from the Capri, the hotel that was about to open. I didn't know much about the other two. Ángel González was a craps dealer, and Alfredo Longa, a blackjack inspector, was "Chiri's" good friend, aide, and probable confidant. I'd had my lucky break the previous day, when I thought I'd never be able to confirm the information Madrazo had given me. I got up early and went straight to the office of the district attorney, ready to devour the world. I wore a very American plaid sports jacket, and with the camera hanging from my shoulder, I thought I'd pass as a legitimate sleuth. The reality inside the place soon brought me down a peg or two. There was a fairly heterogeneous crowd of people: detectives, fast-moving individuals involved in some investigation, men who looked like lawyers resolving issues, and others who looked like authentic sleuths, not ones in costume, like me. Phones rang constantly, several at the same time, and for a while I waited in the line in front of a desk where people stopped to ask for directions. When it was my turn, the guard at the desk was filling out some kind of report and barely looked up. I asked for Sullivan, the name I'd been given in Endicott. He said which Sullivan, there were two working in the office. I stammered that I was a reporter and had come from Havana. I showed him my camera as if I were showing him a fish. I held it up in my hand and knew right away I was being ridiculous; a camera doesn't prove anything, least of all in a place like that, where so many people were weighed down by orders, anonymous phone calls, real or imaginary clues. I lowered the camera and took out my credentials. I explained that I was there to write a report on the meeting at Apalachin, but the guy still didn't understand, not only because of my English, which suddenly had stopped working (all I could manage were broken sentences), but also because the word Apalachin, dropped just like that, out of context, didn't mean anything to him. The officer, with patches at his elbows and fingers stained with ink, gave me the most obscenely bored glance anybody's ever directed at me. He said I should wait; he'd see if one of the detectives could take care of me, but he wasn't promising anything. I sat down on a bench, crushed as I'd never been before, not even in my childhood. I began to wonder if I wasn't too green for this kind of assignment; maybe all I was good for was what I'd already been doing: interviewing sexy girls like Kary Rusi, Toty Estrada, or Gilda Magdalena, the blondest of our vedettes, who had a secret I'd uncovered: in the mornings she sold vacuum cleaners. Maybe the leap had been too premature, or too risky, or both, and since they knew it at *Prensa Libre*, they'd thrown me to the lions—there were the lions again—sending me to New York on an adventure nobody else would have been willing to accept.

"You're from Cuba, right?"

A tall, skinny guy who'd been listening to my conversation with the guard sat down beside me. He had a notebook in his hand, and I saw three or four pens clipped to his shirt pocket. He didn't seem very old, but he was brutally wrinkled; there was almost no room left for more crow's-feet around his eyes. He looked as if the skin of an old man had been placed on the face of a man in his thirties. His eyes were young, still full of life, and his hair oily but dark.

"I'd like for us to talk. I've been able to get some information from Lieutenant Sullivan, maybe we could compare notes."

He looked so shabby, with his worn trousers, faded shirt,

and old, grease-stained raincoat, that I was tempted to ignore him. Dressed like that in Cuba, he would have been ignored by everybody. I don't know if he guessed what I was thinking, but he took out a pack of cigarettes and held it in front of me. I took one, and then I had to answer. I told him my last name, Porrata, and said I was covering two cases: Umberto Anastasia and Apalachin, mixed up together. When he heard this he smiled; I saw his teeth, dirty or stained by tobacco, in any case I was about to admit I had no notes, nothing that could compare with what he had, whatever it was.

"My name's McCrary. I'm a freelancer, doing an article for the *New York News*."

I shook his hand, a trout that was long and too cold. Then he opened his notebook, paused, sighed as if it were hard for him to spit out what he had. He began with Trafficante, arrested in Apalachin: his father, with the same name, was based in Tampa and controlled illegal gambling and the numbers in the Southeast. The son had flown straight to Tampa as soon as he was released. Nothing new under the sun, I said, I knew all that, and a little bit more besides. McCrary looked up, and I realized I had to prove it. Without looking at my notebook, because it was in my pocket and had nothing written in it, I explained that, until very recently, Havana had been a city open to all the families, without territories or exclusive rights, a paradise where you didn't even need bodyguards. But precisely for that reason, anticipating that disputes might arise, the Mafia's high command (the Commission, I emphasized in a very quiet voice) had decided to appoint a mediator who at the same time would act as an informant. Santo Jr. was chosen because he came from a more peaceful mob in Florida, where the internal wars being waged in New York or Chicago didn't exist. Besides, he probably was the only one who spoke correct Spanish. He acted as the link between all the families and

Colonel Fernández Miranda, the president's brother-in-law, owner of the slot machines and head of the Palace Guard, a secret police force that also protected the casinos.

I stopped to catch my breath. McCrary, who smelled old and stiff, like a wet cat put down next to the fire to dry, kept taking notes. When he finally stopped, it was to light another cigarette. Around us the traffic of investigators and prosecutors continued. These were people who ignored us; we were two assholes sitting on a bench, cooling our heels, waiting for a few crumbs. They were used to guys like us. Besides, I must have had the look of a novice, clutching at a camera that dozed on my lap like a quiet cat, a dry, quiet cat.

"Do you know the Warwick Hotel?"

McCrary had lowered his voice. Instinctively I stopped keeping my distance and moved closer. I had a premonition, I felt my luck turning. You can feel that at the right time.

"It's at Fifty-fourth and Sixth, very close to the Park Sheraton. On Thursday, October seventeenth, four Cubans registered there. They'd just come from Havana and were with Cappy, Anastasia's driver and bodyguard. Do you understand what I mean?"

It was my turn to take notes. Between us McCrary and I had raised an extraordinary cloud of smoke that seemed to surround only us and not drift anywhere else. I wrote down the names of the Cubans, and to repay his confidence I briefly explained who each of them was.

"On Friday," McCrary continued, "one day after arriving in New York, the four of them meet in Mendoza's suite. They order liquor, appetizers, Coppola shows up, he's a slippery little toad, and later Anastasia arrives with two individuals, one of them's his partner, Augie Pisano, and the other's somebody named Gus, that's all I know about him. They begin to drink, and finally a friend of theirs, Rivers, comes in with the special guest of the evening: Joe DiMaggio."

Our smoke bubble quivered delicately; we were smoking like madmen. I told McCrary everything I knew about Rivers, whose real name was Silesi, one of the two Silesi brothers who lived in Cuba. They were both professional gamblers and had been brought to Havana by an atrocious character: Nicholas "Fat the Butcher" DiConstanza.

The officer came to tell me that Sullivan, that is, neither of the two Sullivans, could see me that day. I looked at McCrary. I had to send my article to the paper; in it I was going to mention people who were very important in Cuba. How could I be sure the information had already been corroborated by the police? McCrary shrugged. To obtain the official version I'd have to wait around there for at least a week. According to his sources, it had been Coppola, Anastasia's bodyguard, who admitted his visits to the Warwick and invented some lie to justify the presence of the four Cubans: he said they only wanted to meet DiMaggio and hire him for some casino. That's why the police had asked for the hotel register of arrivals and departures; they knew the exact time the four came in and the exact time they left.

"From the hotel they went to La Guardia Airport," McCrary pointed out, "and caught a flight to Las Vegas."

He rummaged through his notes again.

"TWA flight 33. That's easy to check."

McCrary gave me his card. I didn't have a card but I gave him my address and phone number in Havana. As for New York, I was staying at the Park Sheraton.

"That fits!" he exclaimed. "It must have ghosts."

We walked together to Lexington Avenue. He remarked that the Anastasia murder wasn't the first crime committed in that hotel. In 1928 another famous gangster, Arnold Rothstein, was shot in one of the rooms and went down to the lobby and out to the street, wounded and asking for an ambulance, but then he died very quickly. In those days the Park Sheraton was called the Park Central, and he was a young reporter who'd gone there to write an article and take a photograph, though all he found was a large pool of blood at the door to Fifty-sixth Street.

We separated with a handshake and the promise to see each other again, in New York or in Havana; McCrary had never been to Havana. I hurried to the Warwick, but before I got there I went into a bar, wet my hair, and combed it in a different style, with the part on the side, the way my mother combed it when I was a boy. I put on my reading glasses, buttoned the plaid jacket, and hung the camera from my shoulder. I was sure my appearance as a well-to-do blond Cuban was perfect. I went into the Warwick, walked to reception, and a girl asked how she could help me.

"I want to make a reservation," I said. "It's for my father."

She took out a paper and asked when I wanted it.

"For Thanksgiving," I replied, somewhat scornfully. "From Thursday the twenty-eighth to Sunday, December first."

The girl wrote it down. She had beautiful hands. I bet they weren't as cold as McCrary's, that they were soft little trout, and certainly warm. She asked for my father's name.

"Roberto Mendoza," I said, loud and clear, and besides that I spelled the last name. "He wants the same room he had last month."

The girl raised her eyebrows. I'd already imagined what came next: she asked which room.

"He told me, but I don't remember. Can't you check the number? He was here October seventeenth."

She took out the enormous register and immediately found what she was looking for.

"1405," she said with a sigh. "I have to see if it's free."

Then she asked for my phone number. They normally confirmed the arrival of a guest one week ahead of time. I gave her the number of *Prensa Libre* and said goodbye with the formality of an English lord. No doubt I looked like the son of somebody who could afford a room at the Warwick. I left and began to walk toward Fiftieth Street, looking for Chandlers Restaurant. I knew it would be much more difficult to confirm Anastasia's lunch with the four Cubans, but at least I wanted to see the place, write a couple of lines about the atmosphere, the food, how the waiters looked. I felt confident, and that was a good sign. Chandlers has a glass divider between the bar and the restaurant, and on the glass are embossed engravings of the faces of all the presidents of the United States. I sat at the bar and ordered a beer; the bartender looked like an Irish thug, above all like one who didn't care to engage in conversation with anybody. Unusual in a bartender. I asked for a table to have lunch. There weren't many people in the room; the menu was varied but I decided to have a fillet, the euphemism for steak, in honor of Yolanda, who'd promised to cook another one for me when I got back. The story of her love for Rodney, an impossible love, of course, had left me perplexed. At first I didn't know whether to feel anger, revulsion, or jealousy. I knew Rodney, I'd seen him several times at the Tropicana. A few days after I came to work at the *Diario de la Marina* I was sent to interview him. I thought he was awful, a vulgar, arrogant man who'd have been ugly in any case, but leprosy had made him even uglier, to the point where he seemed the last person that anybody, man or woman, could find attractive. Merely imagining Roderico asleep in the same bed that I'd shared with Yolanda caused an uneasiness in me that had nothing to do with either anger or fear. I don't know, maybe it had to do with my inability to understand that kind of passion. When I tried to reconstruct the scene, that incredible scene of Roderico asleep and Yolanda watching him, a macabre song came to mind—"Boda Negra," the "Black Wedding," in which a man digs up a corpse, takes it to his house, and lays it in his bed. The Pinareño Trio sang it, and I remembered a line that was perfect for being in love with Rodney: ". . . he covered the horrible mouth with kisses, and smiling he told her of his love."

The waiter came to serve me a glass of wine. He waited for me to taste it, I made some comment, and he caught my accent. He asked if I was on vacation, and I replied that I was, that I lived in Cuba and had just graduated from the university; the trip was a present from my father. The waiter smiled: he was Cuban too, what a coincidence, recently a lot of Cubans had been coming to the restaurant. I liked the direction the conversation was taking and it occurred to me to say that in fact it was my father who recommended that I be sure to have lunch at Chandlers. He nodded. I bet he thought I was an imbecile.

"Sure," I added, maintaining the imbecilic tone, "Papá was here a month ago. He came in with a man who was killed a few days later."

That was the hook. From the waiter's expression, I knew I'd caught him, but he didn't dare say anything; he just waited for me to go on.

"They killed the man in the barbershop of a hotel, which one was it . . . ? Oh, right, the Park Sheraton."

"Anastasia?" The waiter concentrated on my face. "But you're not Raúl's son."

I thought of that English teacher I'd had at La Salle: reflexes are a primitive attitude, more powerful than courage and intelligence.

"No, I'm Roberto Mendoza's son. They call my father 'Chiri.' He's the owner of the Almendares."

The waiter was mine, I could see it in his expression: relaxed, credulous, contented. The Almendares were probably his favorite ball team.

"I think I know who your father is. Two or three gentlemen came in with Raúl that day. I've known Raúl since we were kids, we grew up in the same neighborhood."

The truth was I couldn't care less: his childhood, the neighborhood, his nostalgia because he lived so far from Cuba, it was the next thing he was going to say. I had to get the conversation back on track.

"The one who was killed, did you know him too?"

"I'll tell you the truth: he was a little crazy. He came in often for lunch. But after that day when he was here with your father and Raúl, we didn't see him anymore."

"Damn," I muttered. There are damns that, said in a certain way, signify the end of a conversation. I knew he wouldn't contribute anything else. And suddenly I had an appetite, I wanted to wolf down my fillet alone and then dash to the prison ward at Bellevue Hospital for my possible interview with Coppola: I had a hunch he'd give me one.

"Another glass of wine?"

I thought I deserved that glass. I hadn't even had time to walk around the city. I would soon. I'd take a couple of days before I went back to the "gorgeous Havana of the great Rodney," which was what I'd read a while back on a Tropicana poster.

After lunch I went to my meeting with Coppola. I was astonished that they allowed me to see him, though it was through a glass, he on one side and I on the other. Each of us picked up his telephone receiver, and that's how we talked. He really was a slippery little toad. He didn't want to talk about the Cubans, he wouldn't even admit he'd been with them in any hotel, but our conversation gave some flavor to the subject of Anastasia: "The words of mutes are so pretty!" was the favorite sentence of his boss, who in fact had left a good number of individuals mute. Since Cappy had no paper, I sent him my notebook with one of the guards, and he wrote it down in that dialect of theirs, in his second-grade handwriting. When it was dark I called *Prensa Libre*. Madrazo said he'd been waiting for my call, he had space reserved on the first page for me, and he hoped what I had was worth it.

"It will be," I replied, with the elusive coldness of somebody who doesn't want to show his enthusiasm but something betrays it, his tone, perhaps, or an imprudent hoarseness.

"I'll pass you to Fini so you can dictate it."

Fini got on, and I dictated to her. She was a woman in her forties who looked a hundred, the soul of discretion, nothing but skin and bone. She said, "Hello, Porrata, you can begin when you like." I read slowly, and she interrupted only to repeat the names and make certain they were correct. I concluded with this line: "For the New York police, the strings that have moved several apparently isolated events, like the attempt on Frank Costello, the crime against Anastasia, and the recent summit in Apalachin, are controlled from the same geographical location: gorgeous, vibrant Havana. The investigation, according to sources, will extend to this city."

I hung up. Fifteen minutes later the phone rang. It was Madrazo, of course.

"I'm not even the one who's going to say anything to you. Carbó will do that. I hope you're sure about what you've dictated."

"Absolutely sure," I said.

Carbó was the editor. I explained that everything had been corroborated personally "by this reporter." Everything except the meeting held Friday night in Mendoza's suite, with the presence of Anastasia and his good pal Augie Pisano, and the former star of the Yankees who they wanted to hire for some casino: Joe DiMaggio.

"We'll do a little editing," said the voice on the other end. "We can change a few verbs to the conditional, all right with you?"

I hated the conditional, or the potential, or whatever the hell you call it. It's a tense that weakens a story. But I avoided contradicting him. I took a tangential tack and said the meeting with DiMaggio that night showed they were deceiving Anastasia, making him think they were taking him into account, that he was participating in decisions, when in reality Havana was by definition closed to him and anybody else who didn't have Lansky's blessing.

"We'll publish it the day after tomorrow," the editor concluded. "Try to get back on time."

Getting back on time meant returning right away, on the next flight, the next day. I decided to take advantage of the few hours I had left in the city. I went down to the lobby and looked again at the darkened barbershop. On the day of his death, Anastasia broke two basic rules for any capo of his standing: he sat with his back to the door, something he never did, and he closed his eyes while he was being shaved. He wasn't suspicious about the peculiar details, like his usual barber calling in sick, or the owner, Arthur Grasso, rushing out of the shop seconds before two gunmen came in. He wasn't even surprised when Anthony Coppola, his driver and bodyguard, decided to go out for coffee instead of staying there as he normally did, getting a shoeshine. It had been a thoughtless death, unworthy of the merciless brain of Murder, Inc. One of the bellboys came over to ask if I was Mr. Porrata and to say I was wanted on the phone. I went to reception and took the call there: it was my mother.

"Your papá and I wanted to know if you're all right," she said in the sharp tone of a mother hen.

"I'm coming back to Havana tomorrow," I replied without indicating if I was all right or not.

"Lucy wanted to ask you for something."

Lucy came on. She wanted a photograph of Lana Turner, the biggest I could find. I promised I'd bring her one. That was my family, that strange mix of individuals: there was no chemistry, no passion, no style. Nothing united us, nothing real, I mean. Mamá said she sent me a kiss, ah, she almost forgot: Julián called and left a message that he wanted to see me. We hadn't seen each other for centuries. My mind blanked for a while. I said, "See you soon," but I think she'd already hung up.

I went out into the New York night. It was windy, and there was that peculiar November smell. I raised the collar of my raincoat and hailed a cab to go to Mario's. I felt sure of myself, and satisfied, in a way. It was the last time I felt like that, the last really innocent page. Nothing made me anticipate the misfortune that was approaching except maybe the calm, the strange stillness of things. Everything normal and fixed. Everything a lie.

A RIDDLE

I offered him my bed, he stripped from the waist up, he took off his shoes but not his socks, and not his trousers, he lay down and I lay down beside him. We didn't say a word for a while, he had his eyes closed but I knew from the rhythm of his breathing he hadn't fallen asleep. It's something else I owe Chinita: she taught me that breathing is what indicates if a person is really asleep or only pretending. You need a lot of practice to learn that, but I practiced enough with Chinita herself, who was expert in pretending almost everything: fainting spells and trances, things that have to do with the mind when it goes blank. The hardest thing, harder than all the rest, is to pretend to be asleep correctly, hardly anybody knows how to do it, not even the best artists in the theater.

Roderico took my hand and I got gooseflesh all over, I practically stopped breathing. Maybe he wanted to know if I was asleep, and it would've been easy for me to fool him. But it was just the opposite: I wanted him to know that I'd never been more awake in my life. I heard his hoarse accent; he'd told me he was worn out when he got into bed, and his voice came out in pieces, as if his sickness had reached there too.

"Don't worry, I can't pass it anymore."

I took in air, a thread of air that would at least let me ask him this question: "Can't pass what, Rode?"

"Leprosy," he answered. "Even though I look like this, it's not contagious anymore."

I noticed that even in the street it was silent, for some reason the noises that always reached my room were muffled. Roderico was quiet, and I was quiet because he'd said the awful word. I inhaled a large mouthful of air: I needed lots of oxygen to say what I was going to say.

"I don't care. If you passed it I wouldn't care."

He squeezed my hand, he raised it to his lips and kissed my fingers, he kept kissing them, and I felt his wet, thick mouth—his crude mulatto mouth that could say more filthy things than any other—but I didn't look at him, my eyes were fixed on the ceiling, and I had a feeling his were fixed there too, on the same spot, which was the light. We were both on our backs, my hand still resting on his mouth, and suddenly I felt him crying, I mean I felt his lips trembling, the horrible whistling that came from his chest with each sob. I was afraid but didn't move, I didn't even try to comfort him. We stayed like that for a while, Roderico shedding tears like he was emptying his eyes, my hand wet with everything, with tears and with saliva, and then, without expecting to, almost without realizing it, I began to cry too. There's a strange peace in the tears that come in complete silence, complete immobility, maybe there's a sign in that. After a few minutes he calmed down and moved my hand away from his mouth and onto his chest, holding it tight the whole time.

"Do you know who I am?"

It was a conversation for the night, the dark, very difficult in that brightness, the daylight coming in though I'd closed the windows; it was after seven, people were going to work and the noises on the street started up again, as if they'd stopped only for one awful moment because of the word "leprosy."

"Haven't they told you who I am?" Roderico insisted. He stopped

looking at the ceiling and turned to look at me, to see my profile because I was still rigid, my eyes fixed on the light.

"You're Rodney," I said. "The great Rodney of the productions at the Tropicana."

"Don't play the fool," he answered, making a hugh effort, like those characters who are dying on the radio soap operas and are about to reveal their final secrets. "Do you want me to tell you? Shall I tell you who I am?"

When I heard that I was terrified he'd get up, get dressed, and leave. I turned in the bed, and Roderico and I were face-to-face, something that hadn't happened in a while. His eyes were red but he was smiling, I thought that deep down he was enjoying the scene. The man beside me wasn't the one who insulted the girls who were dancing or made cruel fun of the poor models. He was something else, naked to me, someone who'd grown up seeing what only the dead could see: his flesh rotting and falling off, by then without pain. When it falls off, he told me much later, it's because it doesn't hurt anymore.

"They're injecting me with gold," he murmured. I sensed he was about to kiss me. "Microscopic pellets, almost invisible, they put them in my vein and that kills the disease."

After he said that, he brought his face close and we kissed. We didn't embrace, it was just that kiss, in fact I expected him to put his arm around my waist and hug me like any man would've done. But he didn't. He kept on talking with his lips almost touching mine, like he was whispering things in my ear, but instead of my ear it was my mouth; after all, it could listen much better than any other place on my body. He said they found out he had the disease when he was twenty-three, back when he was already a dancer in Havana and performing in the Marvelous Revue, that was the name of a show. First comes the itching, the feeling that you have flies trapped in your nostrils, a swarm of flies that goes all the way up to the space between your eyebrows. The disease is very slow in everything: sometimes it takes years to appear after you've been infected, and after the first symptoms, more time goes by before it shows its claws. In Roderico's case, when it finally did, he'd already stopped dancing and was producing cabaret shows. He said at least he'd stopped dancing in time, nobody would've wanted to dance with a man who could ruin his partner with just a scratch. He never knew for sure who infected him, but his mother thought it was his grandfather, his father's father, who came back to Cuba when Roderico was a boy, after spending a few years at the Panama Canal. He didn't come back because he wanted to but because he was sick: he had sores on his skin, which he insisted were infected insect bites, and if the disease didn't gnaw off his nose or begin to eat his fingers, it was because the old man died of a heart attack long before that could happen. He lived with them during the final months of his life, in the same room as his grandson, and with fingers dirty from touching his sores he'd caress the boy's scraped knees.

"I had bad luck," Roderico murmured with his eyes closed. "Nobody else in my family got leprosy."

Soon I knew, from his breathing, that he'd fallen asleep. His hand stayed on mine; it was the only part of my body he'd touched, apart from my lips, of course: after that day he often kissed me on the mouth, we were chaste lovers, maybe I was the only girlfriend Roderico Neyra ever had. I stayed very still, watching him sleep for an hour or two, then I got up to fix lunch. I bathed and put on a lot of makeup to hide the traces of the bad night I'd spent, my eyes swollen from mute crying and my lips bitten: I'd bitten them myself because I was nervous. I woke him at one in the afternoon, we ate together and left together for the cabaret: he'd boss the dancers around and I'd put up with Loretta (of Loretta and Johnson), who had her good side and her bad side, and the bad was invincible. We were silent in the car, and on the way I was touched by a feeling of being a couple, a feeling of intimacy that couldn't exist but did exist, and to top it off a taste of something hidden, as if we were secret lovers. You should have seen how his personality changed as soon as he went into rehearsal. I'm not lying when I say that when he was with me he was more manly, he spoke differently, he even laughed in a more open way, or that's what I believed, the illusion I wanted to see. A week later, Loretta asked if I wanted to work with Rodney. I said I worked for her and didn't have time for anybody else, but in any case Roderico had never made me an offer. "He'll make the offer," said Loretta, "and he'll get a girl to help me so you can work with him." I was openmouthed, trembling in the middle of the dressing room, and Loretta sat looking at me, in the mirror. She'd certainly seen a lot of strange couples in her life, but none like the one we made, or the one she thought we might eventually make, Roderico and I.

Two nights later he came to me to propose a job, knowing that Loretta had already talked to me about it. I accepted right away, because he also asked me to go with him to Las Vegas, where he spent his time—and still spends his time—seeing the shows and choosing the artists he'll hire for his productions. At the Tropicana they've always given him a free hand. My job was to be his assistant. I got his clothes ready, organized his papers, collaborated in everything, and as a prize—I can call it that—I slept beside him at night. He didn't touch me, but sometimes we kissed each other, only one kiss, and then I lay still, waiting for a signal from his body, that little catch in his breath that told me he'd finally fallen asleep. And still I waited awhile before I moved, I waited until Roderico's sleep became deeper, and when I was certain he was sound asleep I'd move close to him, very slowly, breathe in his odor, which wasn't unpleasant though it wasn't the odor of a healthy man either. I'd say it was a little like dried meat, or salted meat, a touch of something that made you want to hold on to it, at least I held on with my eyes open, fixed, in a vacant stare, but absorbing that smell like a thread that took me from one place to another: from the person I always thought I was to the person I turned into when I smelled Roderico. I can't forget that leap in the night.

I was going to fly in a plane for the first time to go to Las Vegas. Roderico warned me it would be a long trip, with a stop in Miami. Two days earlier I'd gone to see my son in the circus; it was in Matan-

zas then. I had to leave at dawn to get there in time to have breakfast with him. Chinita received me with her hair hanging loose, she was aging by the minute. She looked at me with a knowing smile and had me drink her tea instead of coffee. We sat by ourselves; my son was sleeping and I used the moment to talk to her about Roderico, because I couldn't talk to anybody else about a man who was a mystery to me. She listened, looking down at her cup of tea, stirring it with a spoon.

"A queer, a leper, and from Oriente," she murmured when I told her everything. "He must be the best magician in the world."

Yes, the best one: you just had to see what he did with the dancers and the decor, the fantasies that filled his head, complicating everything, mixing bursts of light with fountains of water, palm trees with feathers, princes from other times with gamblers at cockfights, and the incredible thing was that he made it seem natural. As for his disease, it was obvious he had it, he didn't like having his picture taken. As for his being from Oriente, that wasn't obvious, but there was no way he could be anything else since he'd been born in Palmarito de Cauto. Finally, the word "queer," almost as terrifying as the word "leprosy." So far, I hadn't seen anything that made me think he liked men, I'd only heard what Loretta's seamstress had said. Chinita drank her tea, she made a whirlpool because she stirred it so much, she looked at me with the same wonderful, patient look she had when I was little. "The important thing is that he likes you."

I hung my head because I wasn't sure about that. It was true he treated me differently from the other women, but so far, two days before we were leaving on a trip, he'd only given me chaste kisses on the lips, on the lips and on my hand, this poor hand, the only one I could offer him.

"Go with him," Chinita advised. "You haven't seen much of the world, you haven't seen anything out there. Have a good time, that's the magic you'll keep."

I smiled and asked her to wake my son. I simply told him that the famous Rodney, the choreographer at the Tropicana, had hired me as his secretary and I had to go with him to Las Vegas. Chinita left us alone so we could talk in private, and Daniel said he was worried because he never saw her sleep. No matter what time of night he got up, he found her awake, sitting in her armchair, drinking tea or talking to herself. During the day she sat by the radio, listening to soap operas. He never saw her even nod off a little.

"She doesn't close her eyes, Mamá, I swear she doesn't sleep."

I tried to reassure him. I knew he loved Chinita as if she was his own grandmother, maybe he loved her as much as he loved me; after all, she'd been taking care of him all that time. I mentioned it to her privately: Daniel was worried because he didn't see her sleep.

"It's a game," she replied. "Often I'm asleep when he gets up to see if I'm sleeping, but what happens is that I pretend to be awake."

I nodded and didn't say anything else. I remembered that bringing up a child, to her way of thinking, was based on those kinds of puzzles, on difficult ghostly trials a little like the "Chinese torture," the box of tricks magicians used. It's impossible to explain in words, you'd really have to live with her to learn the game; she always said it was all you had to know to grow up with a will, and to win without understanding, which was the only decent way to win.

I don't know if I learned it, it wasn't a lesson you can learn by heart, like multiplication tables. You had to catch the signals—the ones Chinita sent out—and that wasn't easy to do, you had to lift your snout and sniff the air, like those dogs that sense things somehow. In the plane, during the night flight, they turned out the lights and I felt something unknown to me. I was leaning on smoke. It was another game. When I was little I was afraid at night, and the Chinese woman told me that before going to sleep I should stretch out my hand and hold it still; in a little while I'd see how the hand of the darkness took hold of mine, and that was a holy remedy.

I think everybody on the plane was asleep. I stretched out my hand and touched Roderico's. I squeezed it and had the feeling I was touching an anthill, I was afraid it would crumble away. Even so, I drew

that hand toward my chest, I pushed it a little way inside my neckline;
Roderico pressed me gently but immediately left me alone. Dawn was
breaking over the ocher-colored mountains when the plane landed in
Las Vegas. As I went down the steps I was shaken by the gusts of
wind typical of a hurricane, they were so strong! And when I got to the
hotel, it was called the Flamingo, they offered me a welcoming pink
cocktail. In the room, next to the great Rodney, I looked out the win-
dow and saw the same mountains, the same ocher color, the swarm of
workers putting up buildings.

"The riddle of the desert," Roderico said with a sigh.

"You're the riddle" was the only thing I murmured.

"ALMENDRA"

I dreamed about Aurora. About an Aurora who wasn't the one of my childhood, or the arrogant old woman she became in later years. The one in my dream was more the Aurora of my adolescence, "our" adolescence, I include Julián because we were together on that awful afternoon. First we went to the movies, I remember they were showing a Clark Gable picture, *Across the Wide Missouri*, and when we came out he suggested we stop at his house to get some money. His grandfather, the father of his dead father, had given him the money, and the plan was to take a cab to Marina's house, a brothel in the Colón district. Julián was tired of going to bed with whores, I a little less so, though I wasn't a novice either. But he made his grandfather think he hadn't been intimate yet with any woman, and the poor old man, feeling compassion down to his balls—never was a saying more appropriate—and without thinking twice, took out a roll of bills and sent him to the most famous establishment in Havana and even went to the trouble of calling Marina to recommend his grandson to her. He also took into account that no boy liked to go alone the first time, which is why he gave him enough money to invite his best friend. Julián was weak with laughter when he told me about it. Neither of us, certainly not his grandfather, could imagine that in a not-too-distant future, his principal source of income would be whores, with no possible competition from Marina: high-class whores, Latin American and from the Far East. Nobody got him into it, he got into it all by himself because he had a vocation, a gift, the instinct born in a person that makes him fit into something, and he fit in there. He dressed and behaved in a special way, he had a talent for that kind of business. When he demonstrated that he did, the rest came to him free: good advice and, above all, protection.

That afternoon, when we went into the house, we heard music coming from the dining room. Julián said he'd only be a minute, I sat down in the living room to look at some magazines, and I saw him walking down the hall toward his room. Before he left the room he said he was going to get two jackets, one for him and the other for me, because Marina didn't like her clients showing up in shirtsleeves. In recent years our sizes had become similar—he no longer was the portable midget he'd been in his childhood: he'd had a growth spurt when he was almost fifteen. But I hadn't grown very much, so when we turned sixteen we were almost the same size, practically the same weight, the same height, and we had a way of communicating with old signals, gestures only we understood, in the way that real accomplices understand each other.

Aurora's house looked like the rooms she decorated, with vases and table runners, that was the theme. The doors to the balcony had panes of stained glass, and it was the light coming in through those panes, with its reddish tint, that pooled so strangely on the floor, an imprisoned brightness that was imprecise and fatal. I closed the magazine and walked toward the dining room. The music stopped playing for a moment and then immediately started again, like an odor that comes and goes. I stopped in the doorway, and the man looked up. I recognized him right away: he was sitting at the table, smoking a cigar without a band, one of the "perfectos" that blacks in the cigar factories roll for their own pleasure. I said hello, and he moved his head disdainfully, recognizing in me the insect that was a friend of the other insect that was Aurora's son. Julián called to me from his room to find out if I wanted to go to the bathroom; I said yes but hovered in the dining room a few more minutes, trying to put things where they belonged, my misplaced ideas, everything suddenly scrambled together. When I went to Julián's room, he pointed me toward the bathroom. "Go and piss, buddy, put on some cologne." Then he saw that I wasn't moving and that maybe I was trying to tell him something but didn't know how to begin. "Hey, did you see a ghost?" He said those words just for something to say, he understood that he'd hit the nail on the head: I had, in fact, seen a ghost. He turned and started to laugh. "The guy's okay . . . he's a friend of Aurora's." He didn't say Mamá's, and that meant many things. In the past, when Julián complained to me about his mother, he'd use her name, it was a way of imposing distance, of punishing her without her knowing it. Now he hadn't complained, but he was punishing her just the same. I went into the bathroom, and while I was urinating I began to tie up some loose ends—Julián's veiled attitudes, a few lies he'd told me. I picked up the cologne and splashed it on my neck and face. Then I put on the jacket he'd given me and we left his room, too quietly; something had wounded us for the moment, in my case it was rage, a morbid incredulity. I knew what it was to embrace a woman, press against her body, sink into her, all of that and much more that this man was doing with Aurora; it was impossible for me to stop imagining the scene. We approached the dining room again; the music of another *danzón* was playing, I don't have to say which one, it was his favorite *danzón.* Months later Julián got around to telling me that "the old man," as he called him, came to his house two or three times a week, and as soon as he arrived he'd hurry to turn on the phonograph. Julián wanted to strangle him, because he could listen to "Almendra" for hours, and dance to it too, with Aurora. They were dancing now. I was fascinated by the intense couple they made, the muted lust on their faces: he held her lightly, not forcing contact, and she, who was a little taller, lowered her eyelids to feel the rhythm. Tan tan tan taratantan . . . Tan tan tan taratantan . . . "*Son* of the almond, not the guava . . . *Son* of the almond, sweet girl of mine." It was Julián who sang, somewhat cynically. Aurora came out of her trance, saw us standing in the doorway, and gave us a bewildered look, as if she'd only just noticed we weren't children anymore. Julián said: "We're going out for a while." She stopped and moved away from her partner, only God knows how grateful I was that she moved away. "Back here by nine, son, do you hear me?" Julián answered: "Sure, Mamá, by nine sharp," and addressing the man: "See ya later, alligator." The man lifted his hand to say goodbye, he must have been furious because he'd been interrupted in the middle of the dance, he looked at Julián with his gray eyes, and I'll never forget his expression, the self-assurance of that warm, hoarse voice: "See ya, Goombah." We went to a taxi stand and caught a cab, we didn't give the driver the address, we didn't want to hear a knowing little laugh or some anecdote about Marina (all the cabdrivers seemed to know at least one). We preferred to tell him to drop us off on Calle Galiano; from there we'd walk to Crespo, the street where the brothel was located. I admired Julián's confidence; as long as there weren't any animals involved—he was still softhearted where they were concerned—he carried himself like a gangster, king of the mambo in his linen suit, his polished shoes, the bow tie around his neck. Almost seventeen years old, he seemed to have more experience than a man of forty. On the way, the street whores called out to us, paying us compliments, inviting us to go up, you always have to go up to do it. Julián turned them down with his seducer's manner— a seducer of whores, which is an ambiguous kind of seducer, full of femininity. He was the one who knocked at the door of Marina's mansion, three loud knocks and then a black woman opened the door. I learned later she was Jamaican, a real institution at Crespo 43. Marina came out to welcome us; she was effusive with Julián because she knew him very well, she'd seen him there a hundred times but wasn't going to say anything to his grandfather. She took us directly to the courtyard with little tables, some occupied by older men, a few accompanied by women and others conversing with each other, unhurried, as if it were a simple bar. Something was still bothering me: "Why does he call you Goombah?" At that moment Julián was a thousand miles from his house, his mother, the spectacle of the *danzón*. He looked at me in confusion and then realized I was going back to a distant time, back to an hour ago. "Ah, Goombah, well, I don't know, that's what the bastard calls me. Sometimes I call him Goombah too."

Some girls came over, and the conversation had to end there, we were changing our code. Julián asked what they would like; there were three of them and all three said they wanted Materva, an awful soft drink made from the yerba mate the Argentines drank. After that, almost everything's a blur. I know we went up to the rooms with the girl each of us had chosen, and when I locked the door I became reticent; I'd been pretending in front of Julián but didn't have to pretend in front of a whore. An exemplary whore, I must confess, who took off her clothes and realized I'd lost my innocence just a few hours earlier and was bloated, overwhelmed. She was a little languid, a little Chinese-looking, even a little bit ghostly, you could see the veins under the white skin of her belly. Finally she coaxed me because I looked very sad, and I responded. I was pleasant, neutral, but I couldn't get the sound of that couple dancing out of my head. And couldn't for a long time, I mean years went by and it was still there, always pulsing. I realized this when I woke that morning in New York and remembered that I'd dreamed about Aurora, about the image of her I'd taken away with me that afternoon. She was about thirty-five at the time, she'd cut her hair and wore the kind of sheer dresses we'd seen Janet Leigh wear in a movie. When the phone rang I was still in bed, going over the dream and its connections.

"It's McCrary. I'm in the lobby. I wanted to ask you something."

I dressed quickly and went down. I found him at the barbershop, which was still closed, peering in through the glass, just as I'd done the night before. We left the Sheraton to have coffee somewhere else. McCrary asked me if I knew the Hotel Riviera, in Havana. I said I'd only seen it from the outside, since it had just been built. It was Meyer Lansky's last big project; he'd announced that he'd open it in December.

"It'll open before that," McCrary declared, and he took a sip of coffee, looking at the street as he spoke. "They'll open on Thanksgiving for a small group: they're holding another 'summit' there, like the one in Apalachin."

I had a hunch and a doubt at the same time. I looked at McCrary, overgrown and ageless, who smelled of wariness, of stray cat, of a whore watcher: who the hell was McCrary? Why was he telling me about it? He sensed my suspicion; he stopped looking at the street and became confidential: if he was telling me, he murmured, it was because he'd already decided to go to Havana at the end of November, and he thought it would be interesting if the two of us investigated together, like a team. I answered that I'd think about it but that in theory I liked the idea. We walked toward the Park Sheraton, discussing the possible reasons the big fish might have for getting together at another large meeting. At the door, before we said goodbye, McCrary dropped the bomb he'd been saving for me: "It seems Lansky was in New York after all."

I controlled any show of enthusiasm. I used all my willpower not to exclaim that this meant I'd been right, above all not to rub my hands together thinking about the scoop it would be for us at *Prensa Libre.*

"Make a note of this," added McCrary. "His return ticket to Cuba was dated Friday, October twenty-fifth, but he called Eastern and changed it. He left on the twenty-second because he didn't want to be around when they eliminated Anastasia."

Normal, I said to myself. It wasn't going to be difficult for the paper to corroborate the change of plans with the airline. I thanked McCrary, who disappeared into a subway entrance, and I went up to my room to write a long report that I didn't intend to dictate. I'd take it personally to the editorial offices as soon as I got to Havana. This would be not just another article about the war for control of the casinos but an analysis of the situation of gambling in Cuba: in recent years, the plan seemed to have been completed, the government didn't want to do business with newcomers, and the island stopped being the open territory it had always been. Those who showed interest in obtaining a franchise in the new hotels were advised to direct their attention to other establishments in the Caribbean or in South America. This was how a silent little war had begun, waged with a good amount of discretion except for the death of Anastasia, which had been bungled. I had one page almost finished when the phone rang. No one was on the line. I hung up and started to concentrate again on my piece. A few minutes later it rang a second time, and I heard a man's voice

123

speaking rapidly. I could barely understand isolated words, not even a whole sentence, nothing but whispers and then a kind of death rattle. I asked what you tend to ask in these circumstances: who's calling, who did he want, but there was no answer. I hung up and waited a few seconds. The phone rang again and I began to count: ten, eleven, maybe twenty, twenty desperate rings; finally I answered and heard the spluttering of the voice, that and an echo, a ferocious sound struggling, I think, against distortion. I called the operator and asked her not to pass through any more calls, but she said she hadn't passed through any; the ones I was receiving weren't from the outside but came from inside the hotel. She suggested blocking the line to my room, and I told her to do it. I went to the window and looked down at the street. I was on the eighth floor and could see life proceeding normally: people walking, the heavy traffic at that time of day, the fruit stand on the corner. I still had time to eat lunch in New York before going to the airport. I sat down again and reread the few lines I'd managed to write, but suddenly I felt cold, uneasy, more weary than I can explain. I had the impulse to throw all my things—the little I needed to pack, some shirts and dirty shorts and whatever shit I had in the bathroom—into the small suitcase. I picked up the raincoat and looked for my passport, the plane ticket. I counted my money in case any was missing, I understood I was behaving exactly like somebody running away, an irrational man in the vortex. All I could think about was leaving the room, I'd write the article later, during the flight, or when I got to Havana. I went out to the empty corridor and looked both ways; there were no noises from the street, the muffled noises you always hear, no voice, however faint, no sign of life behind a door. I knew I'd never, never be able to describe that emptiness, a sickly oil that clogged one's pores, or that solitude, another untouchable oil. I was escaping, that was true; the feeling of doing so is always in one's bones, flight is always grumbling there, any kind of flight, and especially this one, without rhyme or reason. In the lobby I behaved like a shipwrecked man. I paid the bill and got to the street, my forehead covered in perspiration, my heart pounding. I didn't dare to ask myself what had happened, I didn't even dare to go back over the chain of small flights, the chain of terror. I went into a bar, ate there, and added some notes to my article, and at three in the afternoon I asked a cabdriver to take me to Idlewild Airport. I slept during the entire trip back to Cuba, except for the moment when the stewardess woke me to ask if I wanted supper. I'd read that in first class, inaccessible to a humble reporter from *Prensa Libre*, they served stuffed pheasant from Castillo de Jagua, the famous Havana restaurant. Between yawns, I told her I wanted pheasant. She replied she was afraid she couldn't accommodate me. She was cretinous in her sad little cap. I ended the conversation by saying that if I couldn't have pheasant I didn't want anything else, and she went away, not without first giving me a disgusted look stuffed with dark pellets of disdain. We landed at midnight, nobody was waiting for me at the airport, and I thought of some lines of poetry I'd read about a solitary traveler, who arrives and no one is waiting for him, and he raises his coat collar on the large, cold pier. This was my pier, and without raising the collar of my raincoat, among other reasons because I wasn't wearing it but carrying it over my arm, I decided that instead of going to my house I'd go straight to Yolanda's apartment. I'd show up there unannounced, and when she opened the door I'd throw myself, not into her arms, the impossible plural, but at her entire body with all that she could offer: one arm, two volcanic breasts, a mouth that navigated against the light, like a small enchanted ship. At the age of twenty-two, you are suddenly swept away by these passions; it's the time of life when you run, knock down doors, punch your way through a crowd. I went to the place where I'd left my '49 Plymouth, the faithful Surprise. I put my bag in the trunk, fixed my hair with the little brush I always carried under the seat, and pulled away smoothly. I began to drive slowly, knowing I was happy to go somewhere that wasn't my house, take a bath, drink a good café con leche. It was like beginning a double life. My brother, Santiago, would say that everybody, even cloistered nuns, led a double life. And that night I began to think that the country had one too, and that the city had an imaginary face, more or less its everyday face, with clerks leaving offices, people going into stores, crowded movies, and another hidden face, the face of landings, secret transmissions, homemade bombs, and disfigured corpses on the sidewalks. Between the imaginary face and the hidden face was shifting ground, insidious quicksand that swallowed up everything. Eight months earlier, not long after the attack on the Presidential Palace, my father had come into my room and asked me to go with him to the kitchen. There was a round table where we had breakfast, and that's where we sat. I looked at the clock: it was three in the morning.

"Listen carefully, Joaquín: don't even think about joining the revolutionaries, and especially don't think about doing them any favors. I don't want to hear that you're involved in anything."

I smiled and shook my head. I realized that Papá was furious and my smile was making him even angrier.

"This is serious, pay attention and quit laughing: they'll pulverize you, they'll chop you into little pieces, and it doesn't matter who the hell your family is."

My father was never afraid of anything, maybe that's why it seemed so strange to me to see him like that: sincerely terrified, looking into my eyes and wanting to get inside my head and change everything, or leave everything the way it was, depending on what he found. He acted as if he didn't know who the man in front of him was. And the truth was he didn't know anything about me, but I didn't hang around with revolutionaries, I was too busy feeding my files with information about the underworld.

"If one of those friends you had at the university invites you to a meeting, or asks you to carry a package, or to sell July twenty-sixth raffle tickets, whatever, think about this: the SIM will grab you, hang you up by the balls, and pull out your nails. Then they'll stick a baseball bat up your ass and throw you out on the street. Don't be a damn moron, understand me?"

Then it was true. If Papá got me out of bed at this time of night, and so secretly, it was because he was convinced the horror could touch anybody, even the son of a man like him, an entrepreneur who rubbed elbows with government ministers and the military. I promised him I wouldn't get involved in anything. The fact that during that time I'd be working as a reporter on the *Diario de la Marina* relieved his mind.

On the way to Yolanda's house, I thought again about my father's warning. No revolutionary had tried to recruit me, though the deep waters I was exploring for *Prensa Libre* could just as easily involve my being hung up by the balls one of these days. And speaking of balls, there was no light at Yolanda's balcony, she must have been asleep, and it occurred to me to call from a phone on the corner. It wasn't what I'd had in mind when I decided to surprise her, but knocking at her door at this time of night was out of the question. After a couple of rings she answered in a drowsy voice. I said I was downstairs and had just arrived from New York. There was a sound that seemed like a yawn, and I sensed immediately that she wasn't alone.

"My son's here." She spoke in a different way; gradually her voice began to come out of the fog.

"The aerialist," I dared to stammer. "Then I can't come up?"

The night was cool and I was exhausted. I was sorry I'd gone there.

"Come up," she said, suddenly wide awake. "I'll make you coffee."

I went up with my raincoat over my arm, a sign I'd just come from far away; that and my red eyes were the best proof that without even shaking the dust from my feet I'd hurried over to see her. Besides, I was bringing her a present. At Idlewild Airport I'd bought her candy. I'd never bought candy for any woman, not even Zoila, my fiancée at the university. So far, that was the only formalized relationship I'd ever had with a woman, though it ended abruptly when Zoila tried to ingratiate herself with Mamá; one day I came home and saw them together, I saw a pathetic friendship and saw myself in relation to them. I renounced that panorama and broke the engagement. One thing seemed certain: Yolanda was never going to ingratiate herself with Mamá, my mother would never be her friend, and it was a relief knowing that ahead of time. When I got to the fourth floor, I saw the door partially open and Yolanda standing there, waiting for me; I should say I saw her thin robe fluttering, a night banner the color of war. On the way to her room, I thought I saw the silhouette of the aerialist lying on the bed in the next room. Yolanda had raised her index finger to her lips, asking me to be quiet. I began to undress, and she went to the kitchen to prepare coffee. All I needed was café con leche. The situation was far from what I'd imagined, but I was there already and decided to stay. We spoke very quietly, she continued telling me about her life, then she curled up beside me and fell asleep. But I was wide awake, and I spent some time caressing that little piece of an arm, the stump that gave me gooseflesh. I even asked myself if my fascination with her lay there, in what I couldn't touch. I missed her elbow, her hand, her fingers; I was attached to the irretrievable, the detached arm, where was that arm, the bones at least, the skeleton of her fingers, her skeletal hand? Where did they throw it when they cut it off? Finally, who knows what time it was, I fell asleep.

I woke fairly late in the morning. I half-opened my eyes and looked at my watch: it was past nine-thirty. I tried to get back to sleep, but the sound of voices woke me. At first I thought it came from the street, but then I discovered it was Yolanda arguing with somebody, for a moment I couldn't figure out who. I got out of bed and listened more carefully. I assumed that the other voice, which sounded very young, belonged to the aerialist. At first I caught only isolated words, very harsh words; instinct told me I ought to get dressed, and I looked around for my clothes. That was when the voices changed, grew more heated, and I could hear them perfectly.

"Does Santo know?" shouted the boy's voice. "Have you told him?"

There was a silence and she said, "Be quiet!"

Then I heard a door slam, and contrary to all expectations, my reaction was to return to bed. I got under the sheet and remained motionless, certain that Yolanda would come to see me. And she did. She opened the door and called my name. I didn't move. She called my name again and I pretended I just woke up. "It's twenty to ten," she whispered, her voice trembling.

Another café con leche was waiting for me on the table. I took a mouthful while Yolanda stared at me without touching hers. I tried to say goodbye casually. I knew it wasn't the time to draw conclusions, but I was already drawing them. I went downstairs, utterly terrified, and as I started the car and as I was driving, I was pierced by doubt, that implacable thorn. I

129

bought the paper along the way and was annoyed not to find any trace of the article I'd dictated from New York. I bet that Madrazo was waiting for something else before publishing it: for photographs—they didn't have photographs of any of the people involved—or for confirmation of flights and hotel reservations. When I got to my house, the only thing to do was tiptoe in, like a cheating husband, because I didn't want to run into Mamá. The one I did run into was Santiago, who was leaving for work unusually late. My brother glanced at the wrinkled raincoat but didn't refer to it. He put his hand on the back of my neck and exclaimed: "So, stud, did you like New York?"

I told him I'd hardly had time to see anything and apologized for taking the raincoat without letting him know.

"Keep it," he said in a melancholy voice, not very customary in him. "Now that you're a reporter, you'll have to travel. I can't set foot out of here."

I started to laugh because I knew how much Santiago liked to get on a plane and fly away from Cuba, but he assured me he was serious, he was very busy, and added that he and Papá were selling some parcels of land on Isla de Pinos. He suggested I save part of my salary and buy one.

"What would I do with a parcel of land?" I exclaimed. "Who'd live on Isla de Pinos?"

"There? They'll be weekend houses, people will get there by boat or small plane. If you don't like it, you sell it. In no time you'll get three times what you invest now."

I thought this was why my father preferred him. Santiago had a sharp eye for practically everything: for women and for selling parcels of land.

"Look: they're ninety feet wide and a hundred eighty feet deep. In four or five years some American will come along and buy it from you. The place will fill up with Americans."

I promised him I'd think about it. What I really wanted was to get away before Mamá showed up. I also had to complete the article I'd started to write in my room at the Park Sheraton but hadn't finished because of those strange phone calls. And more than anything else, I wanted to ponder the aerialist's words: "Does Santo know?" Why did he have to know anything about Yolanda, about our affair, about me?

I'd escaped my mother only momentarily. And she, with her good nose for tracking down her pups, knocked at my door.

"The paper called you yesterday," she announced gravely. "They said it was urgent. Weren't you supposed to get in last night?"

She stood looking at the open suitcase on my bed, and then she pointed at Santiago's raincoat, tossed on a chair. "You ought to have that cleaned," she added, certainly smelling the intrusive odor that surrounded me, the citric aroma that was Yolanda's sexual smell. "Your sister Lucy's waiting for you. She asked you for something, didn't she?"

Lana Turner! I'd forgotten the photograph of Lana Turner. But this had a solution, because there had to be one, or more than one, in the files at *Prensa Libre*. And if not, I could always turn to one of my old colleagues in the entertainment section.

"Tell Lucy I'll see her later. I'm going to shower. I have to go to the paper."

While my mother talked I'd been undressing until I was in my shorts. At that point she looked me up and down, my skinny legs and my pectus excavatum, the sunken chest that gave me a tragic air. Then I saw it in her eyes, I saw it as clearly as if I were reading her soul: I was still a weakling, a little blond boy who'd come out of her, something it was impossible for me to change.

"Be sure to wash your ears."

131

Mamá left and I dropped onto the bed. I was exhausted and decided to rest for a couple of hours. I was afraid I'd sleep too long and set the alarm for three. I closed my eyes and thought again about the words Yolanda's son had shouted: I could no longer doubt there had been something between her and Santo Trafficante. Or still was. Maybe she'd been creating a smoke screen with the story of Rodney only to hide the details of this other story, a much harsher and more complicated story, from me. I had an absurd dream about some shoes, and when the alarm went off I got up and put my head under the shower. I refused to touch my ears: I wasn't going to wash them because a devil had licked them. Nobody saw me when I left and headed for the paper, but after a few blocks I noticed that another car was following me. I saw it perfectly in the mirror and could make out the hats the two men inside were wearing. Instead of accelerating, I decided to take it easy and drive slowly through the make-believe city.

SWEDISH LOVE

Roderico knows about casinos but never gambles. In Las Vegas we went up to the tables, and on the sly he told me to look at the ceiling: "Do you see that mirror? There's a man up there, keeping an eye on everything." According to him, an inspector on the second floor watched the players' hands and paid attention to the croupier and every move he made. At that time I didn't like croupiers, I was sure they were taught to cheat. Roderico told me they didn't have to, all the games favored the house, some more than others. We walked through the casino, I put a few coins in the slot machines and was glad we didn't attract as much attention as we did in Havana, where we'd go someplace and people would look at us and keep looking until it made us uncomfortable. In Las Vegas nobody noticed us because they were concentrating on their chips and their bets. That trip was almost a honeymoon, the only one I ever had, though I knew a honeymoon was something else and generally didn't end as badly as ours did. We went together to see the show at the Stardust; Roderico told me it was the place where he'd seen Loretta and Johnson dance for the first time and knew right away they'd be a smash hit in Havana; his intuition was always right. That night, the last one we spent in Las Vegas, we took a farewell walk as far as the huge sign that marks the entrance to the city. I enjoyed see-ing what it really looked like because it was on the postcards I bought for my friends, the only ones I had, the people from the circus.

Roderico was explaining things about gambling; he said it's harder to win at roulette than at blackjack, and harder at blackjack than at craps, and in craps the first throw is the only time the player has an ad-vantage over the house. That's why I said I'd like us to stop at a craps table before we went back to our room that night; he said he'd do what-ever I wanted. He used a secret voice, like a stream of oil, and it drove me crazy. I must have been crazy to do what I did: I put my hand un-der his chin, I moved close to him and asked him to marry me. We were sitting on a bench near an artificial pond, a kind of pool where ducks spent the night. I could hear their wings flapping but couldn't see them, they were almost invisible on the dark water. I just saw the white foam, the wake they left behind them. Roderico lowered his head, and I imagined he was thinking carefully about what he was go-ing to say next. He said: "Yolanda, haven't you ever asked yourself if I infected anybody else with this disease?"

No, I hadn't asked myself that for the simple reason that I didn't care. I didn't say anything and wanted to change the subject because I didn't like the direction the conversation was taking. But he went on and said his disease was contagious, not now, it was true it wasn't catching anymore, but it had been in the past, in the early years, and he was sure he'd passed it on to a good friend of his. My mouth turned dry. I asked him what happened; it was what he wanted to hear. He said he dug his nails into him when he still had nails. "I'm a miser-able bastard." His voice wasn't oil now but mud. "I did it because I was jealous."

The ground of Las Vegas sank under my feet. It was only a mo-ment, I was still on the surface, in the air, and I had to control myself and not swear at him, slap him, shout, die of shame, and disappear right there, so far from my house, my son, the advice of the Chinese woman who'd brought me up. Jealousy, had he said jealousy? Roderico added: "I loved him very much, Yolanda, but then not so much, I ended up hating him. And he ended up hating me too."

I felt like crying. We were alone, it was very late, and he didn't stop smoking. I'd never seen him so determined, or so absent. I wanted to get back to the topic of gambling. I did what drowning people do: I threw my arms around his neck, running the risk that both of us would sink. I asked God to do something, to stop Roderico from talking, but the trouble was that Roderico had made up his mind, and I thought it was my fault because I'd mentioned what I shouldn't have, the rotten idea of getting married. Then I decided that no matter what I said, he'd have told me about his lover anyway because he'd planned to. That lover had a name, Odín, and he met him in Bayate, a town in Oriente near Palmarito, where Roderico came from.

"Some Swedes lived in Bayate," he started to say. "They'd been there for years, they came before I was born."

Swedes . . . Who were these Swedes, how did they talk, how long had they wandered around before they got to Oriente? Even more important, what would happen now with Roderico, and what would happen with me, and the craps table, and the first throw, my only advantage?

"When we were little we played together, Cubans and Swedes, and Odín and I would run around La Güira, a sugar plantation that belonged to another Swede who was a friend of his father. A Jamaican worked at La Güira, an overseer named Brown, and one day this overseer saw us, we were laughing and peeling a cane stalk, he ran into us and gave us a mocking look: Odín was so attractive and I was so insignificant, he said we looked like a pair of dumb lovers."

Lovers! I repeated it to myself and closed my eyes. For the first time in my life I was breathing a sandy breeze that didn't smell of saltpeter. In Cuba that kind of breeze always brings the smell of the ocean or the stink of fish, but not in Las Vegas. I missed my house, I wanted to reach safety, but Roderico let everything go: he talked in torrents, as if he were vomiting up an alcoholic binge. I heard him tell a story that hurt me, destroyed me inside: it was true that the Swede and he were dumb lovers when they ran into the Jamaican overseer, but they weren't a couple of years later. They'd stopped being dumb but went on being lovers. Together they escaped to Havana, and for Odín's father, and for most of the Swedes, who couldn't remember a stain like that in all the years they'd lived in Cuba, it was a tragedy. Roderico's family reacted differently; they were resigned ahead of time to whatever happened, and none of it made them ashamed, or else they refused to show it, they didn't even ask questions. Roderico and Odín began a life together, far from Bayate and Palmarito, the towns that had suffocated them, and far from Oriente. They worked at different jobs and at the same time took dance classes; they were hired as dancers, Odín in better places because he was tall, muscular, and blond. They danced in nightclubs, in cabarets, in movies too. Odín had a small part in Carita de Cielo, and he leaped from there to fame, or almost, because right after that somebody wanted to take him to Mexico. Nobody wanted to take Roderico, he knew he wasn't a very good dancer, maybe that's why he agreed to go on tour with the Marvelous Revue, a variety show that toured the countryside. And the final straw was when he broke out in the first pimples, or the first blisters. It all happened very fast, and it all happened at once: Odín met another man, and Roderico had to confront him to make him confess.

"Let's go," I interrupted, and I said it with authority. "I want to go back to the hotel."

We went back with our heads bowed, we went straight up to the room, we didn't stop at any craps table. When we finally went to bed, with the lights turned off but with brightness coming in from outside, Roderico kept telling me about his friendship with Odín until he reached the end, when his voice broke. Roderico crying for another man was the bitterest pill of that trip, of my whole life. I'd have given my arm, the one I have left, not to hear him swallowing his snot, sniveling like a child. I understood there was nothing to do, and I let him talk without asking questions; it wasn't worth it anymore to ask him about anything. He said the man Odín had left him for was a knife grinder, the kind who goes from house to house, but very refined, with a virgin's hands and profile: nose, mouth, chin, everything delicate and pale. The knife grinder had lived in Cuba since he was a boy but was a native of Spain; his mother brought him here when she got him back—he'd been stolen from the cradle when he was a baby.

"Odín believed that fairy tale," Roderico lamented. "He felt sorry for him, he thought a witch really had stolen him to suck his blood."

In the dark he told me about it, and I trembled from head to toe, not from fear but from sorrow. Odín wanted Roderico to meet the knife grinder. One night the three of them went out, they walked around the Aires Libres, and sat down to have some rum. The knife grinder knew he was killing Roderico, and to finish him off he exchanged glances with the Swede and was brilliant telling jokes. Odín encouraged him to tell the story of the witch again, but Roderico, a little drunk, shouted that he wasn't interested in hearing it, he was sick of listening to lies. The knife grinder said he had newspaper articles that proved it: the vampire witch stole him in Barcelona. The three of them were silent— all you could hear was the orchestra music—they said goodbye quickly, and the knife grinder went in one direction while Roderico and Odín went in another, toward the apartment on Calle Egido where they were living at the time. When they got there they argued, they began to use their hands, and Odín shook Roderico and called him leper, the black word. Roderico grabbed his arm and dug in his nails, and Odín tried to get free and punched and kicked until he did. He hurried to get his leather valise, the same Swedish valise his parents had brought to Cuba; he tossed in his clothes and left with his shirt open, that's how men leave when they're running away from madness, not buttoning their shirts the right way, putting the buttons in the wrong buttonholes. Roderico dragged himself to the balcony, and when he saw Odín go out, he shouted that he'd be a leper too. He was sure he'd infected him.

"I never saw him again," he said, so sad I could smell the odor of his unhappiness. "Somebody told me they'd gone to Spain to live, Odín and that evil queer who sharpened knives."

He took my hand, but I was rigid, unable to move: somebody had sucked my blood too.

"Forgive me, Yolanda," he whispered just before he began to snore. "I forgot to take you to the craps table."

I hardly slept that night. I got up very early, went into the bathroom, and cried as I showered. Then I got dressed and combed my hair, I tried not to make any noise and wake Roderico, but it's hard when you have to do everything with one arm. I put on a lilac hat with a veil that covered my face; I put it on for the trip back, just like the artists who came to the cabaret. That's how Roderico saw me when he woke up: bathed and dressed, my eyes, red from crying, half hidden under the veil. He asked me what time it was, then he got out of bed and went into the bathroom. I thought he was probably crying under the water too, thinking about that Swedish love. I'd never heard about Swedes in Cuba, but I didn't doubt it because in Oriente there was everything, lots of people from the strangest places, some of them working in coffee, like the French. The French loved the circus and took their children whenever we passed through those towns.

The trip back to Cuba was a wake. I was the deceased, it had to be me because I couldn't even feel myself leaning on smoke. I didn't feel any kind of support under my feet or my single hand. Back at the Tropicana, everybody gave us curious looks, as if Roderico had gone crazy or I had gone crazy. We seemed to be accomplices, and in the eyes of other people, the simple fact of traveling together to Las Vegas turned us into a strange couple: the one-armed woman and the leper. How many people must have said that? But in fact, only I knew that our friendship had come to a dead end. Roderico became fretful. Sometimes he talked to me only to tell me about his ailments; leprosy is a disease that destroys not only the outside but the inside too, it was logical that his joints would hurt, or his chest. But more than everything *else there was his attitude: he put distance between us and became very suspicious about all his things. From one minute to the next I expected him to throw me out. I even felt resigned, I prepared ahead of time the words I'd say when he told me he didn't need me anymore. And in the middle of all that trouble, one night I got a call telling me that Chinita had died. Today I say it fast, but from the moment I hung up the phone to the instant they lowered the coffin, my heart beat much more slowly, everything was slower: the way I walked, the way I picked up a cup to have coffee, or started thinking, my thoughts clotted. I couldn't decide, or understand, or imagine my poor son, alone in Chinita's world, a bottomless world. I put a change of clothes into a bag and went out without combing my hair, like a desperate woman, I only wanted to find a car to take me in a heartbeat to Mantilla, the town where she died; luckily the circus was there, so close to Havana. By the time I got there they'd put her in the box, under a second tent they put up inside the main tent. Everybody embraced me, gave me condolences; some of them were new and didn't even know me. My son was calm but pale, fat tears ran down his face, it seemed to me he'd shrunk, he was shrunken in a chair, he was only a boy. "My mother's gone," I heard him say, and at that moment everything that was already slow stopped, my own heart stopped in my chest; I couldn't breathe, or see, or imagine anything but words of remorse. I collapsed from the effect. In a circus they always know how to bring around people who faint, they always have ammonia and salts. The rest of the wake was normal, but the most curious thing is that it made me think about Odín; I thought about his history with Roderico, and I imagined scene after scene, in fixed squares, the way you look at photographs in an album. And I imagined the knife grinder, all the door-to-door knife grinders I knew were fairly old; in Cuba it's a trade for old Spaniards, pedaling their bicycles with the tools they use to grind an edge, but I told myself that at some point they'd all been young, like the little boy whose blood the witch sucked. At midmorning I went to the covered wagon where Chinita had lived. I gathered up her clothing and saw some tiny shoes* on the floor; they looked like two beetles, that's why I remembered what she told me: the spirit never leaves from the chest or the head the way people think. It leaves from the feet, and you have to be barefoot, die completely barefoot. I kept her glasses, the ones she used all her life, they were old and had mother-of-pearl frames; I thought my mother had gone too. I fixed some tea, and while I drank it, I knew nothing would have comforted me as much as having Roderico with me during this difficult time. It was noon when I called his house. I'd never done that before, he'd told me to call only in an emergency, since he lived with his mother, who was old and suffered from headaches. And an old woman answered, Roderico got on the line, and I explained what had happened. He said he was sorry and I should take the rest of the week off. That's all. He didn't ask if I needed him, if I needed anything. We buried Chinita in Havana, in a Chinese cemetery where she had a mausoleum. She told my son about it in her final moments; she explained that almost all her family were buried there, and that the Portuguese magician, before he died, had given her the papers and a little map showing where the pantheon of her ancestors was located. She never told us anything. She had to die for us to know that she had a space in this earth, something of her own among her people, in the cemetery with the pagoda gates.

Roderico came to the house to give me his condolences; he brought flowers, and sandwiches and beer to have with me. He seemed distant, like a different man, especially because he didn't come alone; Cristóbal, a boy with drooping eyes who was studying medicine, came with him. My sadness was so great I didn't even have the heart to turn on him and find the defects in Cristóbal, who was studious and refined, with the manners of a priest, nothing that resembled the world of the cabaret, or Roderico's world, or mine.

Months later, I found out he was preparing another trip to Las Vegas. I knew he wouldn't ask me to go with him on this one, though sometimes in the afternoon he still dropped by the house. Especially when he had a falling-out with Cristóbal; you could see it in his ex-

pression, in how angry he felt about his own defects, about his scars and misshapen shoes. He complained about everything, about being ugly and a mulatto, even about burning his fingers and not being able to feel it. Then he asked me to fry him a steak, and he stayed and slept with me. But he took Cristóbal to Las Vegas. I heard about the preparations for this trip and thought about the one we'd taken just the way I thought about the arm they cut off, the same way, with the feeling I'd lost something made of flesh and bone.

Since he'd be away for a while this time, he suggested that instead of staying at the Tropicana, doing nothing, I ought to go to the Sans Souci and help his friend Kary Rusi. That was the end I'd been expecting all this time. I got my things together and felt a little humiliated because people there knew what had happened. I was alone, but I always had been. I missed Chinita, and above all I missed my son, who stayed in the circus, he didn't want to come back with me, his life was in the troupe, it was the place he belonged to, and he agreed to come to the Sans Souci only for a short time when the choreographer hired him to make the leap.

One day, Kary Rusi told me she was expecting a reporter from the Diario de la Marina, *and that I should stay with her a little longer so the reporter wouldn't see her alone. You came in; nobody imagined you'd be so young. Kary called me later to say that she noticed you were so interested in me you didn't even pay attention to her debut at the Stardust. It made me laugh. I think it was the first time I'd laughed in a long while. You looked less like a magician than anyone I could have imagined.*

THE MIRROR

"They shut down our presses!" Madrazo roared. "Somebody ratted us out."

He was busy reading galleys and barely looked up when he heard me come in.

"Sit down," he said without looking at me. "We'll meet now with Carbó and decide what to do with your article."

I didn't sit down and I didn't respond to what he was saying, I couldn't, I wasn't capable yet of sorting things out. Madrazo realized I'd come in without saying good evening (it was evening by now) and hadn't reacted to his news about the presses. He thought about it and looked at me again: he saw that I was soaking wet and pale, and that one eye was almost closed.

"What happened?"

I moved my head, trying not to fall down, not to shit in my pants after everything was over. It wasn't logical to shit oneself at the wrong time.

"Do you feel sick? Do you want coffee?"

"Coffee," I answered, but my own voice sounded distant, false, as if it were coming out of a sewer.

Madrazo hurried to the door and ordered Niño—a black man with a rotting nose—to run and get some coffee. Then I heard a bustling behind me, the opening and closing of drawers, and the next thing I saw was the glass he placed in front of me.

"Sit down," he said more firmly. "And drink this cognac, it'll help you warm up."

I drank it in one swallow. I could have been drinking bleach, Coca-Cola, slime, it would have all tasted the same to me.

"Do you feel better?"

I made a movement with my head, I stammered so-so. I hadn't seen myself yet in a mirror, but I could feel that my cheekbone was swollen, and my eye, my eye terrified me. The fear of going blind had been one of the specters of my childhood, a mania I'd carried with me ever since. In the fights we had as kids I always made sure nobody touched my eyes, but in this uneven fight I wasn't able to do that.

"Spit it out," Madrazo urged. "Then you have to go to the clinic and get fixed up."

The cognac helped. At first I didn't feel it in my mouth, but now that it had gone down it was having an effect.

"Some guys followed me," I mumbled, my tongue faltering because I'd bitten it. "They were waiting for me when I left the house, and they began following me but I didn't stop, I thought I'd better drive straight here."

Madrazo stood up, patted me on the shoulder, and said, "Go on, go on." He looked for a glass for himself and brought over the bottle. I asked him to pour me another one, and I began to spit it out like he wanted; I was doing that, literally getting that glob of fury and stupefaction out of my mouth. I told him that at first I thought they were only trying to scare me, but when I turned onto Manrique, two blocks from the paper, another car was waiting for me and cut me off. Some guys got out, the two from the automobile blocking me, and they pulled me out of my car.

"That's when they hit me here," I said, pointing to my cheek.

"Fuck," Madrazo said with a shudder. "Go on . . ."

They aimed their guns at me and forced me to get in with them. We pulled away in a Chevrolet, it was a blue Bel Air, and when we drove past *Prensa Libre*, they stopped for a moment: "You work here, right?" We drove away fast, heading for the university; all I told Madrazo was this:

"They stopped where a girlfriend of mine lives . . ."

I didn't want to tell him that the man who was driving, a skinny mulatto, his hair dripping with brilliantine, had said: "The one-armed woman lives up there, doesn't she?" I didn't know if he was talking to me or his pal. "The things that go on. I never fucked a one-armed woman but I've had plenty with one leg, those cripples love to fuck." I was riding in front, between them; the one on the right kept the barrel of his gun pressed against my ribs. He pushed it hard against me and whispered: "Hey, boy, what made you think you could wet your prick where Santo wets his? You must be fuckin' crazy."

"They drove to my house," I continued telling Madrazo, "and stopped. 'You live here, right? With your fuckin' whore of a mother.' "

Until then I hadn't opened my mouth. The only thing I opened it for was to say I didn't know what this was all about. They said I did know, but what a coincidence that we were going to the zoo, because maybe the place would bring back my memory. They said the zoo, and I remembered the hippopotamus, I thought they were going to kill me there and that Bulgado was in cahoots with them.

"Bulgado's the one who wants to go to the Capri," I explained to Madrazo. "Remember I told you about him, the guy who wants to meet Raft?"

He replied: "Yes, sure, sure I remember." Just then Niño showed up with the coffee; there was an obligatory pause. We mixed it with cognac and drank in silence, and when we finished, Madrazo asked me to go on. He still had to take me to be treated—it wouldn't be a good idea to let my eye close up completely, and it was almost closed now. I proceeded slowly, trying to walk with leaden feet because I knew I still had to leave out something else, something I didn't want to tell anybody. I couldn't, especially not Madrazo, who was my boss.

"We got to the zoo. We went straight to the slaughter pen . . ."

I had to explain that at the zoo there was a small slaughter pen where they killed animals to feed to the lions. Madrazo made a slight grimace of revulsion. Bulgado was in charge of the slaughter pen; it wasn't normal for him to be there at that time of day, and yet he was, and there was somebody else pointing a gun at him, though he didn't look frightened, just the opposite, he was smoking, as calm as could be, his clothes stained with blood. There was no way to know if it was his own or the blood of the horse lying there with its head split open. Bulgado and I looked at each other as if we were agreeing to something, but agreeing to what? Somebody else came in, and I knew he was the boss because of the attitude the other men assumed: it wasn't a way of greeting him, because they didn't even greet him, but a way of looking at him, of waiting for a gesture, a subtle change of frequency. The new arrival came toward me, took some papers out of his pocket, and showed them to me. "Tell me something, kid, did you write this garbage?" I read the first two lines of the article I had dictated to Fini from New York. I didn't try to open my mouth. My instincts told me to admit everything but without saying a word, to use only gestures. I nodded yes. He seemed satisfied. I'd have done anything not to irritate him; he had the look of people who lose control when they're irritated. He was white and had a thin mustache and a face like a cracker, an implacable face that had pockmarks and a scar. He turned and walked to the place where Bulgado was standing. "Let's see, who told this faggot about the hippopotamus?" Bulgado pushed his cap to one side and looked up, with tremendous self-assurance. The man with the mustache immediately signaled to the two men who'd kidnapped me, and they both left; he also signaled to the one who was guarding Bulgado, and he put away his pistol and left with the others.

"Stop there," Madrazo interrupted when he saw Fini come in.

The secretary looked at me in surprise. When she saw me in her boss's office, she put on a crafty face, the carefully studied face that traitorous secretaries put on, and I asked myself if she hadn't been the one who'd ratted out the article. I looked at Madrazo, who was hypnotized, not by Fini—impossible to be hypnotized by a scarecrow like that—but by everything I was telling him. He and I both knew we were close to the outcome, but only I—and Bulgado—would know the truth; there are things that can't be told even when they occur against our will, they're too monstrous, too humiliating. In the end, I was grateful that Fini interrupted, it gave me a few minutes to improvise, to invent an ending that would seem logical.

Madrazo rubbed his eyes. I think he didn't even understand what his secretary was telling him, it was a message from the editor: could they meet at ten-thirty? I imagined that the cognac had probably dulled his senses, as it had dulled mine, though my eye, my ear, my cheekbone still hurt, and considering the force of the blow, I couldn't understand why that cheekbone hadn't split open. Fini left, I was tempted to ask Madrazo if she wasn't the government spy who'd been planted there. But I didn't have the heart. Suddenly I was beginning to fall apart. The same cognac that had animated me a few minutes earlier was now pushing me down into an incredible stupor.

"Keep talking . . . What did they do to you then? Did you find out who they were?"

Both of us knew perfectly well who they were. Even Bulgado knew, and he was an imbecile.

"What do you mean who they were?" My tone was insolent, I knew that, but I maintained it. "They told me to be grateful the article hadn't been published. I'd been warned, and he wouldn't talk about it next time; I shouldn't play with people's reputations again."

"Let's go to the clinic," Madrazo insisted. "Let them treat you and you'll get some sleep, take a couple of days and then we can talk calmly."

I said no, you treated a punch in the face like a punch in the face: with ice and warm compresses, it wasn't the first one I'd received in my life, and I was afraid it wouldn't be the last. Madrazo put his hand on my shoulder and asked if he could help me with anything. I thought about my sister; it was very unusual for me to think about her when things were so stressful.

"Would you have a photo of Lana Turner around here?"

He smiled. Lana Turner? I didn't intend to give him explanations or tell him the photograph was for Lucy. He didn't want to find out too much either.

"Well sure, I'll tell them to bring you one right away."

He picked up the phone and talked to Fini or somebody.

Then he asked if I felt strong enough to drive. I confessed that I didn't even have the strength to take a piss but that I'd manage to get home without any problem. Fini brought in the photograph, gave it to him, and he passed it to me: Lana Turner was good-looking. I couldn't blame my sister for falling in love with her.

"I'll go downstairs with you," Madrazo offered.

Before we went out, I asked him to let me make a call. He pointed to the phone and left me alone. I dialed Yolanda's number and said I had to see her right away. Then I went down to the street and joined Madrazo. He looked all around, waited until I was in the car, and leaned over to talk to me through the window.

"Yesterday a messenger from Santiago Rey showed up here," he whispered, repulsed or furious, both have a common root in contempt. "He went straight to Carbó and told him that by order of the Ministry of the Interior, the piece by Joaquín Porrata, special correspondent in New York, couldn't be published. Carbó told him he'd come too late; the next day's edition was on the presses. The guy shouted to stop them. He went berserk and called Interior, and within five minutes the place was full of troops and civil police, who destroyed the papers. Before he left, he warned that if we published anything, he'd close the paper."

Those words were a bucket of cold water, much colder than the water thrown at me earlier, in the slaughter pen. I turned the ignition key, said goodbye to Madrazo, and pulled away in the car that never failed me, the Plymouth of my soul that almost became an orphan. My destiny probably lay in the cabarets, interviewing lifelong whores or falling over myself in praising the productions of the great Rodney, the inexhaustible Roderico Neyra, what a surprise for me that a woman like Yolanda could have fallen in love with a man like him! Not only ugly, not only a faggot, but worse than that, out of his skull, and brazen enough to have presumed to take her to Las Vegas. My destiny was to compete with Don Galaor and the Gondolier, going up and down the canals to find out about idiocy, and who knows, as the years passed, maybe I'd fall into the clutches of Skinny T. again. At this time of night, with my head aching and the wind hitting me in the face—it hit hard, over and over again, like a pie in the face—I couldn't have cared less about my future in the newspaper business.

I was slightly intoxicated. Three large drinks, combined with the mental weakness I was feeling, were equivalent to twice that amount. The cognac had helped a little to lessen the horror, which I hadn't spit out in front of Madrazo because I couldn't. Bulgado and I weren't allowed to reveal how the fiesta ended, but it went like this: the three men who left on the orders of the one with the singer's voice returned a short while later carrying something, evidently a human body wrapped in jute sacks. They cut the ropes, unwrapped it quickly, like diligent traveling salesmen ready to show their merchandise. They displayed a man's corpse in undershorts; I avoided looking at it because I stupidly thought the less I looked the less complicated things would be for me afterward. I didn't realize I was already long past any complications, I was done for. If my irony had been intact, which it wasn't, I'd have admitted that my situation was more compromised than the corpse's; the poor bastard had already lost all hope. He had nothing left to lose, but I did. The one who gave the orders spoke to Bulgado, muttering something I couldn't hear. Then I saw that Johnny Angel, or Johnny Lamb, or whatever that son of a bitch insisted on calling himself, got up and walked to a corner of the slaughter pen. He came back with three or four butcher knives. He was apprehensive, waiting for the next order, and the man with the thin mustache gave it to him in a quiet voice. Bulgado came toward me, stopped in front of me, and showed me the knives. "Choose the curved blade," he whispered uneasily, indicating it with a twist of his mouth. I didn't dare touch it. I looked up and discovered that all of them were hanging on my movements. "Choose one, damn it!" said the voice of the boss. I took the knife Bulgado had indicated. I stood there holding it like an imbecile. The head man looked at me scornfully, put his arms akimbo, with his thumbs hooked inside his belt, and slowly approached the cadaver. "Now you two cut up this piece of shit for me and mix it with the horse meat." I didn't understand. Or I understood, but no, it wasn't possible. Bulgado, who was standing beside me, realized how bewildered I was. "I'll do everything, you follow my lead." I had the sensation of being anchored to the ground, anchored to the odor of blood and to the odor of the corpse, a stink I thought I'd never get rid of for as long as I lived. "If you don't move," the man threatened me, "you'll be the one we cut up." Naturally, I moved. Bulgado suggested I take off my shirt and trousers and keep on just my shorts. He was wearing the zoo coverall, which in a sense was his clothing for cutting up horses, so he could get it dirty; in fact it already was dirty. The boss swore. He shat on God or something like that, I heard him shout: "Strip if you want to go home alive. I won't send you back covered with bloodstains." I stripped. I was a little blue lizard, a little blond worm, a kind of larva with no ambition, humbly observing the remains: the horse's on one side, the dead man's on the other. "I'm going to work," Bulgado announced. He left the knives on the ground and picked up an ax. "When I finish with the ax, both of us will start in with the knives." I heard the first blows of the ax; I closed my eyes and understood that things were spattering me, not necessarily blood, maybe little bits of bone, of cartilage, of human skin and animal skin. "Cut what you can," Bulgado said to me on the sly. He'd put down the ax and was armed with a vicious-looking knife. Four killers—the two who'd brought me there, the one who'd been guarding Bulgado, and the one who gave the orders—watched us. I vomited twice, and they saw me vomit. I waited in vain for their laughter. I assumed they were going to make fun of me, but they remained serious, as if they resented the job. I cut the little I could cut tormented by the smell, by how my eyes were burning, the skin on my neck, my filthy arms, where pieces of flesh, horse fat or man fat, were sticking. "Be happy you're not the one going into the lion's mouth along with the horse," growled the one who did the talking, and I looked at his mouth, small and sadistic, a real chicken's ass under his impeccable mustache. "I hope you stop sticking your nose where it doesn't belong."

Bulgado assured me later that the dead man was an American and this was the punishment they got when they tried to cheat at the casinos. That's why Havana was clean territory, or boasted of being clean: no dead bodies in the bay, no scores settled in barbershops or restaurants. As far as Lansky and the rest of the families were concerned, in Cuba dirty laundry was washed in a more spiritual way: cheats disappeared without a trace, everything cloaked, as it had to be. I realized it didn't matter to the killers if we cut a lot or a little, the important thing was the gesture, the humiliation of having participated in a sickening ceremony. After an hour—an eternity—they told me I could wash and put on my clothes, and that I should consider myself a dead man if I said a word to anybody. In the slaughter pen there was a very primitive shower; I took off my shorts and stood motionless under the stream of cold water. Bulgado was shoveling up pieces of meat and tossing them into the basins that I imagined they used to feed the lions as well as the tigers, all the wild beasts, and the hyenas that gnawed the bones. Standing under the water, I felt like crying and fighting too, like attacking those individuals and beating them with my fists now that they were off guard, smoking so cheerfully. I turned off the tap and realized I didn't even have anything to dry myself with. I stood there a few minutes, shivering, with my arms crossed, the men ignoring me and Bulgado shoveling up meat. I began to dry myself with my own shirt, but with one thing and another, Bulgado became aware of my situation, left the meat, and with dirty hands he offered me a threadbare, fetid towel, a rag really, with unpardonable stains. I put on my trousers, my shoes, my wet shirt. I was breathing in spasms from the cold and my own helplessness. In a sudden impulse of generosity, the one with the mustache said I could go. "But look," he blustered, "remember what I told you: keep fucking with you-know-what, I swear by my mother I'll cut off your dick and throw it to the giraffes."

I didn't answer, I bowed my head, which was enough. I ran along the paths of the deserted zoo, a ferocious place when the animals were asleep. I came out on the avenue, and the first thing that occurred to me was to catch a bus, almost empty, of course, maybe five or six passengers surely lost in their own dramas, since they barely looked up when I got on and didn't see that my hands were trembling. I got off in Vedado, stopped a cab, gave the driver the address of my house, then changed my mind and told him to take me instead to Calle Manrique, the place where I'd left my car. It made me happy to see it, the stupid happiness of knowing that you're returning to objects, and those objects are signs that throw you a line and pull you back. The keys were inside. I started the car and drove the two blocks to the paper. I went up like a zombie, removed from everything around me. Somebody, some colleague, greeted me as I walked by, but I didn't return the greeting because ghosts don't talk, and I was a ghost. I'd been with the dead, I'd smelled blood, human and animal blood mixed, the contact that obscures everything, or that clarifies everything, depending on how you look at it: a mirror is deciphered only in another mirror. I went straight to Madrazo's office, I saw him through the glass, reading galleys. He wasn't a relative, he wasn't even a friend, but I felt relieved to find him there. I went in without knocking. Madrazo looked up out of the corner of his eye; that was enough for him to know who I was, and that was when he shouted: "They shut down our presses!"

RUMBA

I told Yolanda I had to talk to her that same night, but not in her apartment because it was dangerous. She became nervous and lost control a little and insisted I tell her what had happened. I said I'd been kidnapped. She was silent, and when she spoke again, she made an effort to appear calm: Where do you want us to meet? I said the Golden Eagle, a Chinese movie house in Chinatown.

Half an hour later we were together, sitting in the last row. It was a brutal meeting. Two Chinese girls were singing in the film, high Chinese tones that can't be heard by the human ear, but that night I discovered they could be heard in your bones, your eye sockets, that's where they resonate. There was a smell of opium in the theater, of tobacco, of dirty feet, and you could hear coughing, the perpetual hawking of old Chinese men. I began to speak incoherently, running words and ideas together, but she understood. I believe she understood from the moment she heard my voice on the phone. And now she listened in silence, looking straight ahead; the light from the screen illuminated her, and two or three times I saw her grimace, as if she were being infected by the sorrow of the Chinese girls. I practically accused her of being an informer for Trafficante, of giving him information about me and telling him about my movements. I was too weak to continue. She caressed my hair: she had to talk to me and explain some things, but not right then. She thought I was in bad shape and ought to rest. I said I wouldn't rest until she told me everything: if she knew they were watching me, if she'd had any idea they were going to take me by force, if Trafficante had ordered her to go to bed with me. Yolanda gave me a low blow, the one that hurt me most after all the ones I'd gotten: "You're not that important to Trafficante."

There was a dive behind the Golden Eagle, two mulattas worked there and the clientele was varied: blacks from the docks, solitary Chinese, homeless drunks . . . In short, the perfect place not to be noticed. We went in and ordered highballs, we smoked constantly, I mean I smoked and Yolanda talked. It wasn't Trafficante who asked about me but the second in command at the Sans Souci, the fat, bald man named Jacobs. He asked her directly if we were having an affair, and Yolanda's first reaction was to deny it. He said there was a rumor going around that I was "mixed up in something," that was the phrase used to suggest that a person was involved in the revolutionary underground. After that the subject didn't come up again, except for one barbed remark that Jacobs made: no employee at the Sans Souci was authorized to give information about the bosses, whether they were in the cabaret or away on a trip.

It would have been easy for Trafficante to ask Kary Rusi to fire Yolanda, and so far she hadn't tried to. Yolanda admitted that she and Trafficante had "seen each other" briefly, but that was a private "torment" she'd put behind her. She wasn't going to tell me any more, except for the episode of the woman who was murdered in the cabaret; she had seen the dead body, which made her very sad. By this time I'd stopped paying attention, my vision had blurred, and I decided I'd better get home as fast as I could. We kissed each other goodbye, but first she asked the same question as Madrazo: did I feel strong enough to drive. I said I did, and she said she'd take a taxi, I shouldn't even think about driving to her house.

I didn't think about it because I didn't even know if I was capable of getting to mine. I did, finally, guided by instinct. I arrived without mishap and discovered to my relief that everybody had gone to bed. It was almost twelve, and probably the only one who wasn't home was my brother, Santiago, who always stayed out late. I slipped the photograph of Lana Turner, inside an envelope, under the door of Lucy's room, because I knew she was awake, she stayed up late in her own way. I looked all around for an ice bag. I didn't find one and had to improvise with a towel. I wrapped it around some ice cubes and hurried to my room; I put it on my face and fell asleep right away, water streaming onto the pillow. The next morning, predictably enough, I was worse, more swollen, and I had a black eye. I summoned the courage to face my family and went down early, when I supposed they'd all be having breakfast: Papá and Santiago, who almost always left for work together, and Mamá, arguing with Lucy about wearing barrettes and using a lipstick that she called a nice pale pink. At the age of seventeen, in her last year of secondary school, Lucy tore off the barrettes as soon as she left the house and rubbed her lips until there was no trace left of that deceptive pink.

Santiago wasn't there. It was just my damn luck: the only one who would have taken my part was the only one not at the table. My mother looked up and was so shocked that, for the first time, she didn't say a single word, nothing, I even thought she'd choked. Papá did speak, though he behaved casually, without any fuss. "Let me look at you . . . Where was the fight?" I stammered an answer I'd prepared ahead of time; I said I tried to separate a couple of guys at the paper who were fighting over a woman. I added that Madrazo, the editor, had wanted to take me to the clinic but I refused because the way you treat a punch in the face is with ice. My mother came out of her silence, her shock, whatever it was, to say there was still time to call Dr. Doblas, our family physician, because who knew what would happen to my eye. Papá knew my story was a lie, but one man to another he didn't say so; he remarked that if the men who were fighting worked at the paper, the normal thing to do was to fire them. I lied so quickly it seemed real: they'd have a month without pay, though for the moment they hadn't been thrown out.

"They ought to give their pay to you." Mamá poured out all her acid. "I'm sure you got the worst of it."

For her it was unthinkable that I'd have any chance at all to outdo anyone in anything. In her eyes, I was a midway point between a solid older brother and a sister whose solidity was something else: a daily struggle to survive, a courage that turned men into little boys.

"It's like when dogs fight," Lucy interjected. She looked happy that morning. "You should never get in the middle. And thanks for the photograph."

I said it was nothing. I couldn't ask her if she liked it because I knew she did. She'd probably kissed it on the mouth: the expectant, capricious mouth that Lana Turner had in that photograph. My mouth, by contrast, burned, my tongue too, especially when I chewed, and my jaws, though I'd recovered the timbre of my voice. The servant who'd worked for us for years, her name was Balbina, was the most expressive: "Holy God, Quin, look what they've done to you." She'd known me since I was a little boy; she showed me affection—I can't understand why, since I never did anything to deserve it, just the opposite, in fact—and she promised to fix a poultice for me. Mamá had been transfigured, she wasn't even speaking with her usual hysteria but in a calm way that left me astounded, Lucy incredulous, and Papá, I suppose, fairly disoriented. She said she was still going to call Dr. Doblas. I really didn't care if she called him or not. I was tired, the horror was still flowing in my blood, and I wanted to put my arms around Yolanda, who'd convinced me of her innocence, maybe because I needed to let myself be convinced. In any case, I didn't want to leave her, I didn't gain anything by doing that.

I ate soft-boiled eggs, I drank café con leche, I felt relieved at having faced the family, and for the first time in my entire life I think I even felt happy to see them again. I slept until noon, when my mother woke me. She was with Dr. Doblas, a joker to whom, in a way, I owed my life. Twenty-two years earlier, soon after I came into the world, I almost died of asphyxiation. The doctor taking care of me at the time deceived my mother out of compassion: he pretended he was taking me away to give me oxygen. He told my grandmother the truth: she'd just lost her second grandchild, and he put me on a stretcher reserved for babies who had died. But Dr. Doblas, who happened to be passing by, glanced at me (with his wise owl's eyes), discovered I was still breathing, picked me up by my feet, and struggled with me until my color returned. "The little dead blue baby," he said this time when he saw me. "Who turned you blue again, you great dumb bastard?"

More than a joker, he was a skilled fencer with foul language. He prescribed some pills, gave his consent for Balbina to prepare her poultice, and told me to keep sleeping. It was easy for me to obey him, my body didn't ask for anything else, not even food, just that blurred world, I'd wake up and go back to sleep again, remembering the horse's head, its shattered skull, and the dead man's legs: intact but soft, white with blond hairs, the veins silent, like pensive worms. It was almost eight that night when Lucy woke me. She did it gently because she was grateful to me for understanding her.

"A man's here for you," she said. I noticed that her voice was changing, it had become husky, and I was glad for her. "He says his name is Joe Martin and that he works at the zoo."

I covered my face with my hands. It was a spontaneous gesture, but Lucy interpreted it as a gesture of horror, or panic. She tried to calm me: she hadn't let him in, he was waiting outside. She'd told him I was sick.

"He has a bruise like yours," Lucy added. She was so mistrustful. "He's the one you had the fight with, isn't he?"

I shook my head.

"I fought with other people. He was on my side. Let him come in, and try not to let Mamá see him."

Lucy was a perfect accomplice when it was a question of misleading my mother. She left my room, and while she was gone I put on my pajama top, the horrendous pajamas that Mamá would buy and that we wore only when we were sick. I slept in my shorts, and Santiago bragged that he slept naked. I don't know about Lucy. She probably slept however she wanted to, even though Mamá surely bought her little girl pajamas at El Encanto. My sister came back with Bulgado, whose face was slightly bruised but not as much as mine. He carried his hat, a first-class panama that I imagined he'd inherited from his father-in-law, wore a guayabera, and looked like a planter. He wasn't the same Bulgado who washed out the animals' cages with buckets of water. He shook my hand, very ceremoniously, and asked how I felt. I said I was almost better. I told Lucy that if Mamá asked about me she should say I was still asleep; it was also a way of asking her to leave us alone. Bulgado was eager to talk; he said one of the men had come to his house for him, and he had gone with him because he didn't want his wife or mother-in-law mixed up in this business. They didn't take any detours but drove straight to the zoo. Two other guys were waiting for them. They showed him the article I'd dictated from New York, they showed it to him printed on newsprint, which meant it came from the same edition the minister of the interior had confiscated. They said I'd been caught and would be taken to the slaughter pen, where they'd shoot me and throw me in so he could cut me up along with the horse.

I interrupted in the most stupid way: "And would you have cut me up?"

Bulgado answered frankly: "If you're dead and don't feel or suffer anything, and if I can save my skin by cutting you up, then yes, I would."

He told me that after they let me go, and before he could start distributing the food (so that not a trace would be left the next morning), the men had disappeared, not without first giving him the same warning they'd given me: if he said a single word about what had happened that night, he could consider himself a dead man.

I sat up in bed; the pain in my face seemed to have spread throughout my body. I felt literally beaten. Bulgado was surprised to see me with so many bruises. But he'd come for what he'd come for: next Wednesday was the opening of the Hotel Capri, with the presence of George Raft, and he hoped I'd feel better in time to take him.

"One promise for another," I said quickly. "Even if I can't write it, you're going to tell me what's going on at the zoo, how many times you've done what we did last night."

"A few," Bulgado admitted, "but I was always forced to. And who can I complain to? The chief of police? Hell, I'm not that crazy: sometimes they come with an escort of plainclothes cops. I know cops: I just have to see their fingernails."

I was going to ask him what there was in particular about policemen's nails, but Bulgado went on in a quiet voice. His assistant Lázaro, who cleaned cages with him, was the one who had proposed this business to him. A year ago they were eating lunch together when the other man suddenly tossed a roll of bills on the barrel they were using as a table. When it wasn't raining they always had lunch there, a few steps from the slaughter pen, under a tree and surrounded by the odor of rotting flesh. Bulgado looked at the money, and Lázaro said it was one hundred pesos, payment in advance for the work they'd do that night. "I don't work at night," Bulgado quipped, and Lázaro said he would tonight and all the other nights that came along, they both had to because if they didn't they'd be killed.

"Buzzard, Jar Boy, and Turtle," said Bulgado. "Those names sound familiar?"

Of course they sounded familiar: they were the three hoodlums who spooked the hippopotamus on the night this story began.

"They came for Lázaro at his house in the Cayo Hueso slum and took him to a bar on the docks. The men who got us last night were there. They said they were hiring Lázaro and me, and we had to accept whether we wanted to or not."

My sister opened the door without knocking and put her head in the room: she'd managed to keep my mother away, though not for long; she assured her I was asleep, but Mamá insisted on waking me to give me some broth. Bulgado looked at me: he asked if he had to go. I didn't answer but begged Lucy to invent something, slipping and falling down, a stomachache, anything that would keep Mamá out of the room. Lucy shrugged and left, and I concentrated on Bulgado.

"Do you know who those guys from last night work for?"

Bulgado nodded. He gave a crooked smile. "For a Santo who doesn't wear a crown. Be afraid of him."

"Trafficante? Did they tell you?"

He laughed. He assured me that those men, so elegant, with such good cars, didn't talk to guys like him, even less to guys like me. Jar Boy had said something about their working for Trafficante. He was an oddball, of the three who'd messed around so much at the zoo, he was the only one who knew how to read, and the only one who talked like a human being, because Turtle talked through his nose, he had a tumor in his throat, and Buzzard was half crazy, he had fits and bit his tongue and rolled his eyes up in his head. The three of them were resting now.

Bulgado lowered his voice to say this last sentence; he lowered it so much I had to guess at his words from the movement of his lips.

"What do you mean they're resting?"

He looked at the door, leaned toward me, darkened his voice to an impossible point: "I cut them up a few days ago. You were in New York."

I retched slightly and immediately felt a spasm snaking up from my stomach to my mouth. I lay down, looked at the ceiling, and waited until the nausea passed, my mind a blank; I tried to keep it a blank. Suddenly, I sat up again, like those corpses that revive to everybody's surprise and sit up in the coffin. Bulgado leaned back in his chair. I saw the fear on his face.

"You cut them up? Are you serious?"

He hesitated. Three men were three men, no matter what hoodlums they had been.

"They made me do it. When they brought them in they were already stiff, with ants in their mouths. They weren't reliable, you could see this coming. They were spreading the story about the hippopotamus; they told me, they were telling everybody. Well, the days passed and nobody was interested in find-

162

ing them, it's like they never existed, they were pretty close with each other, but outside of that . . . who cared what happened to Jar Boy?"

This was the real world, I told myself. The hidden one boiling under my feet, and Lucy's, under Mamá's and Papá's, under the misshapen feet of the great Rodney; the real world that was the basis for the clamor of the city and the agreeable life of all my friends.

"You won't believe me," Bulgado said, smiling. I was outraged that he was smiling. "Jar Boy had a twin who was born dead. Right after they were born his mother wanted them to put the one who died in a glass jar. The little black baby who lived played with the jar where they kept the little black baby who died; that's where his nickname comes from."

An alarmed Lucy reappeared: my mother was in the kitchen, heating up the broth, and there was no way to stop her from bringing it to me. Bulgado got up to leave, I asked him to wait, Mamá would take some time with the fucking broth, and after all, if she found him there it wasn't a problem, except that she'd start to probe, to ask him questions mercilessly, endlessly, as she usually did. He sat down again, but he wasn't completely calm, Lucy and I had infected him with our uneasiness.

"Who else knows at the zoo?"

He gave his thumb a loud kiss.

"I swear nobody else knows. It's Lázaro's business, his and mine, a business that neither of us likes but what can you do, you saw how they forced us."

I asked him if the names of any of the dead men ever came to light.

"Never," he said very quickly. "It's better not to find out anything about those things. Why would I want to know the name of some poor bastard who won't have a wake or a burial or a grave? Gum for a lion, a hyena . . . just think of it, I can see them chewing."

I felt the breath of one of those animals bouncing off the back of my neck. I don't know what Bulgado was feeling; the truth is that the two of us were shrinking into ourselves, coiling around ourselves like cats. There was extreme cruelty in our conversation, a feeling of disbelief. I had the suspicion we were playing different games. I thought it was time to stop. We agreed that he'd call me Tuesday night at the paper to confirm our appointment for Wednesday, the great day, his only chance to meet Raft, I couldn't even imagine what it meant to him to see the actor in person, maybe shake his hand. I suggested that we meet at Club 21. From there all we had to do was cross the street to be at the Capri.

"Stop right there," he exclaimed. "I take care of lions, but I'm not putting my head in any of their mouths."

Bulgado surprised me when I shouldn't have been surprised. He was very shrewd, he knew more than he seemed to; essentially, he knew who was who in that slippery world, where most names had no faces to go with them. The exception might have been the owner of Club 21. Raúl González Jerez, alias El Flaco, showed his face openly there, and at certain other businesses in which the man who protected him, Luigi Santo Trafficante, was involved. I didn't have to search through my files to remember that: Raúl and Trafficante met in the summer of '45, playing gin rummy at the pool of the Hotel Nacional, where only American big shots went, and other uncatchable members of the Mafia, like Johnny Torrio, and come to think of it, didn't Torrio die a few months earlier in a Brooklyn barbershop? Of course he did, him too, while the barber was cutting his hair. Except that, unlike Anastasia, Terrible Johnny died of a heart attack, like a typical old man, probably dreaming about times gone by, about his first trips to Havana, when he traveled with Al Capone and "Machine Gun" McGurn.

"I passed by the Capri," Bulgado declared, "it's really nice. If you want we'll meet there on Wednesday, outside the hotel."

It was all the same to me, because I planned to get there an hour early and go into Club 21. It was logical that a reporter assigned to cover the opening party at the Capri would arrive early and kill time having a drink in one of the nearby bars, and no doubt that was the closest one.

Bulgado stood and shook my hand. "See you Wednesday, chief."

He was about to close the door when I called to him. "Wait, why did you tell my sister your name was Joe Martin?"

"Oh, I said it because of *Rumba*. Didn't you see that movie? You must have been very little . . . I saw it six, no, seven times; that's how I know Broadway."

Joe Martin left, and Mamá came in. Her broth tasted like shit. Or maybe it was because I had all that crap stuck to the roof of my mouth.

Many years later, I saw *Rumba* one night on television. George Raft was a Cuban who had a cabaret called El Elefante, but they hired him as a dancer on Broadway. It was a mediocre film, with Carole Lombard spitting out stupidities, bursts of stupidities, as if she were Machine Gun Lombard. I watched it with tears in my eyes because all of it reminded me of the abyss, the frontier between one life and another, the world that had remained inside its bubble. It was ironic that after so many years I'd evoke those final hours in the rumba, fatality in its beat, stamping hard as it came nearer.

PRAYER

Do you remember I told you Kary Rusi complained that on the night you came to the Sans Souci you didn't pay attention to her and were only interested in me? Do you remember I said it was the first time I'd laughed in a long while? You didn't ask me why I hadn't laughed for so long, you probably thought it was on account of Roderico. And in part it was. But it was also on account of this: a few months earlier, I saw a woman who'd just been killed, and I don't know why that dead woman made me so sad. She wasn't in my family and I didn't know her. It didn't even shock me to see her lying there where she fell, all covered in blood—when you've been in a circus you learn to deal with things like that—but the next day I woke up wanting to cry, and feeling so down I couldn't drag myself out of bed, and I couldn't explain it, that's the worst part, I didn't know what was happening to me.

When I began with Kary Rusi, I almost always stayed alone in the dressing room after she went out. She's the most orderly woman I know; she likes to have her clothes organized by color, her gloves folded in a certain way, she wants everything perfect. She's exhausted at the end of the second show, generally she changes quickly and leaves. At first I used that time to work quietly; there was a peace in the dressing room that was impossible when Kary was there, and the last thing I did before I left was to put her dirty clothes in a basket and leave it outside, next to the door, where the boy from the dry cleaner's picked it up. I remember on that day I got a card from Rode, that's how he signed it, "Rode," and it touched me, it was a photograph of the sign in Las Vegas, the famous sign we went to see on our first trip (which was our last trip) minutes before I proposed marriage to him and he confessed his Swedish love to me.

I'd finished my work and was about to leave. I put the basket outside and turned to put out the light, and that was when I heard the scream. It was an awful woman's scream, it seemed to last a long time. I might have thought it wasn't important, a joke of one of the models; a lot of them work at the Sans Souci, and some of them talk all night, they order café con leche and sit down and pass the time. Sometimes they scream, not because they're fighting but because somebody tells a joke, they scream with laughter. I wanted to think it was that, but something told me it wasn't; I had a feeling of disaster, a coldness inside. I waited a little while at the door, but everything seemed to be all right, I didn't hear another scream or any voices, and I was locking the door when I saw Jacobs coming toward me. He stopped, and then I understood he was trying to find out if he could trust me. "Did Kary leave?" he said just for something to say, because if I was locking up with a key then she had gone. "I need you to do me a favor." I stood there, waiting, and he was silent. I saw him thinking, until he finally decided to ask me to go to the office of Señor Louis Santos (we never said his real name) and try to help him however I could while he went for a doctor. Señor Louis Santos didn't want any scandal that could hurt the cabaret, and since he'd noticed that I was discreet, he was asking me to go there, bolt the door, and not let anybody in until he came back. "Hurry," Jacobs told me. "There was an accident and a lady's not feeling well."

The lady who wasn't feeling well was dead. I knew it as soon as I walked into the office and saw her lying faceup, in a dress that left one shoulder bare, and on the other a band that looked like greenish tulle was held in place by a brooch. I noticed that, and then the wound on her throat, that's where she'd bled from, a trickle was still coming out. Then I looked at him, sitting at his desk, very pale, staring at the wall; I said: "Jacobs sent me to see if I could do anything for you." He raised his hand, he was squeezing a handkerchief red with blood, I hurried to take the handkerchief, and then I saw he had a deep cut just below his fingers. I looked around, there was a little bathroom, I went in and got a towel and wrapped up the wound. It was the first time I'd been in that office. I'd seen Louis Santos just a couple of times, during afternoon rehearsals, talking to the choreographer. He seemed like a serious man; he had a broad forehead, brown hair that he wore slicked back, and little round glasses. Anybody would've thought he was a professor, though he wasn't wearing his glasses that night and he was in an undershirt, what was left of his undershirt, it was ripped across the top. I saw that he was in a cold sweat, and from his eyes I could tell he was dizzy, that's why I asked him if he wanted me to get him some water, or something else, but he didn't answer. Somebody knocked at the door, and I thought it was too soon for it to be Jacobs. I looked at Santos in case he wanted to ask who it was, but he didn't open his mouth and I had to do it. It was somebody named Bebo, he said he worked at the Sans Souci and needed to talk to Santos. I told him to wait for Jacobs, he was the one who had the key.

After a while there was another knock, and this time it was Jacobs. He had an American doctor with him. The doctor squatted next to the body and picked up a hand; he raised her lids and shone a little flashlight into her eyes. He was saying things in English, he was the only one talking. Finally he stood up and went over to Santos, who showed him his hand. I stood there like a vase until Jacobs remembered about me, looked behind him, and signaled to me to go out with him. It was deserted except for two policemen waiting in the bar area. Jacobs thanked me, he said he didn't have time to explain what had happened, but the man who attacked them was a drunken gambler, and it *wouldn't be good for the Sans Souci if that got out. I shouldn't say a word to anybody, not even Kary Rusi, did I understand? He said those last words in a different tone, it was much harsher. I said yes, and he gave me five pesos so I could take a cab home.*

The next day I woke up sick to my stomach and spent the morning crying. At first I thought it was on account of Roderico, or that I was lonely without Chinita and without my son. I called Kary Rusi to say I'd be a little late, and she asked if I'd heard anything strange the night before. I thought she was testing me. I swore I hadn't heard anything, though she insisted: "Not even a shout, Yolanda, honey, a little noise, you really didn't hear anything?" She told me somebody had called her to say that a woman had attacked Santos, nobody knew who she was, an American who was having an affair with him; in the middle of the fight she pulled a knife and he killed her in self-defense. "How awful," I said. "Did you ask Jacobs about it?" Kary sighed. "Nobody can ask that pig anything." I couldn't tell her what I'd seen, I couldn't talk to her about the dead woman who was haunting me. I thought about her all the time, about her dress with the bare shoulder, about her long arms with spatters of blood, especially about her mouth, slightly open and still wearing lipstick, she'd put on orange lipstick before the fight.

A few days later, Louis Santos sent Bebo for me, what a coincidence. Jacobs had told me earlier that Señor Santos wanted to see me, and that night, when I finished with Kary Rusi, I was to go straight to the exit, there'd be a car waiting for me. I thought we'd see each other in a bar. I was a free woman and resentful about what had happened with Roderico, and so I had no reason to turn down an invitation from a man like Santos, who's elegant and not unpleasant to anybody. As soon as I took care of Kary, I went to the exit, like I'd been told, and saw a blue car. The driver got out and said: "You're Yolanda, right?" I nodded, and he said: "I'm Bebo, I've seen you around here." I didn't recognize him at all; he was brawny, he had to be a bodyguard. He opened the door for me, waited until I sat down,

*and closed it, smiling all the while, and still smiling he drove to Mira-
mar, to the Rosita de Hornedo hotel. They have a bar on the beach; it
was full of Americans, the only Cubans were the boys waiting on tables. Louis Santos was expecting me at one of the tables. He stood up
when he saw me and kissed my hand, this poor thing you see here.
Then we sat down and he asked what I'd like to drink; I said whatever he preferred, and he ordered champagne. He said he'd wanted to
thank me earlier for helping him with his wounded hand, but since the
incident he hadn't gone back to the Sans Souci. Probably Jacobs had
explained things: a drunken gambler who had his wife with him had
wanted to see him and asked for a lot of credit. The couple began to argue over money, and at one point this individual started to hit her, and
then he pulled a knife. Santos supposed he'd gone crazy, or that the
drink had gone to his head, because he didn't have a record in the
United States. Finally, he said it was possible the police would ask me
some questions, but I shouldn't be frightened, I only had to say what
I'd seen. "Now do you think we can forget about this subject?" I said
I thought so. The champagne was iced, and there was that mist when
the surf is high, it smells different at night, I saw the whole ocean in
front of us. I realized that Santos is a silent man, he takes his time between one sentence and the next, he drinks champagne, lights a cigar,
has a calm that seems like magic to me. No, don't think I saw the air
of a magician that I saw in Roderico, or that I saw in you, he doesn't
have that; he's very cold and doesn't know how to turn things upside
down, all he wanted was to take me to his room. We drank more
champagne there, I heard him ask how I came to work for Kary Rusi,
and I explained it was on the recommendation of the great Rodney. He
started to laugh. I thought he was good-looking, and I discovered he
had a wonderful smell: he smelled of tobacco and perfume, all of that
counts, and so does the time I'd spent without being near a man, the
time without that sweet fucking I'd wanted so much with Roderico.
I don't know what I'm saying anymore, I've had a lot to drink and I
don't know how this strikes you: all of Santos's personality, that good*

170

nature of his, it's due to his monster, an animal that takes your breath away. I've never seen anything like it. A circus woman is telling you this.

In the morning, when I was alone in the room, the maid came in to clean. I was in my underwear, and she stood looking at me, and suddenly she said: "Oh, poor thing, you're missing an arm." We talked for a while, and I saw her other times, the few times I woke up at the Rosita de Hornedo, because the affair ended very quickly. One day she told me her husband was in jail, but she'd taken another man. She thought a woman like me, a migratory bird, would understand. The man worked at the zoo, he fed bananas to the monkeys or something like that, he was a bum who looked like a movie star, but he helped her a lot. The last time I went to the hotel, she gave me the address of a santera *so I could tell her about my sadness, about the dead woman who made such a strong impression on me. The* santera *found out that the dead woman's name was Betty, that she'd been hovering over her human body when I came in, and she'd seen the top of my head from the ceiling. That's why I had to do a prayer of the head to get rid of the bad spirits. I slept three nights wearing the white handkerchief, and then I laughed, really laughed, on the day Kary Rusi got so angry with you.*

SNAKE

I left Club 21 with a couple of whiskeys under my belt and a feeling that the night at the Capri would be deadly. I saw Bulgado on the sidewalk outside, looking mistrustful as he waited for me, he couldn't hide his nervousness. He'd taken off his filthy cap, put on a discreet suit—I should emphasize this detail, discreet and dark, I didn't expect so much from him—and combed his hair with a center part and a good amount of brilliantine, an old-fashioned style. All he wanted, he confided to me later, was to resemble Guino Rinaldo as much as he could; that was Raft's character in *Scarface: The Shame of the Nation*, his best role by far. Forget about Paul Muni, and double that for Boris Karloff, Raft really kicked their asses, what a way he had of chewing up the world and spitting out gaskets! Bulgado said that: spitting out gaskets, who knows what it meant?

A few minutes earlier I'd had a brief but friendly encounter with Raúl González Jerez, the owner of Club 21. He was one of the four Cubans who had stayed at the Warwick in New York in mid-October. The 21 was slightly below street level, though not as much as a basement would be. When you went in, the first thing you saw was a bar on the right and some small tables on the other side. I sat at the bar, ordered a drink, and observed what was going on around me. The place was crowded with elegant couples and some Americans on their own, everybody killing time until the moment came to move on to the Capri. That morning I'd received a call from McCrary: he'd just landed in Havana and the next day was Thanksgiving, why didn't we have a lunch of roast turkey with cranberry sauce? Mentioning turkey was code: he insisted there'd be another meeting like the one in Apalachin, but at the Hotel Riviera; we agreed to get together later to discuss it. Suddenly, the 21 was bubbling, and it became really animated when Raúl came in. Somebody told him a joke, and he replied with another, which provoked the guffaws of three or four men who were near me at the bar. Raúl laughed too, but with the kind of laugh that resonates inside and never goes any further. I'd noted in my files that he was the son of an upstanding military man, one of the famous officers who barricaded themselves inside the Hotel Nacional in 1933 to protest the coup led by an obscure sergeant: Fulgencio Batista. In fact, on that November afternoon, when he was ready to go to the opening party at the Capri, Raúl was far from resembling the inspector for the Ministry of the Treasury he'd been a few years earlier. I saw him greeting people as he went from table to table. Like a good host, he was interested in knowing if his patrons were well taken care of, and when he came to the bar, and it was my turn, he shook my hand and asked how I was being treated. I said it was fabulous, but I was careful not to say I was a reporter, much less that I worked for *Prensa Libre*. After a while I paid the bill and went out. In the vicinity of the 21 there were dozens of police, many of them in plainclothes, who'd taken up positions to guard the entrances to the Capri. I avoided them and went up to Bulgado. I could tell he'd poured on a bottle of perfume. If my nose didn't deceive me it was Varon Dandy—some time back my father had used it. He watched me take the invitation out of my pocket, and he stared at it as if he were looking at a diamond and not a worthless piece of cardboard. Two men in livery greeted the guests; one of them, after a few months, would become a key player in obtaining information about what was going on inside the hotel: they called him "Sabrosura," and he sold black-market autographed photos of Ava Gardner.

I was wearing my brother Santiago's dinner jacket; I was doomed always to wear the worldly clothes he knew how to buy. At first Bulgado felt out of his element, since very few guests were wearing dark suits, but gradually he began to relax, as much as he was capable of relaxing while he looked around for his idol with an anxious glance that suddenly became terrified.

"I got fucked over by that one, it's better if he doesn't see me." He bowed his head and signaled to me to look to my left. "Turn around, casually . . . There are two guys talking, you see them? The two who're smoking."

Everybody was smoking, but I saw them. The file in my brain started to operate: the fat one was Nicholas DiConstanza, alias "Fat the Butcher," one of the owners of the Capri; the other was a gorilla whose face said nothing to me, not about anything, any place, any casino. He had purplish lips, a misshapen nose that reminded me of a good piece of Roquefort cheese, and little bat's ears where it was likely he pulled out hairs when he was alone.

"That one . . . the guy who looks like a safe, was the first one who hired me and Lázaro."

My lips tightened, I'd just caught him in a blunder.

"So where are we? Did this guy hire you or was it the three from the other night?"

"I forgot there were four of them." He corrected himself without changing expression. "That animal, he was the one who was missing. We went to a bar on the docks, there was a dog sniffing at the cigarette butts, and do you know what he did? He picked up his foot and flattened it like a cockroach."

I thought of Julián: he wouldn't have been able to tolerate a scene like that.

"So you were in that bar after all. Didn't you say that this Lázaro went by himself?"

"The two of us went," muttered Bulgado, who became aware at that moment of the general excitement, a murmur that increased in intensity, anticipating ecstasy. He looked where everybody was looking: Raft had just climbed to the podium that had been placed in the middle of the lobby, as radiant as a deluxe ghost, much grayer than he appeared in films but impeccable in his dinner jacket, which you could tell from a mile away was tailor-made. People began to applaud, but Bulgado couldn't manage to bring his hands together, he was halfway between applause and a gesture of adoration.

"Johnny Angel," I said to fuck with him a little. "There's the man."

Bulgado didn't hear me, he was in another world. He'd seen Raft only in the movies, and now he was hypnotized by his presence, by the mischievous brilliance with which he saw him rise above the guests, control them with a gesture, just one, and at the same time pretend to be their accomplice. He said we were welcome to his house, that he would be there to attend personally to the patrons of the casino and would try to make this his best role. To demonstrate this, he began to flip a coin he had in his hand, the old low-class trick that had characterized him years before and now excited the people there, almost everyone but Bulgado, who was awestruck, livid; his emotion didn't allow him to enjoy it. Raft came down from the podium and was lost in the crowd, and Bulgado began to walk like a zombie. I followed him because he didn't seem to be in his right mind, and in a sense I was the one responsible for his movements, for any stupid thing he might do. He made his way to Raft. His dark clothes contrasted with the light jackets of the other men, so it was easy for me to follow him. The real Johnny Angel was talking to two elderly people; she was an American with a tremor who wore a diamond tiara on her curled hair, and her husband, very thin and full of emotion, watched the scene as if he were contemplating the twilight. Bulgado stopped next to this couple, and I managed to get right behind him, a strategic position for taking him away whenever it became necessary. But Bulgado waited in silence, his eyes fixed on his idol, who, I must admit, gave off a kind of glow. He wasn't like us, or like the rest of the Americans gathered there. He was paler and, in a way, more virile, a real contradiction.

He finished speaking to the couple, the old woman with a tremor and her husband stepped back to escape the press of people, and Raft inadvertently turned toward Bulgado. Something happened then, because he reacted with surprise. It was a small crisis, as if someone had pulled the pin on a grenade and we'd all thrown ourselves to the ground, all of us except Bulgado, who perhaps took it for granted that it was normal for Raft to suffer a hallucination and look at him as if he were looking at himself.

"Brownie Raft," Bulgado said with delight in a perfect English that left me astonished.

"You can call me Snake," Raft remarked in a somber voice that the other man took in like someone taking in a sublime password. The scene looked rehearsed, and Bulgado dared to add: "Yeah . . . The Old Blacksnake."

It was enough. All the people around Raft held their breath, as stunned as I was, because it seemed that Raft had found a twin brother, a guy who didn't look anything like him but who did look like him, identical in another dimension, another accidental level we all could see. They shook hands, and I'd have done anything to avoid what happened then: Bulgado bent over and kissed the actor's ring as if Raft were a bishop; he brushed the magnificent stone with his lips, the only thing it could be was a star sapphire, the same kind of stone worn by Raft's brothers at the casino. It was a fit of tenderness, a sudden impulse, a joke to the people who witnessed it, though for Raft, and for Bulgado too, the gesture turned into catastrophe. It seemed to me the height of absurdity, but it had already been done. I noticed that Raft had been startled, more by himself than by Bulgado, at what he perceived in his bones regarding an emotion, a displacement: the devastating loneliness of the zookeeper. There were a couple of flashes. I looked around for the photographer and saw he was a friend from my days at the *Diario de la Marina*, one of the guys I played craps with on nights when I escaped the clutches of Skinny T. Later I asked him for the picture, and it's the only one I have of Bulgado, of him and Raft looking at each other, with strangers standing around them, and me, my eyes popping and holding a hand in the air. I don't remember raising my hand, but I did, as if I'd tried to warn somebody. Finally I managed to get hold of Bulgado. I caught him by the edge of his jacket and tugged to get him away. It was going on too long and I was beginning to feel dizzy. I dragged the zombie along, took a glass from one of the trays, and ordered him to drink. I stood beside him watching him down the liquor. I needed to make sure he remembered who I was, where he was, where he'd go when he left the Capri, in short, basic information. Suddenly, a man came up and put an arm around us, both arms, one around Bulgado and the other around me. He bowed his head, and I imagined he was going to tell us a secret.

"Why aren't you cleaning up elephant shit?" he asked Bulgado.

I had a naïve thought: 'I imagined it was a joke. I looked at Bulgado, expecting to see him laughing, but it was just the opposite, his face was contorted and his eyes stared at the floor.

"The gentleman's coming with me," I intervened. "I'm from *Prensa Libre*, any problem?"

The man lifted his arm from my shoulders, looked at me with curiosity, as if he'd just discovered that a fly could challenge him, could rebel or simply pronounce words. He looked behind him; I think he was searching for a sign, a clue as to what the next step was. I looked in the same direction and didn't see anybody.

"Take him out," he said, gesturing toward Bulgado. "Both of you are leaving."

"I have to write a piece about this party," I said. "I can't leave."

I saw him hesitate and look behind him again. "Wait here."

We didn't wait. As soon as I saw him walk away, we went in the opposite direction. Bulgado followed me with a sorrowful expression, and I even reached the conclusion that something in his meeting with Raft had gone wrong or hadn't turned out as he expected, but I couldn't imagine what it was. Raft had been cordial and more than patient with him: what other artist would have tolerated that kiss on his ring, that unnecessary display in the middle of a crowd?

At first I couldn't identify McCrary. I stood looking at him because his face seemed familiar; he waved and then I knew who he was and walked toward him. He was with a woman and introduced her as a photographer from *Life*, and he assured me that the two of them intended to do a report on Havana nightlife. He proposed that when the party was over we go for a drink. I said that tonight was impossible, I had to arrange something with the friend who'd come with me. I pointed to Bulgado, who was leaning against a wall, let's say he was coming out of his trance, smoking with seraphic eyes, still fixed on Raft, who was showing the lobby to the patrons and handing out cards: "George Raft, General Manager, Casino de Capri Corp., Havana." An orchestra began to play, McCrary took advantage of the noise to ask me if I had any more information about the meeting of capos at the Riviera, the second Apalachin in less than fifteen days. I said I didn't, nobody could get near the hotel, it was still closed to the public and watched over by armed guards.

"The war's about to break out," he declared. "It isn't a war between Italians and Jews the way people think, it's something else. Everything's in motion."

In his first few hours in Havana, McCrary found out that Meyer Lansky had moved from the Hotel Nacional to an unknown location, that he'd spent several days secluded in a Havana hospital following gallbladder surgery, and that, faced with an avalanche of Sicilian vultures who'd come to Cuba, he was threatening to go to Las Vegas and let the war be resolved with guns, like it was everywhere else.

"He must be tired," said the little avenger that lived in me, "he's an old man."

I saw that Bulgado had moved away a little; he was heading again for Raft, who in turn was moving toward the casino. People were going to the blackjack tables, waiters were moving around the area—the strategy was to pull in the patrons gradually—and you could hear the first sounds of chips being set down to make bets. I made a date with McCrary for the next day, in the Roof Garden of the Hotel Sevilla, which was the territory of Don Amleto Battisti, Lansky's friend and protégé. I took another drink and stopped to talk with a couple of photographers, one of them the guy from *Diario de la Marina*, that was when I asked him for the photograph of the encounter. In all that time I didn't neglect Bulgado, who was still devising something, certainly a way to talk to Raft again. After a while I went up to him and said it was time to go, the next morning we had to get up early for work, he with his animals and I with mine. He looked at me scornfully, as if I were talking about a very mundane topic in a very spiritual place.

"The croupiers at the Montmartre," he said, starting to walk beside me, "do you know they all came here?"

I said I did, I'd heard something about it. At the Montmartre, a few months back, the rebels had shot Captain Blanco Rico, chief of military intelligence, and in retaliation for his death the government had closed the cabaret. Charles Tourine, alias "The Blade," who controlled that casino, and the croupiers' union both failed to have it reopened within a reasonable time. The union advised its members to look for work in the new hotels: at the Capri, which hired a good number of them, or the Riviera, which was opening very soon, and even the Havana Hilton, which would open early in 1958. No halfway decent croupier was out on the street.

"My best friend was a croupier at the Montmartre," Bulgado said with a sigh. "They call him Trabuco, but he didn't come here."

The same guy who'd told him to clean up elephant shit was circling us again. I became aware of him and gave Bulgado a light push as a warning.

"Trabuco was a bodyguard," he told me in a quiet voice. "Think you can guess who for? The great Lucky Luciano . . . What do you think of that?"

We walked in a leisurely way toward the exit, I told him we

should move naturally, and it was just before I got to the door that I saw them, protected by a wall of men who didn't disguise their mission and who were armed, that was obvious, they even had pistols in their shoes. Meyer Lansky and Santo Trafficante were engaged in solemn conversation, leaning against the wall, both of them smoking, but only Trafficante held a glass. Lansky was encased in a caramel-colored suit, no dinner jacket for him, he had that phlegmatic way of shitting on everything, including the attire that was expected of him. The other man, however, was wearing his white jacket made of cloth that gave off a gleam; on the whole, you could say he shone as much as George Raft.

"Did somebody lose you here?" A muscular young man confronted me; maybe my age or younger, he'd just broken out in acne. "I know who you are, get going, move, damn it."

Something in the way he said he knew who I was irritated me, and I didn't get going, I didn't move an inch. Maybe it was because we were at the same point in our lives, unadorned blusterers, two kids taking each other's measure in all the glitter.

"Did you hear me, faggot?"

He said it quietly, bringing his mouth up to my ear, and Bulgado, who was beside me, gave us a sardonic look, as if he were about to see two boys shoot each other with water pistols.

"Wait for me outside," I told Bulgado, who shrugged; he raised one shoulder higher than the other, and in that gesture I realized he'd become himself again, he'd recovered his own character after the profound impact of meeting Raft. Then I spoke to the thug: "I'd like to interview Mr. Trafficante. I'm Joaquín Porrata, of *Prensa Libre*."

He gave a little laugh and turned all the way around, pretending he was looking through the crowd. "Well, kid, as far as I know, there's nobody here by that name. Do you see anybody with that name?"

"I'll only ask him a couple of questions, it's for an article on the Sans Souci."

He didn't give me time to say anything else; he grabbed me by the lapels and began to drag me, not toward the exit but in the other direction, toward the group of men guarding the two capos. At a time like that, all I could worry about was the dinner jacket and how I'd tell my brother I let a hoodlum rip it off me.

"Let him go . . ."

I looked up, I was tired and a little drunk, but I thought I saw an air of satisfaction on Lansky's face. He wasn't going to waste even half a minute on the insect I must have seemed to him, but maybe a few seconds, enough to realize that he'd met me, then he'd file me away in his memory and close the clouds again, the harmonious mists of his "Almendra" afternoons. Later I learned that he boasted of almost never forgetting a face.

"It's okay, Jaime . . . Let him go."

With sorrow in his soul, this Jaime let me leave. We'd hated each other on sight, and he let me go with an aseptic gesture, as if he weren't releasing a man exactly, but a bag of garbage. I stumbled out to the sidewalk; Bulgado received me without a trace of surprise, he wasn't alarmed at seeing me dizzy, short of breath, or pale, immensely pale: for him, that was my natural state. I asked him to help me get to the car, and on the way I asked if he knew how to drive; he said of course, he drove almost as well as Joe Fabrini. I didn't ask him which picture Fabrini was in, and I didn't remind him that we had a deal because I didn't have the heart to pressure anybody or listen to another word. My brother's dinner jacket was stained, it looked as if I'd rolled around on the ground wearing it, and all I hoped was that I wouldn't run into Santiago now. I'd take it to the cleaner's and return it to him as good as new. Bulgado drove the Plymouth, he was fantastic: not a single hesitation, no sudden stops, there are small minds that can make easy connections, they have an ability to adapt to motors, Bulgado was one of them, so I proposed that he drop me off at my house and drive the car to his. I'd pick it up at the zoo the next day.

When I got out I saw lights in the windows; that meant they were all awake, and I prepared for the worst, having to give explanations or, at a minimum, saying hello. I opened the door very quietly and encountered my mother's agitated face; as soon as she heard the key she shouted "Santiago?" In my usual tone, that is, a tone of boredom that was my specialty, I said no, it wasn't Santiago but the one who borrowed his clothes. Lucy appeared behind her, she signaled to me: "Santiago hasn't come home." I started to laugh: Did he ever come home at this time of night? Mamá shook her head. "He hasn't been home since yesterday." I tried to laugh again, and Lucy gave me a look that stopped me. I told them he had to be with some woman, living it up with his friends, what was so odd about Santiago not coming home to sleep? Mamá turned her back, that night she was in no mood for my sarcasm, and Lucy came toward me, her eyes like saucers, wet, strange, empty saucers. "We think he did show up," she said in a quiet voice. "Papá went to see." Mamá dropped on the sofa, I can't say she sat down; she was something round, stiff, and compact, like a stone that wouldn't move again. I pulled Lucy to my room; we spoke in whispers, leaning against the door, and again I tried to shrug it off and say fuck it. I wanted to break into a terrible guffaw, a laugh that would come out hard, my entire body denying what seemed impossible: Santiago caught at a meeting in an apartment on Calle Humboldt, with other revolutionaries who had bombs, shooting at the police and being shot himself, only one bullet in the leg but it stopped him from running, the SIM caught him, took him away alive, and this morning he'd been found dead. They thought it was Santiago because of an identity card stuffed in his mouth; there was nothing else, no wallet, no papers. Lucy turned into another stone, but one that was a little softer; she dropped on my bed and began to cry. Again I had the feeling I was collapsing, and then I vomited, I didn't even have time to get to the bathroom. I tore off the dinner jacket, it was true it was burning my body, I put on another jacket and asked her where Papá was. "At the Belascoaín morgue," I heard her say, and I recovered my self-control; possibly I already knew she'd be the only sane one in the house. I kissed the hair on the top of her head, it was the first time in my life I'd given her a kiss, and I walked out, horrified. I closed the door at the same moment Mamá screamed.

"... I TAKE REFUGE IN YOU"

Papá was sitting on a bench, his elbows resting on his knees, looking down at the floor in the attitude of somebody leaning over a puddle of water and staring at his own reflection. Much later I understood that he was, in fact, seeing himself, not in stagnant water but in his own mind, in his liquefied brain melted by stupefaction: Santiago was not what he seemed and never would be, not to him, who was his intimate friend, or the clients who bought parcels of land on Isla de Pinos from him, or the house where his mother and sister were waiting for him, or the city that would never again see him stay up all night. I walked over to him and put my hand on his shoulder. I still remember how he looked up, the way in which he absorbed the irony of seeing me alive. "He's a wreck" was the only thing he managed to say, in a voice I didn't recognize. I wondered why his voice had changed, and I began to sweat as if that were the only answer. I took out my handkerchief and wiped my face. I went up to the man behind the counter and said I wanted to see the body of Santiago Porrata. He gestured toward my father, muttered that the gentleman had already identified him. I said I was the brother of the deceased, showed him my press card, and insisted that I had to see him. He thought it over; I don't know what he saw in my face, but I could tell he was softening, it was a way of moving his head and coming out from behind the counter, walking to the back, to the alcove where they kept the bodies, coming out again and telling me to wait a few minutes. My disbelief was as thin and piercing as a needle. I'd said I wanted to see him because deep down I doubted it was Santiago; it was a doubt that allowed me to breathe, I mean a doubt that was in my lungs.

A bald mulatto wearing a white lab coat and an apron over the coat came out for me, not saying a word. It was the man behind the counter who said, "Go with him." I followed him, we walked down a hallway, he opened a door, and a sudden onslaught, an intense stink that penetrated all the way to my soul, wounded me. There were three or four occupied stretchers. We did this quickly: the mulatto raised a sheet, and I saw Santiago's face, his light brown hair gleaming as if he'd just come out of water, and his sunken eyelids, there was nothing under those eyelids, only a few bloodstains. I'd stopped sweating, and stopped hearing; in the face of what surrounded me, the only things in my head that might have been working were my eyes. These eyes of mine felt an awful solitude because those other eyes, the living or dead eyes of Santiago, were missing. I lifted the sheet a little more; his torso was naked, splotched with bruises and burns; I lifted his shoulders and gave him something that resembled an embrace. I felt his icy skin, that coldness unlike any other, and I asked in a quiet voice: "Where did he go?" I don't know if seconds or minutes went by, I do know that the mulatto in the apron took my arm and tried to move me away, but I raised my voice, this time I shouted: "Where did he go?" He tried again to pull me away, and this time he succeeded; he covered my brother's body, pushed me toward the hallway, and returned me to the waiting room, where my father was still looking at his reflection in a nonexistent puddle of water. I sat down next to him. "It's Santiago," I said, and I discovered that my voice too sounded as if it belonged to somebody else.

The two days that followed, November 28 and 29, 1957, were the days on which I came into the world. Like those babies born in the middle of cataclysms, between gusts of wind in a hurricane or under the rubble left by an earthquake. I have the feeling I hadn't been alive until the day my brother died, until that night when we had to go back home, confirm the news to Mamá, who collapsed in a heap, and entrust ourselves to Lucy, who also must have had the feeling she hadn't been alive before, because from that time on she took the reins of the house, put on a man's shirt—one of Santiago's, certainly— picked up the address book, and informed relatives, friends, she called Aurora, and I heard her tell Mamá that Aurora and Telma (another of my mother's childhood friends) had been told and were on their way. Papá turned into gelatin, into a nothing that sometimes sighed. He'd lock himself in Santiago's room and root through his papers. I imagined he was looking for some clue, some information about his clandestine activities, but Santiago, for all of us and even for his fiancée, had maintained an impeccable front, an appearance with no chinks, nothing that could compromise him at home, much less at his office next to Papá's. His fiancée had been to the house only two or three times, and nobody ever took her seriously because Santiago had been engaged so often. She arrived dressed in black, small and blond and wearing a braid on one side; she looked like a little girl to me. The girl assured my sister that she and Santiago had already set a date for the wedding and even bought furniture. She spent almost the entire day with us, crying as if she really were the widow, until her father, who was an

187

army doctor, came to the funeral home and practically dragged her away. My mother's sister came from Santa Clara, and though my father was an only child, he had some cousins who were like his brothers; they took turns sitting with him, and obliged him to eat or at least to try the soup that one of their wives prepared for everybody. Aurora came at noon, walked directly to me and embraced me, explained that Julián was in New York but wanted me to know he'd return to Havana in a couple of days. Aurora had grabbed my hand, and we were joined for a time, my fingers intertwined with hers while she complained that she still didn't know what she would say to Mamá when they saw each other or how she could face my father. Sitting there, in that unexpected intimacy, I thought of Yolanda. Nobody had told her, and so she wasn't imagining anything, and I decided to call her as soon as I was alone again, whenever Aurora found the courage to face my mother. "Frightened of everything, I take refuge in you" was the line that came to mind. I'd read it, when I was a kid at school, in a letter by José Martí and I said it two times, three times, maybe more, as I waited in vain for Yolanda to answer the phone. She must have been working, running errands for Kary Rusi, and I promised myself I'd call her again at night, and take refuge in her house during the small hours. "Frightened of everything," I repeated in confusion and began to cry. I took out my handkerchief and covered my face but didn't need to because at that moment no one saw me, I was in a corner, facing a wall, I needed to give vent to my feelings. A few hours later, Madrazo came from the paper. He whispered in my ear that it was becoming intolerable, that this had to stop because they were doing away with the nation's youth, with the youth that was worth anything. I knew they were merely words of consolation, there was no way to stop this unless it was the way Santiago had tried, fighting it out with bullets. Compared with that, with what he'd done, my work had been an absurd exercise, all that time I'd invested in finding out the name of the tailor shop where Lansky had his suits made (Pepe Tailor Shop, taken care of by an attentive Pepe), or the cars in which he drove around Havana (the Mercedes, the pearl white Chevrolet, the 1950 black Ford), or his Thursday afternoon routine, when he went to Joe Stassi's mansion on the banks of the Almendares River to meet with his staff, all the bosses in Havana.

Madrazo was waiting for me to say something, but I really didn't feel like talking; he understood and patted me on the shoulder. Before he left, he said that somebody named McCrary had called me at the paper. I closed my eyes: I'd forgotten about McCrary. I explained to Madrazo that he was the reporter who'd helped me so much in New York, I'd seen him the day before at the party at the Capri and we'd arranged to have lunch at the Sevilla Biltmore. Of course, I'd forgotten about the article on the Capri; under the circumstances I didn't know when I could write it. Madrazo told me not to worry, there was no rush for the piece on the hotel, and as for McCrary, the operator finally had transferred the call to his office, and Fini, his secretary, told him I'd had an incident in the family. An incident, I thought, what a strange way to refer to horror.

At the cemetery, at the mausoleum where three of my four grandparents were buried, Mamá fainted and Papá left this world. In a way he left forever; he never completely came out of his stupor, not even after days had passed and someone came to talk to us on the condition we were discreet. It was a friend of Santiago's, the only one who knew his plans for an uprising in the Sierra. He brought us a letter my brother had written, it was the farewell letter not of someone who thinks he's going to die but of someone who plans to be away for a few months. Mamá became serene in a way that wasn't typical of her. She remembered Santiago's happy moments, and that was all. She never said another word about his death. It fell to Lucy to organize his room; she came to mine with many of Santiago's clothes hanging over her arm. "It hurts me just to give them away," she said with an exhausted sigh, "and after all, you always wore his clothes." I was exhausted too; I didn't have the heart to tell her to leave them in the closet or take them all away—and when I say "all" I mean the dinner jacket too—because it pained me to see them. I couldn't say either thing; it was a moment of confusion, a fog that was like limbo.

When I finally managed to speak to Yolanda on the day of the funeral, I could tell how affected she was, and I heard her say that she'd leave right away to be with me. I didn't respond, and she corrected herself: on second thought, it wasn't a good idea because maybe my parents wouldn't take it too well. I said yes, they probably wouldn't, and then I reviewed it mentally: a dead son, a lesbian daughter, and the only surviving male involved with a one-armed mulatta who was a damn sight older than he was. Yolanda and I got to see each other two days later. I picked her up at the Sans Souci, and we went to her house. When she asked how everybody in my family was and I tried to explain it to her, I realized that the always absent Santiago, the one nobody ever expected to find in his room, had suddenly moved in; he clutched at that house and it was something physical, a whirling disturbance you felt in the living room, in the dining room, when you went up the stairs. I don't believe in ghosts, but I had the feeling Santiago was shouting to make us hear him, and above all to indicate the things that mattered to him: when it really was time for him to go, he wanted to stay. Yolanda stroked my head and assured me it was only for the first few days, then gradually we'd get used to it. "Not Papá," I remember saying. "They worked together, they were like the nail and the quick." Yolanda murmured these words: "Even the nail and the quick have to separate." When we went to bed, I realized I was frightened and had been the whole time, from the moment I came back from the Capri and opened the door and my mother greeted me by calling for my brother: "Santiago?" Her anguish, compressed into a name, was etched inside me. At that point my fear began; it became unbearable when they lifted the sheet and I recognized the body, and even more unbearable when I went to bed with Fantina, a phantom from the past. From then on I had a past, because for better or worse everything was new. I left behind a way of being, of understanding certain places, of looking at life. Few people perceived this, but curiously enough Bulgado did; it was enough for him to glance at me and he got the idea, I know he did. When I didn't come to the zoo to pick up my car, it occured to him to drive it to my house, where Balbina spoke to him and told him my brother had died. That night he put on the same dark suit he'd worn to meet Raft, and he came, accompanied by his wife and mother-in-law, to offer his condolences. I must have had a sickly look, because Bulgado's mother-in-law claimed I had to have something to eat, and quickly, because fasting at funeral parlors almost always turns into tuberculosis. She offered to fix me some soup, and when she said that I thought about the fish and eyes soup I'd had at the Mercado Único. It was true I hadn't eaten anything for hours, and there was still a conversation I needed to have with Bulgado. I took him aside and proposed that we go to eat in Chinatown, I needed to get something in my stomach and we had to talk; he understood and told the women to take a taxi home. Before they left, Bulgado's wife looked at me through her glasses for myopia, just as if she were looking at a larva, put her plump hand on my cheek, and in her sleepy, retarded voice she said: "Eat something, my boy." I went over to my mother, who was in the chapel next to the closed coffin. I asked if she'd like me to bring her something to eat and she didn't answer.

Telma, her childhood friend, was beside her, and she shook her head. I interpreted this as meaning I shouldn't disturb or interrupt that sorrow even with my voice, which was an insult precisely because it could be heard, and if it could be heard it was still alive. I went out with Bulgado and saw my Plymouth parked in front of the funeral home; it calmed me to see it, as if I'd been expecting a gesture, I don't know, an impossible sign. I felt very weak but thought it would be good for me to drive awhile, and it was, I began to breathe more easily, for moments I had the feeling I was alone, since Bulgado huddled next to the window, taciturn, not saying a word until we reached the Pacífico. We went to the Pacífico because I was looking for what nobody would have looked for under those circumstances: loud voices, strong odors, the buzz of Chinese going back and forth carrying dishes. I didn't ask Bulgado if it was all right, I was imposing my will on something as simple as choosing the place where we would eat, because in a very few minutes I was going to impose it on something a little more complex, obliging him to talk once and for fucking all. I looked around at the other tables: couples who'd just left the theater, musicians ready to go to play at some club, reporters who stopped in for a plate of fried rice before going back to the editorial offices, ready for the frenzy of putting the paper to bed. We ordered highballs. I looked at Bulgado, who knew how to return my gaze; he had an innate shrewdness.

"What a blow," he said.

Silence on my part. I didn't want to think about Santiago, and I didn't want to think about Papá either, but what came to mind was the night my father introduced me to his mistress in this restaurant: "I want you to meet Lidia," he declared, in front of the other couples sharing their table, and Lidia surely felt constrained, because she already knew Santiago (all my father's girlfriends were screened, tacitly, by my older brother), but I was another story, younger, not as close to my father. And speaking of Lidia, had she heard about the death of Santiago? Had her lover, Don Samuel Porrata, called to explain that nothing was as he thought and that the world had fallen down around him? Frightened of everything . . . I was afraid my father wouldn't take refuge in anything or anybody, except maybe in the memory of the deceased, in running the same movie over and over again: what my brother said or didn't say, the comment he never let slip, a strange package, a call at an odd time. Much later I came to the conclusion that Papá blamed himself for not having guessed what no one could ever have guessed.

"Begin at the beginning," I said to Bulgado; weariness must have been coming out of my pores. "When did you find out that what happened to the hippopotamus was a message?"

Bulgado leaned across the table. He seemed a little weary too. "When they told us to let him out. 'Let him out and push him toward the woods.' That's what we did, we scared him a little, we threw sticks at him . . ."

"Do you mean to tell me you did it?"

"I did, yes, along with Lázaro. They forced us to, you know those people force you. They had it all arranged with the police so that they'd kill the animal. I'll tell you something else: just a week before that we cut up a guy, an Italian from Anastasia's mob. And that Italian, after he was dead, carried the message, what do you think of that? But Anastasia said fuck that, fuck the dead Italian and their warnings, and then only the hippopotamus was left. It was the final warning, but I don't understand why it came so late."

Another highball. Chinese soup with a poached egg. No fish and eyes. No eyes at all.

"I know he was Italian because they said he was," Bulgado continued, "and when he was dead they took his picture. I swear it by Elvira; I don't have a mother and I swear by my wife. They made a sign, some guy wrote it in Italian and told Lázaro to put it on the stiff's chest. It was a message they were sending to Anastasia. I knew that because the sign said 'Anastasia' and then there were things I couldn't understand."

"And the blacks? Turtle and Jar Boy?"

"The hippopotamus was our work. Lázaro and I did it; it was a shame, such a big animal, but we had no choice."

Bulgado drank his highball, breathed in the aroma of the soup, and tucked the napkin into the collar of his shirt, like a baby ready to be fed his pap.

"Let's go, start to eat," he encouraged me in a tone of voice used to rouse lions. "The trouble with you is that you're dying of hunger."

He began. I watched him sip at the Chinese beans.

"Why did you tell me, Bulgado? Why did you tell me about the message when I went to the zoo?"

"I don't know," he replied. "I think it just slipped out."

"I don't believe you. They wanted it in the paper, they wanted people to know it wasn't an accident, they told you to give me something, tell me the truth."

He chewed the egg. Watching him chew, I felt hungry and picked up my spoon; it trembled in my hand. I really did need to get something hot into my stomach.

"I am telling you the truth, compadre," he said, irritated. "I tell you the truth but you don't pay attention to me. Eat your soup."

I swallowed a few spoonfuls. I'd have gladly grabbed him by the lapels, shaken him where he sat, demanded that he tell me everything.

"And if I let the thing about the message slip, so what?" He smiled in an insolent way, he seemed to have read my mind. "What difference does it make? I don't talk about those things with anybody, just with you; you got into this because you

194

wanted to, and you can't put it in the paper, how could you put it in? Colonel Fernández Miranda came in a car with his escort and parked at the entrance to the zoo, waiting for them to take the picture of Anastasia's Italian buddy. Are you going to write that? What the hell, they'd burn you alive."

Bulgado's bowl was soon empty. Mine seemed like a trick bowl: I took spoonful after spoonful and the bowl stayed the same, full to the brim.

"Aren't you going to eat?" Bulgado offered me a cigarette. "Don't forget you have to get back to the wake."

"We have to get back to the letter," I said. "Where did you get that letter?"

"I told you the truth about that. A friend of mine who's a chambermaid at the Rosita de Hornedo gave it to me. Trafficante lives there, or it's the hideout where he takes his women, the truth is I don't know. Just between us, the chambermaid thinks my name is Vince."

He still pronounced it "bean-say." We ordered our last highballs.

"I gave it to you because it was no good to me, and it seems it won't be any good to you either. It's a stolen letter, but even if it wasn't, it smears the friends of General Batista. This whole country is smeared. I think fat Anastasia thought something like that when I gave him the photograph."

It was the masterstroke at the end of the night, the currency he paid to me for taking him to meet his idol. Bulgado was keeping his part of the bargain.

"Anastasia? You want me to believe you went to see Umberto Anastasia?"

"Well, yes, a little while ago. I went to the Nacional, and I brought him the picture of the dead Italian with the sign on him. They told me to take it to that hotel, ask them to call the room, and say I had a delivery for him from Señor Lucania; they made me repeat the name a few times so I wouldn't forget it: Lu-ca-nia, Lu-ca-nia . . . Anastasia's bodyguards came down and opened the envelope; they saw what it was and they made me go up, they took me to him, you could see he was bad-tempered, he looked at the photograph but didn't say anything, his expression didn't change, he stayed the same, he had these shadows under his eyes. I held my employee's card from the zoo in my hand, he talked to his men in Italian, they opened the door and told me to leave, a bodyguard went with me back down to the lobby. And that was it. Nobody asked me any questions."

Bulgado signaled to the waiter for the check. I let him pay. I don't know if we were finished, but as far as I was concerned we were. For a while I'd managed to concentrate on something that wasn't Santiago's dead face and what still lay ahead of me, several more hours at the wake and the burial the next morning. On the way back—maybe it was the effect of the highballs—Bulgado didn't stop talking, he said he believed the dead Italian was a bat Anastasia had sent on ahead to size up the situation (bat, I said to myself, why bat?), and the meal we just had at the Pacífico reminded him of *Background to Danger*, a movie in which Peter Lorre interrogates George Raft, whose name is Joe Barton.

"I'd like to be named Joe," Bulgado said, on a whim, pronouncing it "yo-ey." "What do you think?"

Not a thing, I didn't think a thing. My eyes were closing, and he added that, after eating, what I needed was to sleep awhile; he encouraged me to find a sofa and lie down now, while there was hardly anybody in the funeral home. He left, and I dragged myself to the chapel. My father was there, sitting between a couple of friends, the three of them silent. I didn't see Mamá or Lucy anywhere. I took Joe Barton's advice and found a sofa where I could lie down, deposit all the horror in my bones, without any possible refuge.

GHOSTS

I never liked Fantina. It sounds like the name of a ghost, and I'm afraid of the ghost I see in myself, always telling the same story: a magician who comes into a house, using some excuse, casts his invisible hook into the air and fishes for the heart of a woman. That magician was the man who pulled in my mother, but Roderico was one too, the great Rodney of the Tropicana's Paradise Under the Stars, who's never bothered again to find out if I'm alive or dead. I tried to get out of this story about magicians when I met Louis Santos, so icy and fierce, he has a tool that can melt a woman, but he isn't interested in people and that ruins everything. Later you showed up, and at first it scared me that you were almost as young as my son; then it occurred to me that maybe this would help me, that the difference was a way of destroying time.

One day when I was feeling very bitter, thinking about the bad luck I'd had falling in love with Rodney, somebody knocked at the door. I put my eye to the peephole and saw a short Chinese wearing a suit and black hat, one of those old-fashioned hats that are round on top, like Charlie Chaplin's. Two girls were with him, and when I opened the door and asked how I could help him, he answered: "I'm

Benjamín, Lala's son." I didn't understand, I had no idea who Lala was, I was going to tell him he'd come to the wrong apartment, but then he added: "I went to the circus and your son, Daniel, sent me here. I'm the son of the Chinese woman who brought you up, and these are my daughters, Lala's granddaughters." The younger one was about eleven, and her name was Lupe, and I estimated that the older one was about thirteen, and her name was Carmen Luisa. I was wearing a sleeveless blouse, and the girls didn't take their eyes off my stump, they were in a state of excitement, surely because they'd never seen a woman without an arm before. I invited them in and went to the kitchen for cold drinks, then I thought that if this Benjamín was like his mother he might prefer tea. I came out with the drinks on a tray; by this time I was used to carrying it with one arm, balancing the weight, necessity makes you learn a lot of things, but the girls looked at me with their mouths open, and then they looked in their father's eyes for an explanation. He had the kind of watery eyes that looked straight ahead, just like his mother, just like all the Chinese. When their father didn't answer, they looked at each other; they'd probably never seen a one-armed woman who was so efficient. The one named Lupe was more Chinese looking, I saw a resemblance to her grandmother; the other one's eyes weren't as slanted, though both of them were pretty, each in her own way. I thought Benjamín was a little old to be the father of such young daughters, and the first thing he said, very gently, was that he understood he and I were brother and sister, since he knew his mother had an affair with a Portuguese magician who was my father too. I had to explain to him that my mother didn't have children with the magician, that I was born much later, when she fell in love with the man who trained dogs, which was normal in a circus. Benjamín didn't show either disappointment or relief at this news. But he did give me a big smile when I offered him tea, and he said it was the only thing he liked to drink. While I put water on to boil, the girls went to look at the photographs on the sideboard of Daniel at different ages, doing acrobatics. They'd just met him in Camagüey; the circus had passed through there, they'd seen him perform, and they felt proud, especially because they'd been told that Daniel was their cousin. Carmen Luisa looked at him with her almond eyes, beautiful, fascinating eyes, she could hypnotize anybody if she wanted to, she must have inherited them from the magician, her real grandfather. Benjamín took a sip of tea and bowed his head in a sign of approval. He had Oriental gestures, though he'd been brought up not by his mother but by a family from the Senado Sugar Mill, a schoolteacher and his wife, who took him a month after he was born. He'd grown up at the mill, married and been widowed young, and when he was much older met the woman with whom he'd had the two girls. She'd stayed behind in Camagüey because she wasn't well, and he'd come to meet me, but above all to ask me—he said this calmly, very coldly, not upset or angry—if Lala ever spoke to me about the son she had when she was fourteen, and if I knew why she threw him away and never asked about him again. He used that phrase: "threw away." He used it in front of his daughters, who surely had heard him use it before, because it didn't surprise them, just the opposite, while their father was talking they whispered together and giggled, arguing over Daniel, they both liked him.

I told Benjamín the truth: I didn't even know her name was Lala, she never mentioned it, and from the time I'd met her nobody called her anything but Chinita, and we learned her real name—the Cantonese name was on her papers—only when she died. And she never mentioned that she had a son, but I said that she'd grow sad when she talked about people who couldn't remember their mothers' faces. I told him about the time we lived together, about how much she taught me, and that thanks to her I became the partenaire of another magician, one whose name was Sindhi. Benjamín listened to me with attention, sipping his tea and thinking; he didn't ask any questions while I was talking, he just listened and nodded very politely. He had a sparse mustache, like a little trail of ants, and as I looked at him I realized he resembled Chinita, not because he was Chinese, he wasn't completely Chinese after all, but because of how he moved his lips and the way he drank tea, the things you learn from living with your mother, touching her and having her close. It was strange that he was so like her when he'd never seen her, not even in photographs. I asked him if he wanted to see her, he said yes, and I brought over the box of photographs; the first one I took out was of Chinita at one of Daniel's birthdays. "Here she is," I said and handed him the picture. He took it delicately and sat there looking at it. The girls were quiet, I realized it was an awkward moment, and it was lucky that Lupe, the younger one, said in the most normal way: "I want to see her, let me see my grandmother." She took the photo from her father's hands, he warned her to be careful, and the two girls put their heads together and concentrated on that face, the expressionless face of the Chinese woman holding my son's hand. Benjamín calmly returned to his tea, and I began to look through the box because I wanted to find the photograph of the magician in one of his shows. I wanted to give it to him, what did I want it for, and I had to take out a lot of pictures until I finally found it. "Look, here's your father, you can keep this one." For the first time I saw him react with emotion, he looked at the photograph and his hands trembled, he looked up and his eyes were stormy. "It can't be!" The girls, Carmen Luisa and Lupe, were a little frightened; later, when I thought about everything that had happened, I understood that they weren't used to seeing their father so nervous, or so diminished. "It can't be," Benjamín repeated, and I wondered what it was that couldn't be, what in the photograph could have upset him. "It's Horacio," he muttered, "this man is Horacio." I thought the girls would burst into tears, and I couldn't think of anything else to do but to get the man a little more tea and bring some cookies for them. When I came back from the kitchen they hadn't moved, they were still in that state of surprise, the father because of what he saw in the picture and the girls because of what they saw in their father. "Horacio was the doctor at the mill," Benjamín murmured, "he's the man in the photograph." Then he explained that the doctor, who'd died a few months *earlier, had been a good friend of his adoptive parents and had brought his two daughters into the world. "He was this man," he insisted, pointing at the Portuguese magician. I explained that it was impossible because the magician died before I was born, and it had to be coincidence that he looked like the doctor, or who knows, maybe the doctor was the magician's son too, a son he'd had out there somewhere; the life of circus people is like the life of sailors, sometimes they pass through a town, the men take a liking to some girl, they're in love for as long as the circus is in town, and then they pack up the tents and pack up the romance, but a little seed's been left behind, a child's been planted. The girls calmed down; it wasn't an explanation they could understand, I didn't even realize I shouldn't talk about the subject in front of them, but I saw that in their innocence they understood I was comforting their father. They returned to their giggling and began to eat the cookies, but Benjamín was numb, he even seemed to be breathing differently. The girls moved away a little to look at Daniel's photographs again, and he looked at me, his small, penetrating eyes filled with questions: "I swear to you it's Horacio, he had the same wart, here, near his lip, and this bent finger, look at this finger, and the nose, everything. It's the same man, but I don't understand." He explained that the doctor's widow, after burying her husband, had sold the house and moved to Matanzas, where she had family. "I don't know where Señora Gertrudis lives," Benjamín murmured, "if I knew I'd go and ask her: why was my real father, who was this magician, identical to your husband, who was the doctor?" He took a sip of tea. "No, not identical," he answered the question as if he were talking to himself. "I'd ask her how it happened that her husband was a doctor and a magician at the same time." The visit had ended, we both knew it was ended at the same time. I had to go to work, and he had to go back to Camagüey. He came to find a sister and the only thing he found was a mystery: he'd make the trip home with that mystery, eight or ten hours on the bus turning the question over and over in his mind. I gave the girls some copies of a publicity photo of Daniel; they gave out photos of the* performers to the audience at the circus, and this one in particular was very good, the boy was leaping from one trapeze to the other. Benjamín put on his Charlie Chaplin hat and said goodbye by bowing his head, the way the Chinese say goodbye. I went to my room, changed my clothes, put on rouge because I looked pale, and when I picked up the lipstick and went to the mirror to put it on, I had the impression that my face was beginning to melt; it was only for a moment but it seemed like my eyes were sinking, my nose, my mouth; I looked like a monster, it was the effect of fear, of the tears that were filling my eyes, the feelings that made me see myself this way. The wife of the doctor who was identical to the magician was named Gertrudis. That's what Chinita's son had said. They call every Gertrudis Tula, and this Tula, as soon as she was widowed, packed up her house and hurried off to Matanzas, where she was from. It seemed like too many coincidences, I felt the emptiness that forms around a whirlpool, I felt like I was floating in a dream, or floating on the line that divides two waters: on one side the living, and the normal things that happen every day, and on the other side the dead, and the ghosts that no one should get involved with, or try to learn why they do what they do, much less find them out, catch them in their returns to this world. Between the two of us, Benjamín and I had taken the lid off a hell, the way you take a lid off a pot. I still can't explain it, they're the things nobody can ever explain. Tula was my mother, and at that point I didn't know if she was alive or dead—today I know she's dead—and when I took the bus to go to the Sans Souci and sat next to a window to catch the breeze, it occurred to me that Benjamín and his two daughters weren't who they said they were. I asked myself if it wasn't one of Chinita's tricks; in life she'd been a woman of tricks, and her ghost had to be the same: she'd come to my house in disguise to warn me about something or show me something. Chinita divided in three: a man almost her age, who looked like her, and two girls who meant something else, two old paths, each with a little piece of the spirit of Lala, the name I never knew.

On the bus that day, when I passed the dance halls on Calle Nep-

tuno, which were always so brightly lit, I was afraid I was dead. Suppose I am? I asked myself, suppose I'm dead and don't know it. I felt the terror right there, looking at the brightness, the swarm of people, a lottery ticket seller who'd fallen asleep beside his lottery tickets, and a very funny-looking oyster vendor in a green cap. Later, when I got to the Sans Souci, I went to Kary Rusi's dressing room and began to put her clothes in order and take her cosmetics out of the boxes, doing everything I did every day before the show began. And suddenly I stopped cold, I felt afraid again, I wondered if I wasn't part of the trick too, like Benjamín and his daughters, part of the game played by the magicians on the other side. I shook my head to shake out my name, the name not only of a bearded lady but of one who has the mark of a ghost. That's the most difficult part, because my mother failed me, she fell into the vice of magicians. My father failed me, a poor bastard with his poor dogs, they suffered together, I didn't know that until it was too late. And Chinita failed me, even though I loved her so much and she loved me too.

After you called me, I lit a candle for your brother. I didn't remember his name, maybe you never told me, but it's all right, I wrote Porrata on a piece of paper, put it in a glass of water, and said a prayer Chinita taught me. That gave me some peace. I realized that the living are the only ones who don't understand anything, something like that got into my head, and at the same time the joy of knowing I was alive and kicking . . . Don't misunderstand me: your brother dead and me happy to still be here. No, it wasn't that, let me explain it again: your brother dead and me awake, seeing so many differences in the candle flame, in the water in the glass, even in the jabber of the prayer, lots of words that make no sense, Cuban and Chinese, I learned it by heart because I thought it was funny. When I was little I wanted to say the prayer for one of my father's dogs that died, the one that danced with balls, the one he loved best, and Chinita wouldn't let me, she said the prayer was for people. I resented that and thought I'd never think about it again, but see, I remembered it and recited it looking at the water, feeling sorry for your mother, it's terrible to lose a child, and feeling sorry for you, now you were going to have a moment like mine, when you passed by the dance halls that were so brightly lit, you probably would wonder: Suppose I'm dead? Sure, my love, listen to me: nobody's dead until he looks out from the water, looks out from the candle flame, looks over to this side and sees somebody else praying and hears the jabber like he was hearing a tune, like he was seeing music, like he was breathing cotton. They're two worlds that breathe together, that's the conclusion I came to, and I'm not a fanatic, I don't believe in miracles, and I'm not a pious churchgoer. I'm Fantina, struggling with phantoms. You have to struggle with them.

BUICK SPECIAL

For Yolanda everything was ghosts. For me, everything began to be a reason to be suspicious, which is another way of agreeing with the idea that the people around us aren't real. How much truth was there in Bulgado and in what he confessed to me that night, that strange parenthesis we made? I felt as if we'd come out of one nightmare—the nightmare of the wake—only to fall headfirst into another: the buzz of people in the Pacífico, that endless soup, a madness dampened with highballs. I thought about McCrary, that slippery individual announcing war; to what extent was he a phantom, a vision, a shade? When I went back to the paper, I was surly with my colleagues; I began to mistrust Madrazo and showed it. I don't know what kind of comment I made that he cut off, roaring that I could shove my fucking insinuations up my ass, and then he softened when he saw my face. I must have been very pale, very startled, he said not to worry. I'd had too many blows and it was logical for me to be on edge. I sat down at the typewriter and was hitting the keyboard with my yellow-stained fingers. I knew I looked like somebody who's been gravely ill. I hadn't eaten well, and my cheeks had hollowed, even my hair stuck to my skull, like dry straw. The first thing I did was write the article on the opening of the Capri. I still remember how it began:

> Anyone who expects to see in Raft the bad manners he exhibited at the Barbary Coast saloon in *Around the World in Eighty Days* is in for a pleasant surprise when he sees him as an irresistible host at the Capri casino.

It was a repulsive opening, followed by a stupid story that had some information about the cost of the hotel, how many employees had been hired, the number of guests that were expected. When I reread it, I thought it was cloying, in the style of Don Galaor, the standard-bearer of the magazine *Bohemia*. But later I decided my piece was worse than that: it came dangerously close to the faggotry of Berto del Cañal. I felt that anxiety when I turned it in to Madrazo, who didn't change even a comma and published it just as it was, but rather than encouraging me it made me feel a certain bitterness.

I was practically alone in the house. Telma, Mamá's childhood friend, took her away. She invited her to an apartment she had on the beach. I saw them leave one morning in a taxi. Telma was a diligent blonde, she arranged my mother's life in the same authoritarian way she had surely treated her when she was a child; as girls they must have been the classic pair of friends in which one imposes the law and the other simply enjoys herself. No one intervened when she ordered Mamá to get her things together and spend two weeks with her and her husband in Guanabo. Nobody was interested in keeping anybody in that house. Papá went his own way, supposedly to put in order the business of selling parcels of land on Isla de Pinos. I suspected he was with Lidia, in mourning—and not obliged to see us. As soon as Telma left with Mamá, Lucy told me she was going away for a few days too, to Irma's house; Irma was a teacher at her school who was advising her about which course of study to follow. I received the teacher when she came for my sister. I took her to the living room and said that Lucy would be right down. There was a tense silence, and I noticed she had the same hairdo as Doris Day in *The Pajama Game*, and a light, warm voice in which she explained her intentions: my sister ought to take it easy, study the future calmly, and not be sorry later that she had matriculated in accounting if her vocation was really in pharmacy. She spoke respectfully, as if I were the family's representative, the principal custodian of the jewel she was about to abduct. Because what she had planned was a perfect abduction, carried out with the clever complicity of Lucy, who finally appeared before us, fresh from the shower, carrying her intimate diary in her hand and pulling a flowered overnight bag, the gift, no doubt, of my mother, a mother will always keep trying until the end. She apologized to the teacher for having made her wait. Irma got up to help her, and I realized I was witnessing the birth of a great romance, like someone witnessing, from a heated observation deck, the eruption of a geyser.

They left, and my routine simplified. I ate breakfast alone, and Balbina, who fixed it for me, spoke very little but observed me intently; she was a distrustful Galician who guessed I was deeply involved in my own world, which was where I wanted to stay. When I came home from the paper late at night, she wasn't there, fortunately, but she'd leave a plate of food for me on the table, almost always breaded steak with boiled potatoes, a stiff, tasteless mess. Balbina was an economical and joyless cook; she liked serving us that shit. Usually I ate before I got home: sometimes I'd invite Yolanda for supper, and if not I'd drive alone to some cheap little restaurant. There were magnificent cheap restaurants in the city. On one of those nights, I ran into Julián when I got home; he'd just come back from a trip and was parked on the street, waiting for me in his Buick Special, an enormous copper-colored car. We embraced, and a lump came to my throat. We went in together and I told him the family had stampeded. Nothing ever scandalized Julián, you could tell him anything: that my father was with his mistress, that Mamá had been dragged away by the only friend who could stand her for two days in a row, and that Lucy had found happiness, in a teacher no less, a woman who was the image of Doris Day in *The Pajama Game*.

"Fuck," Julián muttered, "are you sure it's not Doris Day?"

We sat at the little bar on the terrace, the one where Papá and Santiago had drinks when they were home. Julián told me he liked New York so much that all he thought about was how he could stay there. Then he brought up the subject of Santiago, he had to bring it up at some point. By this time, the first whiskey had calmed me down and I found the courage to tell him everything: they'd called my father from Colonel Ventura's office to come and get his son. That was the entire message, and he ran to his car and drove like one possessed to the morgue, taking it for granted that the body they were going to turn over to him was mine. But before he got there he had a premonition: it worried him that there'd been no signs of life from Santiago since the previous day. It was normal that they hadn't heard from him at home, that he hadn't remembered to let his mother know where he was, or that he didn't see his brother and sister for days. But he never left Papá in the lurch when it came to work, and he didn't stay out overnight without letting his buddy know. They were buddies in almost everything. That's why it was hard for me to imagine how my father reacted when they lifted the sheet—a ragged cloth stiff with dried blood—and he encountered Santiago's face, the sad face he hadn't expected, with the lock of shining hair on his forehead. But I knew how I'd reacted: I confessed to Julián that I felt guilty, that at first I attributed his death to revenge for my troublemaking, my inquiries into the death of Anastasia, and into the war between the families that was moving to Cuba.

"What the hell do you care about Anastasia?" Julián responded. "Do you know who that fat son of a bitch was?"

Papá went to see Colonel Ventura, who, they said, collected the nails he pulled off the fingers of the prisoners he interrogated and kept them in jars. Ventura's wife was famous for breeding canaries; according to *Prensa Libre*, her house was filled with them. When they died she cut off their beaks and kept them in jars too: nails and beaks, it was a delicate home of unspeakable mementos. A friend of Papá's, an army captain, arranged for the interview and accompanied my father to Ventura's office, and the colonel said he was sorry but Santiago was in it up to his neck, his name had been mentioned during several interrogations, they'd been watching him for some time, he was head of a cell, he collected money, he'd been distributing weapons that had been sent by boat to the Isla de Pinos. Finally, he'd shot it out with the police, and there was nothing they could have done to save him. Papá knew it wasn't true, knew Santiago had been taken to the dungeons of the SIM alive, probably wounded, but alive. He didn't ask Ventura for his eyes; who knows what happened to my brother's eyes, when we picked up the body they were no longer in their sockets.

Julián poured himself half a glass of whiskey, drank it down in one gulp, and with a burning mouth he murmured: "His eyes, shit . . ."

We left in his car. The only thing that tied him to Cuba, he told me, putting on the distance glasses that made him look like a serious man, was how well his establishments were doing.

The two he'd opened were strong competition for Marina. He'd just brought some girls over from Indonesia who were different colors. He swore by his mother. From the time they were little they were put in colored dressing gowns: pink, light green, blue, and they were kept wrapped up tight, that was the only clothing they wore, and the cloth bled a dye that was like a tattoo. As the years passed and they reached puberty, you could see the color on them, it even had a gleam, especially on their tits, their smooth bellies, it was incredible. He said "tits," "bellies," and I wanted to ask about Aurora.

"She's okay" was Julián's obscure answer.

"Is she still with that man?"

"She's still with him."

Another obscure answer. We stopped at the Monseigneur; there was no room for anybody in the dining room or at the bar, but for Julián a table appeared. Bola de Nieve was singing an almost providential lyric: "You, who see ghosts in the reflected lights of evening . . . ," and when he finished and saw Julián in the audience, he turned back to the piano and intoned the chorus of another song: "I'm Monsieur, but Monsieur . . . Julián." It was his way of greeting him, and I realized that Aurora's son had become a popular figure in Havana, always very well dressed—his tailor was Pepe, the same one Lansky used— with the roguish, gallant look of pimps of distinction, that ability to come out with a witticism in the least expected place, the right phrase always on his lips, and he had a great sense of timing and entrance, like a veteran actor. I thought of how different he was from the boy with whom I'd slipped into the gangsters' meeting, that afternoon when we were the only witnesses to Anastasia's humiliation. I remembered Anastasia perfectly, an obedient hippopotamus, turning on his heels and heading for the room he'd just left only because Lucky Luciano had called him back, harshly and despotically, from the door. I also remembered Luciano, and the ratlike dog he carried in his arms. It was Christmas 1946, they'd just agreed to the death of Bugsy Siegel, and Aurora, unaware of everything, was preparing the ballroom where they were going to have a party and eat roasted breast of flamingo. Eleven years had passed since then. Julián was still tenderhearted about animals (did he remember the pink birds piled up on the kitchen floor?), on the street he'd bend over to pet mangy dogs, and he picked up stray kittens and gave them to the whores to take care of. When we left the Monseigneur, I invited him to have the next-to-last drink at the bar next door, which was in fact Club 21. By this time I was half drunk, but not a hair on Julián's head was out of place. He said it was impossible, he'd just come back from a trip and had to look in on his establishments. He repeated that he worked at night and I shouldn't forget it, and when he said that he winked at me, he threw his arm around my shoulders the way we did when we were kids. We drove away in his Buick Special, a car that resembled a palace. I closed my eyes, and I think I had dozed off, or was about to, when Julián suggested we have lunch the next day at the Boris. I said I hadn't been there for a thousand years, not since the Russian waiter threw me out.

"Constantino?" he said, laughing. "That hog kicked you out of the Boris?"

I began to tell him the details: the thugs who occupied the street, the mysterious conclave held in the restaurant less than twenty-four hours after the death of Anastasia . . . Suddenly I stopped talking because I saw a police car signaling us to pull over. Julián slammed on the brakes and muttered: "God damn it to hell, I forgot to put on the light." Three men got out of the patrol car; one of them approached while the others shone their flashlights at us.

"Be quiet," said Julián. "Don't even think about opening your mouth."

The police officer asked him to identify himself. Julián leaned out the window and used a cold tone, a haughty sarcasm that fascinated me. "I work at the Capri, I just left there, I was having a few drinks with this guy . . . I have my identification card from the Capri in my pocket, and there's a pistol in the glove compartment. The permit's in my wallet."

"Give me the card."

Another officer came over to whisper to the first, and then he came around to my side, glared at me, and opened the glove compartment. There was the gun, he pulled it out, and I began to tremble. I couldn't help it. I was high and supposed that at any moment I'd have to throw up. Two or three minutes went by, and the one who'd taken the pistol returned it to its place, closed the glove compartment, and brushed off his hands.

"Go on." They were the magic words.

We went on. I looked at Julián. I asked if it was true that he worked at the Capri.

"Hey, don't be an imbecile. Don't you know what I do?"

He added that this had happened because he hadn't turned on the car's interior light. He'd been told always to turn it on whenever he drove late at night; it was a signal to the police, it meant he had nothing to hide, and it also let them see inside. We got home, and I stumbled as I got out. Julián asked me if I needed help getting to bed. I told him he should take a good look at me, I wasn't drunk, only a little high.

"Quin"—he'd called me that ever since we were boys— "now that you say you're not drunk, is it true you were in love with Aurora?"

I raised my head and saw his profile; he was looking straight ahead, as if he hadn't said anything important, or as if he weren't expecting any answer at all.

"When we were boys," I confessed.

"We're still boys," he reminded me, mumbling; it seemed to me he'd become sad. "I'll pick you up tomorrow at one, at the paper, okay?"

He turned on the interior light of the Buick and drove away without turning it off, visibly alone in the speeding showcase.

CHULITA

The Boris was full. Julián said he didn't feel like waiting until a table was free but still felt like eating chicken soup with kreplach, and so we went to Moshe Pipiks, the other Jewish restaurant; there were a few empty tables and I liked the strudel, the only dessert they had on the menu. While we ate, Julián gave me his new phone number, the one for the apartment on Calle Infanta where he was living with an American girl. He asked if I was seeing a woman, I told him about Yolanda, he thought it was an incredible story and added that I was a lucky guy, since any man's dream was to go to bed with a contortionist. I explained that she wasn't a contortionist, and he said it was all the same, you needed rubber bones to get inside a narrow box and dodge swords.

"The truth is she didn't dodge them completely."

I told him Yolanda was missing an arm. Julián was dumbfounded, he concentrated on the checkerboard floor at Moshe Pipiks. Almost everybody around us was speaking Yiddish.

"You're hopeless, friend," he said with a sigh, staring at the steaming food, "you don't even like the girls I bring in. The ones who have that color I told you about yesterday, I had to baptize them. Not even God could pronounce the names they bring with them from Java. I called one of them Aurora."

"You gave a whore your mother's name?"

Julián shrugged and attacked the first kreplach. I attacked my own food and thought about McCrary. By now he was on his way to Oriente Province; his intention was to get to the foothills of the Sierra Maestra, write about the insurgents, with any luck take photographs and talk to them. That morning he'd come to see me at *Prensa Libre*; he wanted to give me his condolences and say goodbye, since he and the photographer had rented a car and were leaving in the afternoon. We went to a café and ordered two glasses of rum; we drank them without ice, breathing fire from our mouths each time we swallowed, like dragons, but looking straight ahead, talking with our eyes on the mirror behind the row of bottles. McCrary let me know they'd called him from New York, there were indications that the meeting at the Riviera had taken place—though they wouldn't let him near the hotel—and that, far from settling problems, it had produced a degree of chaos. Lansky made it clear that nothing agreed to earlier was now valid, and he again put on the table the possibility of his leaving. He didn't raise his voice to make his point, because the truth is that Lansky never shouted; he didn't shout and he didn't take notes, everybody knew that. But the other capos gathered there got the message loud and clear: the agreements made in Apalachin—the few that had been made before the police interrupted—and a handful that had been ratified recently in Havana, at the meetings in the house by the Almendares River, were no longer in effect. Apparently it was a decision backed by Lucky Luciano, who by then was confined to his house on the Via Tasso, in Naples, but from there he'd sent an emissary to the meeting at the Riviera. As far as McCrary knew, that had been the end of the meeting.

"What do you think?" I asked Julián. "It looks ugly, doesn't it? They say there'll be a war."

Julián spoke with his mouth full, something that irritated Aurora so much. "With the beards? . . . Frank Costello just sent them $250,000, I have it on good authority that he gave orders to put the money in Fidel Castro's hand: in case there's a change, they won't interfere with the casinos."

"I know that. But I'm referring to the other war. Lucky Luciano broke some agreements, the ones made in Apalachin, did you know anything about that?"

"No, Quin, I don't know anything and you know I don't talk."

His answer was so cutting, and his tone so full of resentment, that I felt embarrassed. I didn't feel like eating my strudel anymore, and I had a hunch the war was going to be bloodier and dirtier than I had imagined. Julián had made that point clear, and after that there was no point in going around with long faces, and so he made a joke about the other part of my question.

"And hey, one other thing: don't ever say Luciano again, you'll find yourself with a mouth full of ants, remember he doesn't want to be called that anymore. Not even his friends have the nerve to do that. You have to call him Don Salvatore. Do you remember the little dog he had that day?"

The tenderness that dogs inspired in him dispersed once and for all the shadows that had fallen over the chicken soup with kreplach. We left Moshe Pipiks the same good friends as always and walked for a while along the Paseo del Prado. I almost asked him to take me to say hello to his mother, but I couldn't, I knew I shouldn't. I said I'd take a cab back to the paper, he insisted on driving me, and I insisted on leaving everything on that happy note of childhood memories. On my way back to the paper I saw the first store windows with

Christmas decorations and felt uneasy, and above all uncertain. Mamá would call from her friend Telma's beach house every other day, she knew Lucy was spending a few days with her teacher, and she was so naïve—or so grief-stricken—she said it reassured her. Generally she talked to Balbina, asked if she was taking good care of me and if Papá was sleeping at home. I don't know what pious lies the Galician told her, because the reality was that Papá hadn't come back, at least he didn't come back to sleep, only to pick up papers or change clothes. I took advantage of the situation to invite Yolanda to the house. On several nights we slept in my room, and then we'd eat the food Balbina left; we'd get up at the crack of dawn, set the table, and drink highballs made with the ginger ale kept in the little bar on the terrace, a corner of the house that had become absurd, totally desolate. When we felt hungry, we'd lift the checked napkin Balbina used to cover her dishes: steak with boiled potatoes, inedible roast chicken, often an omelet. Yolanda wanted to cook something else, but I avoided the complication, I didn't like to see her working with only one arm, and it wasn't a good idea for Balbina to find out I was bringing home a woman at night. She was an old fox capable of scheming with my mother, arranging a surprise return, and catching us there, naked in the dining room, smoking in a knowing way, watching the final dawns of 1957, which had been the worst and best year of my life.

During this time I distanced myself from Bulgado. I'd almost succeeded in uprooting from my mind the night of horror at the zoo, and I supposed he wouldn't have anything else to offer me. He left a couple of messages for me at *Prensa Libre*. In the first he obliged the operator to repeat several times his nom de guerre: Steve (which he pronounced "eh-stay-bay"); in the second he simply said he was expecting me for lunch at his house on Christmas Eve. I looked at the small piece of paper on which the operator had written down the message and thought I'd rather be dead, with ants in my mouth as Julián predicted, than sit at a table with Elvira, that fat apricot with the mental age of a flea, and Sara, the long-suffering mother-in-law who was the real contortionist, but a mental one: she lived in a circus world with that peculiar woman, her daughter, and that mixture of magician, clown, and lion tamer, her son-in-law, Bulgado.

Mamá came back in the middle of December. By then Lucy had come home like the prodigal son, never a more apt description because her male transformation was complete. When I saw her she looked a little like Santiago; they looked like each other more than I looked like either one of them, and the way she wore her hair, how she smoked (she was smoking too much), and that movement she made with her shoulders, like a masculine tic, brought her closer to the brother we'd lost. My mother accepted her defeat and didn't display surprise or anger. Papá did resent the change, I could see it in his face, in the sudden rapid blinking that was a way of chasing away phantoms, because it hurt him that Lucy had become a false copy of the deceased. The hardest days were approaching: the head of Christmas at home had always been Santiago; he was the one who took out the tree and decorated it, with Lucy's help, and who went with Papá to the bakery to drop off and pick up the roast pig. Nobody went out that Christmas Eve, not even Papá wanted to leave home; all of us were enclosed in ourselves and in our rooms. In the small hours of the twenty-fifth, I couldn't sleep and had the sudden impulse to go to Santiago's room and smoke a cigarette. I opened the door and was hit by a cloud of smoke, I saw the burning tip of another cigarette, and my father's silhouette, outlined against the dim light that came in through the window as he sat on Santiago's bed. He held a handkerchief and I realized he was crying. I understood I ought to leave him alone; I closed the door softly and wandered for a few minutes around the house. I went to the kitchen and poured a glass of milk; as I drank it I felt like crying too but couldn't. I let out a dry sob and asked myself where the hell we'd be in a year, on Christmas of 1958, how would Papá and my mother be then, how much would they have stopped missing Santiago and how much of him would be left in the house, on the table in the dining room, in the reminiscence of him that was Lucy, who'd become a good boy.

At the paper, Madrazo had been moving me back and forth between Financial and Police Reports. He confessed he wasn't sure in which of the two sections he'd place me permanently, a confession that irritated me a lot. In fact, what I considered untouchable were the roughly two hours a day I invested in updating information about construction of the new hotels, profits at the casinos, and the prodigious attacks of the Banco Financiero, which, thanks to the swindles and backstabbing inflicted on its own shareholders, was overflowing with money for investments and placing it wherever that obscure individual Amadeo Barletta—a close friend of Santo Trafficante—thought it should be placed. One afternoon when I was buried in the secret (and not so secret) papers of my investigation, Madrazo came over to tell me that a fully confirmed rumor had reached *Prensa Libre*, stating that this Barletta and Sam Giancana had eaten lunch together at Ranuccio, a little restaurant on the east side of Chicago. "Generals make alliances," I remember saying, returning instinctively to my papers, "when there's a war that's what they do." Madrazo left and I made a note of the information. I made a note of everything because I felt like it, though in the long run they didn't let me publish much of anything.

On the last day of the year, which was a Tuesday, Julián called me at the paper to say he wasn't going to let me stay home; he added that Santiago, given his character, would've been the first to urge me to see in the new year the right way, and we didn't have to celebrate with those assholes who put on little hats and blew whistles, we'd just sit down to have a few drinks and listen to some music. I told him I'd think about it. He said not to think about it, people who think so much have no balls, I should find a woman and we'd all go to the Ali Bar. I reminded him I didn't have to find one, I already had her, and so it was all arranged. I called Yolanda, but she suggested we eat at her house before we went out. I agreed, and it was a strange meal because her son, the aerialist with whom I'd never exchanged a word, was there. I was four or five years older than he was, at that age the difference is fairly apparent, but he had an immediate advantage over me: the precision of his movements, the tension in his body, an imperious agility that crushed the next man, as if muscle, all his muscles, were another brain, or the only brain available. He was a boy who thought with his biceps; his head appeared to be empty. He made several very stupid remarks that Yolanda celebrated with no misgivings, and there was a moment when reality turned around, in a hallucination: I had the mad idea that thousands of lightbulbs, like the ones in a circus, had been turned on, and Fantina, waving her countless arms, had turned into a Hindu goddess, an unembraceable goddess, hadn't I thought when I met her that she was the perfect wife for Tamakún? I was engrossed as I swallowed a mouthful of white rice and black beans. Yolanda asked if I wanted a little more, she said it just to have something to say, I still had food on my plate. I thanked her and said I'd had plenty. Daniel was a perverse imp between us, ruining everything, including my appetite, as if he had a magic wand for creating havoc. After that night, difficult to forget, something changed in my perception of Yolanda, and I suppose in her perception of me as well. Our romance had lasted about two months. We stayed together for a while longer, with sporadic visits to restaurants, an occasional trip to the interior, kisses and shows of affection that have nothing to do with passion, that perplexing stone that is both pit and stone at the same time. The aerialist got up and left without saying goodbye; Yolanda and I drove in my car to the Ali Bar, where Julián was waiting for us with his American girl, a real goddess with two arms. Blanca Rosa Gil was singing "Kisses of Fire," and Beny Moré went from table to table having drinks with his friends. I saw him give Julián a hug, they whispered to each other and laughed out loud, their own business. Aurora's son, who gave whores his own mother's name, was king of the night and of shady deals, and in that environment, it seemed, he was something else: he was that precious jewel, a man you could trust. We saw in the new year together. He liked Yolanda and his girlfriend had me hypnotized. She was a little older than we were, everybody was older than we were. She must have been twenty-six or twenty-seven, and her name was Leigh. When they shouted twelve o'clock and we drank to a prosperous 1958, I thought of Santiago. I felt a lump in my throat and exchanged a glance with Julián, who supported me in a way that was visible only to me: he pushed out his lips, in one of his typical gestures, and nodded, as if trying to tell me yes, we were connected. Neither one of us could imagine that barely two weeks later, on the most ill-advised night of that month of January, we'd exchange another glance, but one that was very different, a glance of survival: abject fear on my part, icy anguish on his.

Early in January, Madrazo said he was arranging an interview with George Raft and had me in mind to do it. He'd spoken several times with Raft's assistants at the Capri, and the actor's secretary had promised it for after the fifteenth, since Raft was in New York. One thing was certain: the interview would be held in a suite at the hotel, not in the penthouse at

Twenty-first and N, where he really lived, a place I'd have liked to see. The logical thing would have been to give the interview to Berto del Cañal, the head of Entertainment, but Berto didn't speak English well enough, and the paper wanted to focus on Raft as a businessman: it was said he had at least a half-point share in the casino, and that in addition to being "floor man," he was an intermediary who flew to Miami every weekend with two suitcases filled with dollars.

"He goes in the morning and comes back at night," Madrazo said in astonishment, as if he were watching the movie. "He keeps playing his own character."

He keeps playing Snake, I thought, and I bet Bulgado would have given an arm—only images with arms occurred to me—to go with me to the interview. And it wouldn't have been very difficult to oblige him, but I must confess that, after the opening at the Capri, I'd become afraid of him; he wasn't normal, and I couldn't imagine how he'd react when he found himself in a much more intimate situation with Johnny Angel, Johnny Lamb, or that last character, Steve, whose name he took to leave me a message at Christmas; as I learned much later, it alluded to Steve Larwitt, a nightclub owner played by Raft in *The House Across the Bay*.

In any event, I'd changed my opinion about Bulgado's not having anything else to give me. Thinking it over, I concluded that, as the war for control of the casinos intensified, it was possible they'd entrust him and his assistant with more jobs, with severely chastised meat for the lions. And so, on January 6, the Day of the Three Kings, I decided to go to see him. Not to tell him I was going to interview Raft, but to reestablish communication. Elvira received me; she got fatter every day and, to judge by her smile, more retarded too. I told her the Kings had left a present for her, and I gave her a box of candy. She didn't say anything, it's a sign of total imbecility:

when they ought to speak they're quiet, and they chatter when they should keep their mouths shut. Maybe it was surprise that left her mute; she stayed like that for a few minutes—for me they were eternal—and then she called her mother. She screamed for her as if she were being raped; the old woman came running and was reassured when she saw me at the door. She told me to come in, Bulgado wouldn't be long, he'd gone to check on the lions. I waited an hour, she offered me coffee, I said goodbye to the women and said I'd come back another day, and at that moment Bulgado appeared. He wasn't surprised to see me in his house; instead I had the feeling he expected to find me there. He suggested we go out to have a beer, I realized he wanted to talk to me in private.

"When are you interviewing Raft?" He laughed when he asked the question, he came out with it not knowing he'd hit the nail on the head.

"Next week," I answered frankly, "I'm going to see him at the Capri. I came to find out if there's something you want me to ask him."

Bulgado opened his mouth: I was his idol but also his torment. I was getting ready to talk to Raft, to sit beside him and hold his attention.

"I'd have given this arm, look, this arm to go with you to that interview." And he raised his right arm, covered with scars, old caresses from a Manchurian tiger. "Ask him about when he was a boxer, about the time Frankie Jerome left him half dead, bah, I bet you won't ask him that. Jerome broke his nose, closed both his eyes, almost tore off an ear."

He changed when he said this, he'd become very fierce and his mouth was trembling, that tremor so characteristic of an attack of jealousy.

"I'll ask him," I said. "Have they brought you any more stiffs at the zoo?"

He lit a cigarette before he answered. "Why do you say that?"

"Because I know, kid. Because they're having a fucking little war and I know there'll be more bodies."

Bulgado drank, smoked, didn't say a word for a while. Then he went back to boxing. "They carried him out of the ring on a stretcher, ask him about it, with his jaw hanging, look here, with his jaw like this."

He opened his mouth and half-closed his eyes. He looked comical to me: envy was eating him alive. I'd meet with Raft, and I didn't know shit about his life, and he'd have to settle for what I wanted to tell him after the interview, nothing but crumbs.

"There'll be two or three jobs next week. They told us to be ready for two or three. You won't put it in the paper, right?"

The question was heavy with irony, even despair. There was nothing to do: he couldn't refuse to cut up corpses for the Mafia, and I couldn't write about it in the paper, take the lid off the matter and shake up the country. Two or three stiffs were too many for one night. If Bulgado wasn't lying—and it was a shame he lied so much—they were cooking up a minor massacre. Before we said goodbye, at the door of his house, I assured him I'd call him again as soon as I heard Raft's confession.

"Press him," he advised, "but be careful, he has a bad temper. He beat up a truck driver a few years ago, ask him about that and you'll see."

I didn't go to Yolanda's house anymore without calling first. I didn't want to run into her son again. He made me uneasy, as if he were the true magician, the only one really in her life, an imperturbable creature, somebody who went around spreading slime. He couldn't have made a worse impression on me. That night he wasn't in the apartment, he almost never was, and Yolanda and I shared an intimacy very similar to what we'd had at the beginning, though a shadow was swinging over our heads, a trapeze moving by itself, like in the movies about cursed circuses. At dawn, when I was getting dressed to leave, it occurred to me to ask her a bitter question: on the day we weren't together anymore, what would she say about me?

"You don't have leprosy," Yolanda replied from the bed, it was dark and I couldn't see her expression, "you don't like men, and you don't burn your fingers when you smoke, that's what I'll say."

It wasn't very much. It was horrible to hear that this was the only thing she could say. I decided to change the subject and told her that at the paper they'd asked me to interview George Raft. She got out of bed and asked if I was serious; she used an adolescent's distrustful voice to confess that the first movie she ever saw in her life was one of Raft's, Raft playing a bullfighter, can you imagine that? She drew a blank for a few minutes trying to remember the title of the film, or the name of the bullfighter, but no, all she could remember was that his girlfriend was named Chulita.

"Nobody's named Chulita," she said with a yawn, leaning against the doorjamb, a tragic image that I still have of her. "That's worse than being named Fantina."

"OH, LIFE"

Some sticks of incense here. Shredded paper here. Flowers here, black-eyed peas, sesame candies. They're Chinese customs, do I have any left? I don't know what else to set out for you so you'll forgive me, so you don't turn over in your grave when you hear what I'm going to tell you. My regrets, my secrets, very serious things, Lala, will you let me call you that?

I'd never dare reproach you for anything, least of all here, looking at the earth where your relatives are, or as they say in the soap operas, where your ancestors are resting. I don't know what you've told them about Daniel, if you've boasted about your false grandson, if you've said he's the best boy in the world, the greatest aerialist in Cuba. I won't talk about the bad things: that what he has for a heart is a stone, a ball of jade—didn't you teach him to play with jade balls?—and it softens only when I mention you, and it almost broke when you died. What did you do to him, old woman, what did you give that boy to eat? I confess that at night, after I go to bed suffering because of how he treats me, I'm afraid this is your revenge. Sometimes I think that, like a good Chinese, you fooled my mother, you pretended you didn't care about the Portuguese magician. But it must have hurt you like crazy when the circus passed through Coliseo, that dusty little town, and he met Tula and took a liking to her, and then he grabbed her and took her away forever. And I think that to take your revenge on her you kept me, and to harm her you didn't let me marry Daniel's father, and you put the idea into my head of helping the magician with the Chinese torture until I lost my arm and ruined my life. When I go to bed sad, desperate on account of the hatred that boy has for me, I ask myself if revenge could have gone so far, all the way to this belly he came out of: Daniel's spiteful, a devil that jabs at you and fills you with poison. It hurts me to say this to you, but I don't have anybody else to talk to. I can fool Kary Rusi, Roderico, Joaquín Porrata—the poor boy's all wrong about life. I can fool the choreographer at the Sans Souci, who thinks Daniel's an artist—along with his work on the trapeze, it seems he's starting him as a dancer—and he's promised to use him in another production. I can fool everybody, because mothers know how to do that, but not you, Chinita: you know all too well what grew up with you.

That night, when Joaquín came to my house, just back from New York, Daniel opened his bag on the sly, looked through his coat, and went out to see what was in his car, that green car Joaquín says is named Surprise. He took out some papers and read them, I couldn't stop him, he doesn't pay attention to me. He had a grudge against Joaquín because he thought he was too young for me, and because I think he envied him a little: a good-looking reporter who wears nice clothes, who's blond and has light eyes. He never acted this way with other men I've been with, I've never seen him so resentful of anybody. Among Joaquín's papers, by some damn coincidence, he found one that mentioned Louis Santos and Santos's friends, and the strange business that goes on in the cabarets. I said coincidence, and who can tell me it wasn't Santos who told him to search through everything? While Joaquín and I were in bed, Daniel was taking notes, copying those papers, and in the morning he took them to Santos at the Rosita de Hornedo. The two of them hit it off, because after Daniel came to the

227

Sans Souci, Santos made sure he was comfortable and well-paid, I think because we had that affair, and when he learned Daniel was my son he gave him a dressing room so he could concentrate on the somersault that's the finale of the show, and he paid him a lot of compliments. Daniel lashed out at me when we broke up, he thought Santos left me because I didn't measure up. I even think he despised me because of my arm, how it hurts me to say it, Chinita, that my own son thinks I'm worthless because I'm missing an arm.

They almost killed Joaquín because of what he wrote; they abducted him and gave him a beating, they gave him a hell of a scare, I know because I saw him that night, with his face all swollen. I swear I thought I'd die knowing my own son was behind it, that the tip-off had come from him, and to top it all off, that Louis Santos must have been furious because my new boyfriend was his enemy. I knew Joaquín was finding out things about a man they killed in a barbershop, and it was his bad luck that Daniel saw what he wrote down. Then Louis Santos found out, and he ordered his men to pick him up, knock him around a little, and take him to the zoo; Joaquín swore they took him to the lion cage, it must have been to scare him. The worst thing was that they stopped here, right outside, they told him I was Santos's girlfriend, and when they finally let him go, he met me in a movie and threw it all up to me, then we went to a bar, I don't even know what I said to him, I was out of my mind and didn't want him to find out what Daniel had done.

A few days later, on New Year's Eve, my son and Joaquín finally met. They'd never spoken, but I prepared a banquet with this one damn arm, I asked a neighbor to help me put the meat in the oven, you can't imagine the tightrope I was walking. Daniel's bad-tempered and that night he outdid himself, but I think Joaquín got the better of him. Because he's a few years older and was sleeping with me, the boy's mother, he tried to pretend and smooth things over. But he didn't do enough, and that disappointed me. At the table, with an angry face,

228

mashing the black-eyed peas with his fork, he had to put up with an aerialist who insulted newspapers and the people who wrote for them, who said terrible things about women who became involved with younger men, and mulattas who were idiots because they believed that white men really loved them. He painted a full-length portrait of me, and I tried to make a joke of it. But the moment came when I saw that they were toe-to-toe, provoking each other with gestures and looks, and I even thought they'd come to blows. That terrified me, because if it happened, what could I do with only one arm to separate them? Joaquín barely tasted the food, he was self-absorbed, I was ready to tell him to go to his New Year's celebration alone, but then I said to myself: be calm, he just lost his brother, I mean: be calm, he's still alive. Daniel didn't even say goodbye to me, or give me a kiss, nothing. Before he left he told me he'd go to the Chinese cemetery. I said I thought it would be closed. He looked at me in a rage, I swore he was going to spit at me, and he shouted in my face how little I knew the Chinese. Even if it wasn't their New Year, the cemetery would be open all night.

I cursed you and your mother, Chinita. I'm giving you incense, I'm giving you candles, I'm giving you a glass of water so you'll want to forgive me. But when I saw him leave, rubbing my face in it, saying he was going to see you, I thought you'd stolen him from me. Tula took your husband from you, that damn Portuguese, that old shit, I hate him now, I don't know what he gave you to make you both be so in love, even if he had a diamond in his prick it didn't give you the right to take my son away from me. I'm not saying take away because he doesn't love me, I could stand that, I mean take away because you made him strange, you made him the bad person he is, and I say it and fall apart, people will think you died yesterday, Chinita, when they see me here crying like Mary Magdalene.

I confess I felt relieved when he finally left. I have to live, do you understand? My son is my son and he's what I love most, but I'm thirty-five, I'm not an old woman, and I need air. Like Kary Rusi, when she comes back from the second show she suffocates inside the dressing room, and I was suffocating inside my feelings. So I fixed myself up and went with Joaquín to the Ali Bar.

I met his best friend, dressed like a pimp because he is a pimp, and the American girl who went out with him and who I thought was showing off her arms: long, slim, suntanned arms. I'd never been in that place before, Roderico once said we should go, he told me that as soon as Beny saw him come in he'd sing his favorite song, which always was: "Oh, Life," and he felt like dying when he heard it, but we never went, there were lots of places I still hadn't visited with the great Rodney of Cuba. Joaquín was distracted all night, he'd look at the American girl from time to time, but she was looking at me. I think when she saw me come in, she didn't realize I was missing an arm, that happens to lots of people, they're so used to other people having two arms that at first their minds fool them, they don't realize I'm missing something, and it's not until some time goes by, when I stand up or change position, that they discover I have a stump, a little chunk of flesh I don't cover up because I don't want to, because I think that would be the greatest betrayal I could commit, not only of the good arm buried in a place only you know about, here in this cemetery, but also of my memories, the sawed woman I was for so many years, the partenaire run through by swords, which isn't the same thing as being a contortionist; the pimp was so ignorant he told the American I was a contortionist. She stopped staring at the stump and looked into my eyes. She wasn't going to forget the last night of 1957 either, because after midnight Julián asked me to dance and then Joaquín asked her to dance too, and while we were dancing, both couples pretty close to each other, I saw a peculiar little movement, it caught my attention right away, they were touching each other, I mean she was touching him but he didn't respond, Joaquín, after all, is a good friend to his friends. As we walked back to the table, the two men were behind us, talking to each other, and I grabbed her arm. I thank God for Roderico Neyra, I remembered a phrase he'd shout at one of the dancers he brought in for the show about the paradise of Asia, she was half-Indian and spoke only English, and he'd scream at her: "You bitch, move your ass!" It was the only thing I learned in English, but I was sure it would work. I shouted it at the American, I could let myself raise my voice just then because there was so much noise, people blowing their whistles and all the uproar of New Year's Eve, and at the same time I said those words I dug my nails into her. Nobody who hasn't been pinched by a one-armed person can know the strength that develops in the hand that's left on its own. She tried to get free, she screamed and looked behind her, I imagine she was looking for Julián. I blessed Rodney again: "You bitch, you dirty whore, don't you see Joaquín's with me?" I'm sure she understood me, she was in a daze, stunned, she sat down looking sick and rubbing her arm above the elbow; a welt was starting to appear in the place where I'd grabbed her.

Beny Moré came to the table to say hello to Julián; they hugged and I realized that Beny was whispering something to him; I never imagined he could like me even a little with all the great-looking women there in that room. I'll never forget those first minutes of 1958, when the people quieted down and he began to sing. It was a current I felt that night, a shock that made me wonder what I was doing at that table with these three assholes, three little shits, two Cubans and the American slut. When I stood up and saw Beny following me with his eyes, I thought of something I'd never thought of before: what a lunatic magician fate is when you're not looking for it! I was a little high, and I went up to him to request "Oh, Life," I did it not to flirt with him but to please Roderico, who was far away, but what difference does that make? I was thinking about him and wanted to dedicate the song to him, inside I dedicated it to him and I think he probably heard it; wherever he was, I'm sure he felt like dying and didn't know why. Beny sang it for me; he didn't know my story and he didn't know where to find me, but I sent him a paper where I wrote Yolanda and the number of the cabaret. In a few days, when we were together, I told him my real name was Fantina. It gave him a laughing fit. He was *smoking marijuana, and he told me it sounded like the name of a crazy queer. I asked him for a drag, you'll die again when you hear this, he took out another joint and I smoked the whole thing, and while I was enjoying the taste, I whispered: "It isn't a faggot's name, honey, it's a bearded lady's."*

THE MONEY MESSENGER

"I told a colleague of yours a few years ago," George Raft recalled. "I told him I'd come to Havana in '58 to take charge of
the Hilton casino. Instead of the Hilton I came to the Capri.
Not bad, I was wrong by only three blocks."

He'd said it to Rai García in '56; he was a reporter about
my age, I'd run into him at a few press conferences, but he
soon had the chance to leave Entertainment and devote himself
to what he really liked: writing about baseball. There are guys
like that, bursting with good luck. During that interview, Raft
had promised that, along with taking care of the casino, he'd
dance for the patrons if he had to. I asked him if he still
planned to dance.

"I already am." He spread his arms in an easy-to-understand
street gesture. "There's no way I can live in Cuba and not shake
my butt."

He used that expression: "and not shake my butt." He had a
heavy, dry voice, as if he chewed stones in his spare time, and
he spoke quickly, his lips almost closed; it was torture trying
to understand each word, sometimes I could only guess at a

phrase. Fifteen minutes earlier, when I walked into his suite, I was afraid the interview would be ruined by all the people fluttering around him, among them a kind of secretary who showed him papers, and an older woman, like a housekeeper, who walked in and out of the adjoining room. Once she walked in with a suit hanging over her arm and asked Raft: "Is this the one?" He said it was, and she examined it right there, it seemed to me she was looking for a stain. Behind the small bar a couple of waiters were arranging glasses, and I breathed a sigh of relief when Raft asked everybody to let him take care of the press, pointing at me; I must have looked to them like a kid lost in a jacket that was too big for him. My mother would have said it needed more man to fill it.

They all left and Raft stood up to pour whiskey; he did it in an unnatural way, as if he'd studied every move. He didn't ask if I'd prefer something else, he only said: "How many ice cubes?" I said three. When he came over to hand me the drink, I noticed he was wearing a strong scent, an intense sandalwood, I don't know if I could have stood it for more than two hours in a row. I jotted down something about the perfume and added: ivory cigarette holder, dark silk smoking jacket over a white shirt, two-toned shoes. I began with the classic question of a starstruck pen pusher: I asked him to tell me how he'd acquired his taste for gambling. It's what anybody would have asked him: Don Galaor for *Bohemia*, Skinny T. for the *Marina*, or Berto del Cañal himself, who'd confessed to me the day before how angry it had made him when he heard they'd given me the interview, but he understood he couldn't do it because he didn't know enough English. Raft said that in the neighborhood where he grew up, which wasn't called Hell's Kitchen for nothing—his voice may have made it sound more hellish—there was an old man they called Killer Gray, who'd been a sheriff, a gunslinger, and an Indian hunter. Since his parents were so busy bringing up eleven other children, Killer took charge of him: he taught him to use a knife, drive trucks, and play poker. You couldn't survive in Hell's Kitchen, or in the Gophers, the gang where they named him Snake, if you didn't know all those things. As he was speaking, he looked at me two or three times out of the corner of his eye, and the way he did it, tilting his head slightly, keeping in character, reminded me very strongly of Bulgado. Then I told him. I said I knew an individual who took care of lions at the zoo and was a great admirer of his movies; he'd seen them all and even remembered the names of the characters he played.

"Oh, sure," Raft replied without hesitating. "I know who he is, he looks just like a friend of mine."

I didn't have the nerve to ask who his friend was, but I tried to find out where the hell he'd met Bulgado.

"They told me about him here. And then he came on the day we opened the hotel, I met him and they took a picture of us together."

I was about to say I was the one who'd brought him, but I didn't want to complicate things. I thought it wasn't the right moment, maybe later, when we finished the interview. Before getting to the point—the point was the Capri, the fortune made there every night, already so unmanageable he was obliged to make a weekly trip to Florida with the money— I asked about his memoir that *The Saturday Evening Post* was publishing at the time; he grimaced and said he hadn't bothered to read it, I reminded him that he'd dictated it, he replied with another street gesture, as if he were saying: So what? And surprisingly he returned to the subject of Bulgado, he wouldn't let another day go by without calling his friend Madden (he said it through closed lips, but I heard Madden perfectly), who lived in Arkansas, to tell him he had a double in Havana, a guy who had his mug, but younger, obviously; Madden was over sixty, and how old was the lion tamer?

"Much younger," I said, "and he's not a lion tamer, he just feeds them."

"Ah, and you don't think you have to tame them to give them food? You try it."

He was a quarrelsome man. A cynical Raft. He didn't lose even when he lost. I thought we'd had enough of nostalgia, of comments that would have interested only an asshole like Berto del Cañal, and I said I wanted to know how difficult it was for him to manage a place like the Capri, which was full on opening day, had to turn away patrons during the whole month of December, and was a madhouse in January, with a waiting list for rooms and gamblers who came from other hotels to try their luck in the casino where Snake ruled.

"I'll give you a scoop," Raft announced, ignoring my question, "so you can tell the lion tamer: I'm making a movie with Marilyn and Tony Curtis. I've already seen the screenplay, my name will be Spats Colombo."

And he started to laugh with an old guy's little sibylline laugh, because nobody laughs like a young man when he's sixty-two, well-fed and better dressed, maybe that's why he didn't look his age.

"*The Saturday Evening Post* already published that scoop," I said to annoy him, so he'd show a little respect.

"They published the part about the movie"—his face hardened, even his eyes hardened—"not what my name would be."

I gave him a humble smile, afraid he'd lose his temper, and returned to the subject that had brought me there: it was said that, in view of the casino's success, they had to put in more craps tables, and Colonel Fernández Miranda, President Batista's brother-in-law (it sounded so painless in English: the president's brother-in-law) had to take slot machines out of the Nacional and rush them over to the Capri to satisfy the demand.

"I don't know anything about that," he lied shamelessly, then stopped to light his second or third cigarette. "I only try to keep the people happy; last week I brought breakfast in bed to a woman. Believe me, she wasn't mine."

Again the laugh, a little harsh, lightly wrapped in phlegm. Skinny T. had told the story in his column: a couple from Texas had come to the Capri for the first time, the husband said his wife was Raft's biggest fan (he didn't consult the magic mirror: a better-looking one at the zoo would have appeared), and the next morning somebody knocked at their door and said "Room service!" and then the actor walked in with a tray—according to Bulgado, the scene could be traced to one he played in some movie with Ginger Rogers—placed it on the woman's knees and, looking at her with a serpent's eyes, spread the toast with ardent jelly. I felt hungry, and I felt above all that Raft was playing with me in the clumsiest way. I asked if it was true he had at least a half-point share in the casino. He licked his lips and murmured that it was his business, but he'd taken a liking to me and would give me an answer. At that moment, the secretary came into the suite without knocking: he wanted Raft to read a cablegram and didn't even apologize for interrupting us. Instead, he spoke to a waiter who'd come in with him and told him to bring more ice; even the woman who seemed to be a housekeeper, when she saw the open door, entered silently, with lowered eyes, and walked through to the adjoining room. The flutter around Raft resumed, I had the suspicion it had all been planned so that I'd get out, but he said to me: "Wait just a minute."

I asked for the bathroom; if this was going to be prolonged, I at least needed to piss out the couple of whiskeys I'd had. The secretary indicated a room on the other side of the suite, which was the guest bathroom. I left my things on the chair, there was nothing secret: the notebook where I was making notes, empty except for this interview, the pen I'd been using, a Parker with Santiago's initials, and the jacket I'd taken off a while ago. After emptying my bladder I washed my hands and looked around; I opened the medicine cabinet and saw razor blades, a soap dish, caffeinated aspirin tablets. There were bottles of cologne and some women's things: boxes of face powder, lipstick, pink rouge. The rouge filled me with nostalgia, it was the same as the one I'd seen on the dressing table in Aurora's room many years earlier, when I sneaked in to touch her things. I smelled it so that nostalgia could claw at me all over. Then I let the water run, wet my hair, and used somebody else's brush, full of blond hairs. I came out of the bathroom and went back to the room where I'd left Raft, but he was no longer there, there were other people in the suite: a very good-looking American woman in her thirties wearing the blue dress of a governess, and, next to the window, two fat men talking who didn't even bother to look at me. The waiter said Raft would be right back and asked if I wanted something to drink. I ordered another whiskey, I'd already peed out the first two and thought I'd handle the third with no problem. I noticed that the American, in spite of her modest dress, was overflowing with sensuality. I looked at her a couple of times and sized her up conscientiously: skinny and in-tuitive, a veteran of the wars. I looked over my notes, picked up a magazine, and killed time looking at the photographs until Raft returned and we were back where we'd been before, with me sitting in one armchair and him in another, and the table between us. The two fat men talking next to the window left, and so did the waiter, but the American didn't move from the sofa where she was talking on the phone, an interminable con-versation about a flight to San Francisco. To the sound of that background music, I asked Raft three or four questions related to his new life in Havana; it's the kind of rubbish women like to read, he had a wonderful time answering them, he was a specialist in pretending to be accessible. Then I thanked him and said that was all; the photographer would stop by the casino that afternoon to take his picture in his element, like a fish in water next to the roulette wheel. He walked with me to the door, we shook hands, and I went down to the lobby. I don't know why I noticed the rarefied atmosphere. I detected what I supposed were three or four civilian police, and some individuals who looked very different and seemed to be bodyguards, probably placed in key positions. I started the Plymouth, thinking that Bulgado didn't look like Raft's best friend or like anybody else who wasn't Raft, though maybe he was better off not knowing him, adoring him in the shadows. There are disillusionments that have a diabolical side, and Bulgado's could have been one of those. Before I put my jacket on the seat beside me, I took out the pack of cigarettes and matches I kept in the pocket, and a folded piece of paper came out with them. I didn't remember putting anything there except my "smoking apparatus," as Julián called it, and so I was curious as I unfolded the paper and saw lines in English written in a clear hand and dark ink:

"Voloshen, Skip, are gonna get whacked by Fat the Butcher."

I moved from curiosity to disquiet. For a few moments I thought that the paper belonged to Santiago, that he'd left it in his jacket pocket. But I realized immediately that Fat the Butcher, also known as Nicholas DiConstanza, was one of the shareholders in the Capri, and I was still there, and so my instincts told me I ought to get moving, get as far away as possible as soon as I could. When I looked behind me in the rearview mirror, I saw two of the guards who watched the doors to the hotel; they both had seen me take out the paper, read it, and then speed away.

I went back to the editorial offices; first things first: I had to write up the interview before I thought about the anonymous note. I sat in front of the typewriter and filled four sheets, but it also occurred to me to play a joke on Madrazo, and above the title I put this line: "George Raft, The Money Messenger." For the title I chose a sentence that I took from one of his answers: "I can't conceive of living away from Cuba." As I was writing, I kept turning over in my mind the contents of the paper that somebody had put in my pocket. I had no idea who Skip was, or Voloshen, but it didn't matter, somebody was warning me that they'd be killed; true or false, they were the names of two condemned men. I took the interview to Madrazo's office, but he hadn't come in yet. I read it over before leaving it on his desk and came to the conclusion that nothing's more pathetic than a gangster who breaks out in hearts: Raft in love with Havana, Raft in love with the women of Havana, Raft madly in love with the ocean. How did I have the nerve to criticize Skinny T? And with what morality could I ridicule the vulgarities of poor Berto del Cañal? As soon as I left Madrazo's office, I forgot about the interview and took out the anonymous message to read it for the hundredth time: "Voloshen, Skip, are gonna get whacked by Fat the Butcher." It had all the characteristics of a little trap for a little idiot, like those spring traps used to break the necks of mice, and somebody had put it in my pocket so I'd catch my fingers. That's when I made the first mistake in what would turn out to be a series of humiliating mistakes, inexplicable in someone who had spent at least ten of his twenty-two years soaking up the tactics, warnings, secrets, and habits of the Mafia residing in Havana. I approached Castillo, the best investigative reporter in the country, who was threatened and bitter, feeling useless because he couldn't write two lines anymore without becoming involved in difficulties. We had a cordial relationship, but I knew he saw me as an upstart out to steal his glory. I showed him the paper, explained how I'd obtained it, and said I was almost certain it was intended to trick me.

240

"But look," Castillo observed, "Voloshen was Anastasia's lawyer, I don't know who he represents now but he's in Havana, he's been seen at the Hotel Nacional, and Skip is Shepard's nickname, he's one of the owners of the Capri."

Castillo held the note between his fingertips; I didn't take my eyes off it, I was dying to get it back.

"Know what an American who knows all those lunatics at the Capri told me?" He'd been chewing on a toothpick, and he took it out of his mouth to imitate the nasal voice of his confidant. "He said: 'Shepard made a mistake going in with a gangster like DiConstanza . . . DiConstanza will eat him alive.' So whoever wrote this note is not far off the track."

I practically tore it from his hands, I was sorry now I'd shown it to him, but at the same time I knew nobody else could have given me that precious information: Voloshen had worked with Anastasia, and Skip was a stone in the shoe of Fat the Butcher. I went back to my desk and wrote what I'd try to have inserted as a box in the Raft interview, with this title: "Who Wrote the Anonymous Note?" Then I typed:

As if it were a scene taken from one of George Raft's gangster pictures, shortly after leaving the Hotel Capri, this reporter discovered that someone had slipped an anonymous message into his jacket pocket. The message warns of the imminent deaths of two men, Voloshen and Skip, supposedly at the hands of a certain Fat the Butcher. Having made the pertinent inquiries, we have been informed that Voloshen could be Jay Voloshen, one of the lawyers for the late capo Umberto Anastasia, murdered three months ago in New York. Skip is the nickname of J. J. Shepard, one of the Capri's owners. The question is: who wrote the message, and why?

I took the text of the inset to Madrazo's office. He still hadn't come in. I clipped it to the interview and left him this note: "I have the anonymous letter if you want to see it." I went back to my desk, and on the way I ran into Castillo, who was looking for me.

"I found out something else about Voloshen," he said. "His wife raises big dogs, St. Bernards."

I looked at him, not understanding. What the hell did I care if his wife had dogs?

"Listen to this: the day Anastasia died, that same morning, Voloshen and his wife woke up terrified, they felt something strange in the sheets. When they pulled back the covers, what do you think they found? The heads of the St. Bernards, still bleeding."

"I saw that in a movie," I managed to stammer.

"No, you didn't," Castillo challenged me. "What movie could you have seen it in? Nobody knows about it."

I thought of Julián. A story like that would have broken his heart. I thanked Castillo, didn't mention the inset, and kept working on the things I'd left hanging before I went out to interview Raft. Half an hour later, Madrazo came over to see me; he assured me he loved both things, the interview and the cryptic message, and he asked me to show him the note. While he was reading it, I told him I suspected it was a trick, a joke on me. They still hadn't forgiven my going to New York to stick my nose into the mysterious visit of the four Cubans and their meeting with Anastasia a few days before they killed him. Madrazo said that even if it was a trick, the anonymous note gave a special flavor to the interview, and in the long run we'd be the ones playing a joke on them.

That night I went to Bulgado's house. As always, he avoided our talking in front of his wife and mother-in-law, and we went to the café on the corner, ordered a couple of rums, and I began to tell him what Raft had said about him.

"He knows perfectly well who you are," I said, as serious as hell. "He says you look like his best friend."

He swelled up with pride, but the best was yet to come.

"He wants me to tell you he's going to make a movie with Marilyn Monroe and Tony Curtis. He's seen the screenplay. In the movie his name will be Spats Colombo."

"Eh-spahs," he said two or three times, "what a hard name."

"A gangster's name. Any news about you know what?"

He shook his head; it bothered him to discuss that subject. "Nothing, they can call us any time. Probably they'll call us tomorrow, or the day after . . . They'll call when they want to, when they have the sausage ready. One of the lions is sick."

It seemed horrifying to me that he'd compare a corpse and a sausage. As for the lion, it was a detail like the one about the dogs that belonged to Voloshen's wife. For the moment I didn't understand why the hell the lion made any difference.

"The veterinarian will have to see it, and with the veterinarian there you have to be careful about the food. They always ask what the animals are eating, understand? They ask about everything."

I did understand: what they ate was relevant. We had another couple of rums, and I went to my house, which was becoming gloomier by the day. Sometimes Lucy would spend the night at her teacher's house. Papá wasn't working as much, he was beginning to drink excessively, and my mother went out often, visiting the neighbors or her friends, maybe she wandered around on her own, I don't know, I think she couldn't stand seeing us anymore. I was a normal guy until I walked in that door; Santiago was making all of us sick, his spirit or whatever it was. It was ironic that a happy guy like him would torment us this way after he was dead.

At eight the next morning, Balbina knocked at the door to my room. I knew who it was because I heard her shouting: "It's urgent, urgent!" I threw myself out of bed, opened the door sensing the end of the world, and it turned out to be something along those lines. She said they were calling from the paper, they told her it was urgent and she should get me out of bed. I ran to the phone; it was Madrazo, until that moment, when he opened the paper, he hadn't noticed the supertitle I'd given the interview: "George Raft, The Money Messenger." He asked how I'd had the nerve, it would cause him problems. I stammered that it was a joke, I meant to tell him, I imagined he'd see it himself and delete it. Madrazo was barking at the other end, he became nasty, he shouted that I had the brain of a mosquito and that conditions in the country were no joking matter. He hung up, and I stood there with the phone in my hand. I never believed the line would go through, but I'd completely forgotten about putting it in, and since it was so small, Madrazo and the proofreaders didn't notice it, it's the kind of slipup that happens only on newspapers. I felt humiliated and was probably going to lose my job as well. And, of course, I'd never again be able to set foot in the Capri. I went up to my room, fell onto the bed, I didn't have to be at the paper until noon, and I was afraid. At the age of twenty-two, this kind of disaster inspires too much fear. It must have been close to eleven and I was still in bed, thinking about what I'd say to Madrazo, when Balbina knocked again: she said the same man was calling me, and it was urgent again. Balbina was funny: she watched me come out of the room with her sad-looking face; I made people feel sad, and she could smell my ruination.

"This is worse," Madrazo's leaden voice indicated. "I'm going to say this fast: Voloshen was found dead this morning with a bullet in his head. They think he was killed in the middle of the night. The police came looking for you because they want to see the anonymous note, and Castillo says there are other individuals down there waiting for you too. Hide out for two days and then we'll see."

I hung up. I ran to get dressed. Hide out where? They knew all about Yolanda's apartment. The ideal thing would be for me to get out of Havana and go to Santa Clara, to my aunt's house. But just then I thought about Julián and his new apartment on Calle Infanta. I found the telephone, and the American with the beautiful arms answered; she murmured "Just a moment" and passed the phone to Julián. I told him what I could, the best I could, I don't think he understood much of anything: the interview with Raft, an anonymous message in my jacket pocket, a title that was a joke and was published by accident, and most serious of all, the man in the anonymous note was really dead. Julián told me to calm down and go to his apartment, he'd be waiting for me at the entrance. I didn't take anything because I thought Lucy could bring me some clothes. I flew out of the house, dazed by the sun and by my own confusion, my hands trembling slightly when I opened the car door, and it wasn't until I started the engine that I discovered somebody sitting up in the backseat.

"Surprise, kid, drive out of here fast."

I felt the touch of the barrel on the back of my neck, like an indestructible ice cube.

"Go straight. Don't even think about doing anything dumb."

Not at all. I wouldn't think about anything. Suddenly I felt an emptiness that terrified me, I had an idea it was the proximity of death. What indifference, what a damn calm in my head, when in fact my whole body was shitting with fear.

"Head for the Almendares."

GOOMBAH

Nobody who hasn't seen Fat the Butcher up close could understand that right then, when he was in front of me, I didn't think about my situation or the risk I was running, much less about the possibility that my body would end up in the expert hands of Juan Bulgado. I thought about that later. At first, when he came into the room and leaned over to look at me, breathing hard, smoking with ferocity, I thought about strange things; I wondered, for example, what his newborn face could have been like, the defenselessness of the first few months. I was observing him, intrigued by what I saw, when I had an attack of something like mental hiccups: one question came up, then another, then one more, and I couldn't help it, all of them related to the infancy of Fat the Butcher: his hands when he came into the world, his first cry when the midwife picked him up by his feet, the slight fever he ran when his baby teeth came in. There was an aberration in my mind, I obsessed over the most absurd details. I realized it and couldn't help it: I went on asking myself questions, one after the other, his presence made me an idiot, turned me into a fearful wreck. I turned into a wreck when he spit the first gob of phlegm in my face.

"You're a piece of shit," he roared in Spanish; he had a hard accent, like a hook he used to split ears open. "Where's the paper?"

I asked what paper he was referring to. He gave me a slap that almost broke my neck. Next to him, in that room full of light with a view of the Forest of Havana, was the grotesque little man, probably a dwarf, who'd forced me to drive to this house. I remember that when I got out of the car and saw him full-length, I felt embarrassed at having been at the mercy of so small a man for so long, even though he was a small man skillful with a revolver. A short time after he told me to drive to the Almendares River, he ordered me not to make any detours and to take the usual route from Vedado to Marianao, all along Calle 23 until you get to the bridge. That street had never seemed so long, so full of secret signs that recalled other times in my life. We passed the Carmelo, a cafeteria where I used to eat with Zoila, my fiancée at the university, and I clung to the sight of the little tables that were where they'd always been when it wasn't crowded, as if they were expecting me. When we were close to Jalisco Park, the guy moved the revolver away from the back of my neck for a moment; he did that because there were other cars nearby and too many people crossing the street all around us. I'd passed by there so often, and not until that day had I thought again about the last childhood excursion Julián, Santiago, and I made together, accompanied by Aurora, who took us to ride the bumper cars. The visit to Jalisco Park was the episode marking the start of Santiago's adolescence, I have no doubt about it, because after that day my brother noticed that he had tastes very different from mine and Julián's, he was no longer a little boy, and from then on he didn't go out with us anymore. Aurora was too young to contend with three hungry wild animals, and the worst of them, at that age, was Santiago. Jalisco Park was a frontier: she became a widow a few days later, and I was sent to her house to stay with Julián and cheer him up a little. Nobody knows how happy I was during that time of mourning, mentally occupying the dead man's place, even though we couldn't play the radio, or shout, or laugh out loud. Or even run, but it didn't matter: I ran in my imagination.

"I want the paper," Fat the Butcher insisted. "Where is it?"

If my head was a ball of useless rags shaken by hiccuping questions before the slap, after it I couldn't coordinate or plan anything, least of all remember where I'd put the anonymous message. I breathed heavily, because I felt as if I needed air; I looked at the ceiling and tried to remember. The paper . . . Castillo had read the paper, and when I could take it back, I folded it and put it in my jacket pocket; later Madrazo wanted to see it, he returned it to me folded, and automatically I put it back in the same place. The hiccups in my head moved down to my diaphragm, where all hiccups normally come from: it was as if a thought had become disconnected, and I was sure the paper, the anonymous note that blamed Fat the Butcher for the death of Voloshen, was still there, in the jacket I inherited from Santiago, and that fortunately was the same one I grabbed when I left the house.

"I think I have it on me," I said, gesturing with my chin toward the pocket.

"You have it on you or you have shit on you?" the dwarf said with a smile.

"I have the paper on me."

I didn't dare reach for it. My neck was almost broken, I was dazed, my mind was vacant, but not to the point where I didn't know I couldn't move my hands without prior authorization.

"Give it to me."

I was terrified I wouldn't find it there. My chest began to

hurt at the same moment I put my hand in to take it out; it was so hideous a pain I wanted to throw up, and it was disgusting because I did throw up but it didn't come out, I made an effort and swallowed it down again. Finally my fingers brushed the paper; it made me happy, a humiliating delight that lasted until I took it out and handed it to Fat the Butcher.

"Take it . . . let me go."

He took it with his left hand, and with his right he hit me again, maybe a little more slowly than the first time, but he knocked me off the chair. The vomit I'd swallowed a short while before came back up to my mouth and I choked on it, I coughed and rolled around on the floor. At the same time I felt a kick in the crotch, I opened my eyes and saw the dwarf. He was the one who kicked me, and since it came from him it shouldn't have been too powerful, and yet it was, I twisted with a dreadful pain like a knife; I lost consciousness and didn't come to until they threw water on me. Fat the Butcher wasn't in the room, just the dwarf, he was the one trying to wake me up.

"Somebody else wants to see you," he announced. "His name is Navajita, and I think he's mad at you."

Navajita was "The Blade" Tourine, the worst American to come to Havana in the past thirty years, more bloodthirsty than Al Capone, more independent, and crazier. At least fifty-four murders were attributed to him, all of them committed with a knife.

"Get up, or you want me to give you another little kick to get you going?"

He pulled me by the arm, and I was sitting on the floor, trying to orient myself, then I leaned on the chair and was able to stand. I felt embarrassed again that a guy like him had controlled me; it was just what Gulliver must have felt. I remembered the illustration in the story of the Lilliputians jumping on his nose. This one didn't jump, he just kept aiming the revolver at me, indicating that I should walk to the door; he knocked three times, and somebody opened it from the outside. It was a mulatto wearing dark glasses—he looked just like Burt Lancaster, but in dark skin—and I heard him say to the dwarf: "Hey, wait, people are in there." I heard voices in what I imagined was the living room, a conversation in English, fairly heated. My belly hurt, my cock, my stomach, but most of all my neck. I touched it and thought a vein had swollen. I staggered, and the mulatto said: "Get him back in, he's going to shit himself here." With the barrel of the revolver, my jailer indicated the way, and at that moment the discussion got louder. I could hear shouting, but they were talking very quickly and I could barely catch a few isolated words, almost all of them obscene. The mulatto closed the door so I couldn't hear, and the dwarf stayed with him on the other side, so that for a moment, finding myself alone, I thought about running to the window and jumping into the trees. I would have if my legs had responded, but they were made of wood, just like my neck; I could hardly move it. These were wretched minutes, during which I resigned myself to the idea of dying. A strange silence fell, and the singing of the birds was the only sound. I was dying of thirst, and again I longed to jump into the trees, not to escape but to find the river. I could hear the water running, a delicious bubbling. I think I dozed, hypnotized by the sounds of the countryside, and didn't even hear the door open; I know that suddenly I looked up and saw a man in a hat. He had an absurd mouth, a pitiless or simply a disgusted face, but his words were kind: "Do you think you can walk?"

I said I could. No voice came out, only a humble rasping sound in reply; the swelling in my throat kept me from talking.

"Let's go then." He touched me on the shoulder though he kept his distance, it was obvious he didn't want to dirty his suit.

We went into a hallway, crossed two or three rooms and a

little courtyard where two dogs were chained; I think they were mastiffs, both of them followed us with impenetrable eyes. We went out the back to the same sloping ground where I remembered coming in with the dwarf. My car was still there, as dusty as if months had gone by, and maybe they were months, or was it only hours? Maybe minutes? I stepped forward to open the door, and the man stopped me. "No, no . . . Let's go in mine."

He pointed to another car, a gray Mercedes under a lean-to. I understood I wasn't free. They wouldn't let me go after what I'd dared to write. They'd warned me several weeks earlier, when they forced me to become a chopper of flesh: they wouldn't tolerate another article. Now they could wipe me out whenever they wanted, in whatever way would be easiest for them, without worrying about a scandal or somebody being mentioned in the papers. After all, if Santiago had been killed for being a revolutionary, nobody would be surprised if I was killed too. And they wouldn't even have to make use of Bulgado's services: they'd cut me up mercilessly and toss me in some ditch. Let them ask Colonel Ventura what happened to Santiago Porrata's brother, the one who wrote for *Prensa Libre*. He'd say he could see it coming, since I was part of the same cell. Of three siblings, only one—Lucy, the universal heir to all my inherited clothes—was destined to survive. I thought about all this while we were driving back, going toward Vedado; we crossed the forest bridge that leads into Calle 23, we passed Jalisco Park again, and the restaurant with the unsteady tables, the Carmelo, where they served the best club sandwiches. At times I closed my eyes and kept them closed for a few minutes, sinking into the drowsiness caused by the blows I'd received, and then without warning I'd give a start and open them, I saw fragments of the city: La Rampa, Infanta, then Carlos III, and farther on the columns of Calle Reina, and suddenly, without my realizing it, we were in the Parque Central: where were we going? The man didn't answer, he didn't even bother to look at me. But I didn't close my eyes again until he went down the Paseo del Prado and stopped in front of Aurora's house.

"Get out," he ordered, not looking at me.

My stupor vanished. I thought about running down the street; that man hadn't shown a weapon, he gave me orders expecting me to obey without a word, without his having to use force. But he kept a close watch on me, he wouldn't have allowed me to escape, and surely there was somebody else watching us, I could swear we hadn't been alone on that drive, and I concluded that any attempt to run away would have been useless. I walked up the steps suspecting that what was going to happen when I reached the top would be the most painful of the blows, more subhuman than the slaughter pen. The man rang the bell, the eternal bell that had been on the door for so many years, the one I'd rung so often from the time I was little and stood on tiptoe to reach it. Julián answered the door, looked avidly into my face, and lowered his eyes because he couldn't stand what he saw, the swollen neck that choked me slightly, as if the hands of a ghost were giving me no peace, and a closed eye again, and split lips, and a nose full of blood. For the first time I saw Julián moved by another human being; he became tenderhearted, as if he were seeing a suffering animal. I saw in his eyes the same helplessness, the same affliction I'd seen when we were looking at the wounded flamingos. The man who'd brought me there told me to sit down in the reception room and went to the interior of the house, but I wasn't alone with Julián for even a minute. I couldn't say a word to him because Aurora appeared right away. I think she came in planning to slap me, I don't know, her hand was raised, she was determined not to feel compassion, and still she felt it. I saw her stop, gasp for air, and give me a devastated look. Then she turned that look on her son, who was smoking, looking down at the floor, and she said to him: "Go get an ice bag."

Julián got up, and I took the opportunity to ask for water. I don't know what kind of voice came out. I have a hunch it was a kind of watery sob, as if a blowfish, or any of those species that puff themselves up, could produce words, that was the tone. Julián asked if I preferred a nice whiskey (my friend was a simple bastard, he said "a nice whiskey"), but his mother cut him off: "Go get the ice and the water, don't be a pain."

When he left, she decided to talk to me, she certainly wasn't going to renounce that. She came fairly close, and I looked up because I wanted to take away this image of her even though I was half dead. I knew this would be the face, the voice, the angle of the body I would keep.

"Listen to me, Quin." I liked it that she called me by my old name. "I know you don't love your mother, or your father, and I don't think it mattered to you very much when they killed Santiago. I'm not doing this for you, I'm doing it for her. How can I let them kill another of her sons?"

The man who brought me there interrupted. He came back from the interior of the house frowning. He exchanged a look with Aurora and moved his head; it was a message that she understood immediately.

"Now you're going in," she said. She seemed ready for everything, to kill me as long as other people didn't do it. "You're going to hear what he has to say, and don't even think about being rude to him, do you hear me, because if you are, I'll be the one who attacks you. It's a miracle you're not dead, but I'll kill you myself if you waste this chance."

Just then Julián came back with the glass of water. He was also carrying an ice bag, but I didn't have the time to put it anywhere. It would have felt good in my crotch; my balls were burning, it terrified me to think about the consequences. The water, I gulped that down in one swallow, half of it dribbled out of my mouth and the sight must have shaken Julián, who couldn't stay on his feet, he was incapable of that. He dropped onto the sofa that had been there since the time of our adolescence and lit another cigarette.

"You know the way," said Aurora, "go straight into the dining room and keep your ears open."

I obeyed, I headed for the dining room, dragging my feet. As I approached, the music began to envelop me, so rhythmic you could smell it: "*Son* of the almond, my honey . . . *son* of the almond, not the guava." I even wondered if he was going to hit me in the neck too, and if he'd do it with that music in the background, with that rhythm, the indecent enigma of street dancing: "*Son* of the almond, the pineapple . . ." The door was half open. I tapped on it, but with the music it was impossible for him to hear. I stood still, deciding if I should push it open, or knock again, or simply wait until the *danzón* was over to become visible. None of that was necessary because he opened the door, looked me up and down, and gestured with his hand for me to come in. There were two armchairs in front of the balcony, and he indicated that I should sit in one of them, but he remained standing. How skinny and faded he was, dressed only in undershorts that fluttered around him like kites, and with no trace of modesty. From the shorts, which came down almost to his knees, a pair of awkward legs emerged, and it seemed that a cloud of talc still floated around him. One day, many years ago, Julián had told me that Meyer Lansky liked to use talcum powder.

"Sit down," he said in Spanish, something very unusual, bound to be a bad sign. "Don't you like that music?"

I couldn't smile or respond, and so I turned toward the phonograph and pretended I was enthralled listening to it. He didn't do anything until he heard the final chords. Then he went to the phonograph and turned it off so he could talk. He continued in English; that gave me some hope: Aurora had told him my mother had just lost a son, and she wanted to keep the other one from dying. It had been difficult, extremely difficult to convince Nick (I assumed he was referring to DiConstanza), and even more difficult to convince Santo, who was very close to Mr. Raft. He didn't understand why I enjoyed offending his friends so much. It had also been hard for him to get Joe (I learned later he was referring to the capo named Joe Stassi) to take me out of his house on the Almendares River and bring me to Prado. Seeing how many people had gone to great trouble to save my skin, did I think I deserved it after all the garbage I'd been writing? Finally, he wanted to tell me this wasn't the first time he'd managed to avoid something serious happening to me. Aurora, my mother's good friend, had interceded earlier. Or did I by some chance think that what happened in New York hadn't raised any bruises and that Santiaguito Rey himself (he pronounced it "Santguitorey"), minister of the interior, hadn't asked for my head? Julián, who loved me like a brother, had begged him to save me, that time and this.

"But they both know you won't be able to do it again." He sighed as if he were lamenting this; his bones were prominent, and he had the nipples of a newborn. "It's true, my boy, believe me: next time you die. It'll be fast, and I promise that nobody will lay a finger on you again. But lead, yes, in the only place where it doesn't come out the other side, didn't you know that? If they shoot you here, there's no exit wound. You're so drawn to these curiosities, I thought you'd like to know that in the world where my friends operate, that kind of shot has a name: '*cu sgarra paga*.' "

He walked out of the dining room and left me alone for a few minutes. From where I was sitting, near the balcony, I saw the tops of the trees, the great caobo trees on the Paseo del

Prado. Beneath them were the bronze lions, but those I couldn't see. Lansky came back with Julián, ordered him to sit in the other armchair, and said he wanted the two of us to hear something important.

"Do you see this?" He indicated the view, the old tile roofs where the last red rays of the sun were setting, and the Roof Garden of the Hotel Sevilla, where they were beginning to turn on the lights. "All of it is collapsing . . . It doesn't look it, but it's all ruined, I'm telling you, I can smell it; the same thing happened to me in Poland. That knowledge, that memory stays with a person. Sometimes I'm here, listening to the music, and I look outside, I see everything changed, like time had already gone by, not too much time, I see the world down there, changed so much, and I'm sorry it has to end like this. This is fucked up, Goombah; take care of things in time and get out."

Julián stood up, went to Lansky, and put his arm around his shoulder.

"We don't have much time left," muttered the old man, shaking his head.

Then Julián said he'd take me home. We went into the hall-way, we hadn't taken three steps when we could hear the chords of the *danzón* again. Lansky was playing it at top volume: "*Son* of the almond, my honey . . . *son* of the almond, not tomorrow." Aurora watched us leave in silence. I thanked her. She looked up, and I saw that her eyes were filled with tears. We drove away in the Buick Special, and when we passed the Aires Libres, where you could hear the music of the orchestras, the sound of glasses, laughter, everybody walking back and forth as if nothing were going to change, Julián stopped the car. "What do you think, Quin? Can what Goombah told us be true?"

I shrugged.

"I don't know. I need some soup."

"You should have said so, damn it . . . Let's go to Chinatown."

EPILOGUE

Three months had passed since the death of Umberto Anastasia in the barbershop of the Park Sheraton in New York. In less than a year Batista's government would fall. I didn't last very long at *Prensa Libre*. In retaliation for the joke about the "money messenger," and the subsequent letter of protest and threat of legal action sent by George Raft, they put me back in Entertainment. I didn't think there could be a boss worse than Skinny T. until I had to follow Berto del Cañal's orders. He tanned my hide during those months. Among other nightmares, he sent me to cover the "excursion" organized every Thursday from Miami to the Tropicana, in a plane crowded with Americans who were motivated in flight with champagne and a mini-show by Ana Gloria and Rolando, Rodney's favorite dance team.

I had to interview Rodney in connection with the opening of his new show, *On the Way to the Waldorf*, and with every question I asked I had vivid memories of Fantina; I was on the verge of talking to him about her, I was going to say her name at the very moment Roderico Neyra interrupted our conversation: he was very sorry, but he had to go, Joan Crawford was waiting for him in the dressing room, they were going to have their picture taken with Nat "King" Cole, thanks for everything, thanks for the interview, baby, "You have the prettiest hair." Statements that I reproduced word for word, except the compliment Rodney paid my hair. I added a kind of wink for Yolanda in the interview: it was a little crass, but I said that Rodney, more than anything else, had reminded me of a prodigious magician.

When I reached the limit of my patience and was about to blow up at Berto, they offered me a job on *Crisol* covering Police News, which I liked. Curiously enough, I made my debut on that paper writing about the death of Boris, riddled with bullets in the doorway of his restaurant. Julián and I had eaten there at about that time. It was a farewell meal because the young Goombah had decided to follow the advice of the old Goombah and was leaving for New York. The only witness to the death of Boris was a five-year-old girl who'd come into the restaurant with her grandfather. The grandfather went to the kitchen to say hello to Dimitri, the Ukrainian cook, and Boris called the little girl over to give her candy. At that moment the shots were fired and she saw him fall with a pile of caramels in his hand. I wanted to interview the little girl in her grandparents' house, at Compostela 611, a few steps from the Boris, but they didn't let me even talk to her or take her photograph. I only saw her from a distance, and sometimes I wonder what memory she has of that day in March.

Juan Bulgado continued to give me clues about crimes in Havana. Some of them I used and others I rejected with an aching heart: I didn't want to be sent back to Entertainment. I still have the letter he once gave me, written by Santo Trafficante on Rosita de Hornedo letterhead. It's a strange memento that I'll keep forever.

Early in the morning of January 1, 1959, everything changed, just as Lansky predicted. Enraged citizens invaded the hotels, overturned the gaming tables, pulled out Colonel Fernández Miranda's slot machines and tossed them on the sidewalks. Only one casino in Havana was respected. George Raft came out of the doors of the Capri to face the mob. He was still wearing the dinner jacket he'd worn for New Year's Eve, his temples were throbbing, he put on a terrible face and shouted: "This is my casino! Not in my casino!" Outside was a man who knew about his life, knew all his films by heart, and adored him in silence. That man raised his arms in front of Johnny Lamb, in front of Nick Cain, in front of Johnny Marshall, in front of Joe Martin, in front of Guino Rinaldo (his name in *Scarface*), but also, and above all, in front of the man who'd already played Spats Colombo. "It's Raft! George Raft! Nobody touch him!" A strange silence fell, two or three of the militiamen who'd accompanied the crowd removed their berets as a sign of respect. They dispersed without setting foot inside the casino. Only Bulgado remained for a few minutes, alone in front of the grateful actor. I saw that photograph. Raft's kingdom, and no other, had been saved.

Not long afterward, Aurora left for the United States. I found out that she spent a few days with Julián in New York and then settled in Miami. Meyer Lansky also left Cuba at about the same time; in reality he left Havana and came back several times, they say with false passports, but after the summer of 1959 he considered it extremely risky. According to Julián, his mother and Lansky continued to see each other in Miami, they were friends until he died in January 1983.

Santo Trafficante, alias Louis Santos, ended up in the Castillo del Príncipe prison. Steps taken by his great friend Raúl González Jerez, who in his youth had been a member of the Unión Insurreccional Revolucionaria and still had some contacts among the rebel leaders, succeeded in having him released. I saw him again only once, shortly before his death, at a restaurant in Fort Lauderdale. He was walking from one corner of the parking lot to the other, in the company of two other old men, arguing about something. Until the end he maintained his habit of not talking about problematic subjects except in garages or in open spaces, where he could be sure of not being taped.

My father committed suicide in '61. Mamá left with me and Lucy. We had some money saved, in addition to a large sum that Papá had taken the precaution of keeping in a Miami bank. With that we got ourselves settled, and I found a job selling structural steel, a chaotic line of work for somebody who knows only how to write. In an ironic twist, I often had to meet with my best customer, Charlie Trafficante, Santo's brother, owner of a company in Davie that manufactured trailers and trucks. Lucy continued her friendship with the teacher who looked like Doris Day. When Mamá died, they moved in together, and not long ago they were legally married in Cambridge. I was best man, and they were beside themselves with happiness.

Julián still lives in the suburbs of New York. He never married. According to his last count, he lives with about fifteen dogs and twenty cats. He feeds squirrels and raccoons. Sometimes the squirrels die in the jaws of his own dogs. A neighbor does him the favor of picking up the dead bodies. Julián can't: he's still tenderhearted.

I saw Yolanda again in a photograph. I was already living in Miami. I opened the paper and ran across an article about the funeral of Beny Moré. I saw her in the crowd accompanying the coffin. I felt a kind of disillusioned emotion, a tenderness that had to do with me, with what I'd been back then. She wore a black sleeveless dress, and I looked for the stump, that harsh, arduous symbol; I found it, half blurred in the photograph, but more faithful than ever to the abstraction of her name: it was the phantom of Fantina. A year later, in '64, I learned that Rodney had died in Mexico. It was a sudden death, in the midst of preparations for a large *tournée*. I thought again of Fantina. And I thought, above all, of a picture I had seen while I was in Cuba: Roderico with his arms around Joan Crawford but looking tenderly at Nat "King" Cole.

I married Leigh, the American I had met in the Ali Bar on New Year's Eve, 1957. I ran into her again at a party in Miami Beach. Time had passed and it was almost impossible that she'd remember me, but I remembered her. I placed her right away: though nobody believes me, I recognized her from the shape of her arms.

Abelardo Valdés could never surpass the great success of his first *danzón*: "Almendra." His last attempt to displace "Almendra" was a total disaster, an insipid *danzón* that he named after the almond drink: "Horchata."

AUTHOR'S NOTE

Many people offered me information or collaborated in some way in the research that was the basis for this novel, but I should like to express particular thanks to the following:

In Puerto Rico: the Cuban choreographer Víctor Álvarez, creator of the shows at the Sans Souci cabaret, and his wife, the dancer Ada Zanetti, the fairy godmother of dates and memories; the actress Ángela Meyer, who spoke to me of her days as *partenaire* to the magician Richardini; and the musicologist Cristóbal Díaz Ayala.

In New York: Kenneth Cobb, director of the Municipal Archives, who constantly facilitated my work, carried back and forth the eight immense and dusty boxes concerned with the Anastasia case, and had an affable smile that encouraged me on a particularly sad journey. For the present edition in English, my gratitude to John Glusman and Edith Grossman. And, of course, to Susan Bergholz.

In Miami: the invaluable assistance of a person whose name I am not permitted to mention, but who knows how indispensable his observations, information, and patience were in the face of my poor questions, which sometimes led him to exclaim: What a weak mafiosa you've turned out to be!

In Cuba: Eliades Acosta, director of the Biblioteca Nacional [National Library], and the staff of that institution, for the diligence with which they responded to my requests.

Enrique Cirules, whose book *El imperio de La Habana* [The Empire of Havana] was a valuable research tool and who kindly allowed me to read one of the chapters of another book, *La vida secreta de Meyer Lansky en La Habana* [The Secret Life of Meyer Lansky in Havana], which had not been published at the time.

The efficient Ciro Bianchi, for his learned responses.

Vivian Martínez, Dianik and Mario Flores, for patiently putting up with a barrage of questions, some of them absurd, and others too.

And the philosophical Armando Jaime Casielles: Meyer Lansky's friend, bodyguard, and driver, with whom I drank a nostalgic Pernod in the Hotel Riviera. Through him I learned that Lansky fell madly in love with a beautiful Cuban who lived on the Paseo del Prado. Late in 1957 he moved in with her. Her name was not Aurora.